GREETINGS
from
ASBURY
PARK

GREETINGS
from
ASBURY PARK

DANIEL H. TURTEL

**BLACK
STONE**
PUBLISHING

Copyright © 2022 by Daniel Turtel
Published in 2022 by Blackstone Publishing
Cover and book design by Luis Alejandro Cruz Castillo

Printed in the United States of America

First edition: 2022
ISBN 978-1-7999-5676-1
Fiction / Small Town & Rural

Version 1

CIP data for this book is available
from the Library of Congress

Blackstone Publishing
31 Mistletoe Rd.
Ashland, OR 97520

www.BlackstonePublishing.com

GREETINGS
from
ASBURY
PARK

CHAPTER 1

White Horses

The funeral was over quickly because nobody had much to say. Aside from the priest, Davey was the only one who spoke, and the main substance of his eulogy was to invite everyone to a nearby bar following the service. He found me once we were there and we moved away from the others who had come along.

"There's probably no better way to honor the man's memory," he said. He had lost his tie but still looked uneasy in a suit.

"That's probably true."

We had a drink. We had several. I always felt a certain stiffness speaking with Davey and the drinking helped that. I turned my back to the bar and looked around the room, where the mourners had become interspersed with the bar's usual patrons. Most of the crowd probably knew Davey, but I had not been in a very long time and turned back to the bar.

"It was a nice service," I said.

"It was good of you to come."

The bartender came back with the drinks and I lifted my glass before speaking and then put it down again.

"He was my father too."

Davey nodded, but I am not sure he believed it. I'm not sure I believed it.

"It was a good turnout," I lied.

Davey took an orange bottle of pills from his pocket and shook two out into his palm. I watched but did not say anything as he swallowed them dry. Into his drink, he hardly more than whispered: "My mother didn't come."

"No," I said. "Mine either."

"That's alright." Davey finished his drink. He had stopped himself from saying that my mother hadn't really been expected. His, at least, had been married to the man. There was not much more than that to say and so we drank. Before long, Davey focused on a table with two girls and eventually they noticed him.

"Let's give it a go," he said. He finished his drink without taking his eyes from the girls. "I could use something to bury my grief in."

"A real prince charming."

"Well," he said, "you don't ride in on a white horse for a girl who doesn't care much what she mounts." It was a familiar line and I repeated the end of it with him in a half whisper.

"Besides," said Davey. "There's probably no better way to honor the man's memory."

"You've used that one already."

Davey shrugged and shook his head and sauntered off toward the table.

You don't ride in on a white horse for a girl who doesn't care much what she mounts. I remembered the last time I heard my father say it, the last time I heard him say anything. He was drunk as he ever was when I brought Angie home for the first and only time because she thought it was important that they meet. She had cooked because that was the sort of thing she could do in strange houses. Although it was a larger and emptier kitchen than she had ever seen, she had done it and he seemed happy because he was always happy with the smell of food in the house. Probably no one had cooked for him in a very long time.

And then when she served it he had confused his hungers or maybe just suffered an abundance of them and reached out and squeezed her while she bent over to put plates on the table and she had looked for a moment like she might cry and then looked to me and ran from the house. And then he said it, screamed it so violently that it made Angie turn and look to me as if I should do something. And I did do something. I drove my fist into his face and he was so filled with liquor and with sadness that he had not bothered to fight back and only lay there. And through the screen door, rebounding on its hinges, Angie was watching and so I threw my fist again and again until his lips were slick with saliva and blood and he lay there sobbing and when I looked again she was no longer in the doorway.

It was the last time I saw my father and nearly the last time I saw Angie. None of that mattered now. He was dead and she might as well have been. There was something vulgar about recalling lost love after such a funeral but it ought to be somewhere, lost or otherwise, and anyway I did not have much say in the matter. It was not my father's fault that I lost Angie, and it certainly was not Angie's fault that I lost my father. When you drew it out practically you could see the sense it made but it didn't convince you. It didn't convince you and so it didn't stop you from hating her. It didn't stop you from loving her either, and that was the more serious problem.

The best thing to do would be to think of nothing at all. I watched Davey at the table, drowning his sorrow in women and whiskey and suddenly I envied him. I envied him and thought that he probably envied me and probably everybody envied everybody else when they are caught up in such things as confusing a girl you used to fuck and a dead father you used to beat. I envied how correct Davey was—there was probably no better way to honor the man's memory.

At the table I spoke to the one that Davey had lost already. She was not pretty, not exactly, but if a long time from now you would think of her as being pretty and remember her always as being pretty and never have to face her and argue with fact, then she might as well be. Why the hell not. I had drunk to the point where my face and skin were hot and the whiskey on my tongue did not feel sharp or bitter. I lost the present for a bit, but when I caught back up I could tell that disinterest was the sort of thing that worked with the girl. Her name was Lena.

"Do you play pool?" she asked.

"No, but I'm willing to give it a shot."

"That's very good," she said. "I'll teach you a thing or two about shooting."

The table was empty and I found the wooden triangle and racked. Lena rearranged the balls so that the perimeter alternated between solids and stripes. "It's all that matters when racking," she said. Davey and Lena's friend came over and asked to play doubles. Something about being one-on-one with a girl always tightened him up, and you could tell by the way they had come over that conversation had gone south the moment they'd been left alone.

Davey broke and was very good. The girl he was with was not. Lena was and I was not. It equaled out. I missed my first shot by a little and when my turn came around again Lena wrapped her arms around my body from behind and showed me how to shoot correctly. Her slight breasts were firm against my back and she pushed my right arm. The target ball was on the edge of a pocket and I would have made it with closed eyes but I let her guide my motion and when it sunk she got excited. I missed the next shot badly and scratched.

Davey's side won and he demanded that we buy them a round of tequila. It set a precedent for the night that I was all too happy to play along with. After seven games we were roaring drunk and the crimson felt looked like the inside of a coffin and the music seemed dull and far away and I wanted to be closer to it and so I asked Lena to dance.

I was not much of a dancer and no one else was dancing. We stood close to the speaker and the near volume seemed to dull our graceless steps. I twirled Lena around and dipped her and she kicked up her leg and we did it a few more times because there was not much else either of us could do.

"You're a very good dancer," she said.

"You'd be a terrible critic."

"No, really. You're very good."

"I'm better drunker."

"So let's get you drunker."

The bartender was not there and Lena grabbed a bottle of pouring red wine from behind the bar. "Let's get out of here," she said. "Tuck this in your pants."

"Tuck it in yours."

"Isn't any room." She lifted her blouse to show the waist of her white jeans and pulled at one of the belt loops to illustrate her point. There was a glimpse of lace beneath and I took the bottle and slid it into my waist. The air outside was calm and warm and once we were a few blocks from the bar we slowed down.

"You can take that out now," Lena said.

I stopped walking and hooked my finger into one of her belt loops and pulled her toward me. "You take it out for me."

She laughed and pushed me away. "Does that ever work for you?"

"Of the girls who have me steal wine or just all the girls in general."

"Just the ones with stealing wine. I don't want to know about the others."

"Yes, they all fall for it."

"Well I won't."

"You'll come around."

She laughed and I took the bottle out myself and gave her my free hand.

"Let's go to the water."

We walked between the lake and the ocean. The far side of the lake was abandoned and dark but for a perfectly spaced row of streetlamps. A thin fog hung low in the air and the halos of lanterns on our side of the lake sunk into the darkness and turned the world a very pure yellow. We walked on the pavement until there was a break in the seawall and we turned toward the ocean and walked down the wooden stairs onto the sand and left our shoes. It was dark and the lazy waves of the Atlantic lapped against the white sand and we walked until our feet touched the water and then retreated onto dry sand again. Neither of us had a corkscrew so we pressed the cork down into the bottle.

"Is this wine any good?" she said. She tried it and handed it to me.

"I couldn't tell you."

"Well then it's very good. Let's pretend it's very good and that you paid a whole lot of money for it."

"All right then. It's a very good wine and I paid a whole lot of money for it. What's the occasion?"

Lena found a shell in the sand and tapped it twice against my ring finger. "An engagement," she said.

"I think I'd make a lovely trophy husband." I took a fistful of sand and let it slide through my fingers and when it was all gone I took the bottle and drank.

"We'll see about trophy."

"You'll concede on the lovely then? I'll take lovely."

"Yes. Take lovely. You're lovely."

Lena took the bottle of wine and twisted its base a few inches into the sand. I leaned back onto my elbows and she pressed her body down onto mine and kissed me.

"Come on," she said, jumping up, "let's swim."

She stood and undressed and I followed her. The ocean was cold and Lena gave a soft sound of surprise when our toes touched the water.

"It would be very romantic if it were warmer," she said. She was very thin and either I or the red wine or both were convinced that she was also very beautiful. Even as a silhouette against the yellow glow of streetlights I could make out the smooth, lean curve of her hips. We shivered together in the bay. She came close and wrapped her arms around my neck and her legs around my back and she came down softly onto me and we shivered.

I felt married that night. Lena lived in a rented room above a stand-alone garage. It was an old building that had once been servants' quarters, but the upstairs was large, and it had been furnished with a working kitchen and bathroom that faced the street and a small bedroom in the back. The scarred wooden floors of her bedroom had that poor softness to them which translates to a feeling of being home.

"I'll leave very early," I told her. My head was against her shoulder and I whispered even though there was no one there to hear us. "You won't be awake."

"That's all right."

We were quiet for some time and I listened to the sound of her breath going in and out. Or maybe it was the sound of the ocean crashing down against the sand and then slithering back again. I was drunk and half-asleep and it was difficult to tell.

"Listen," she said, long after I thought she had gone to sleep. Her fingers began moving in my hair. "I have to be up by nine. Could you call me from wherever you are then?"

"The alarm would be more reliable."

"It's not as lovely as your voice," she whispered. Her fingers had stopped moving.

It was good to be in love for a night. We were tender in the way you can only ever be with strangers. I would leave in the morning and it was good to be so unmistakably in stringless love with such definite expiration. It was the fervor with which a runner sprints that final stretch because the end is something he can see and will only have to come to once more. It was a short race, but a good one to have competed in, even just to have heard that starting gunshot. There was comfort in knowing that you could say just what you wanted and not worry about what the words meant because in the morning they would be gone and so would you.

When I woke the sky was gray and barely lit and I crept out from her room into the kitchen. I had not eaten since the funeral and was overcome with hunger. I found some eggs and cooked them on Lena's stove. I could not find a plate and my head was filled with sound and so I set the skillet down on a paper towel and ate directly from it. The kitchen table ended in a window of old, warped glass and the white gulls were gracefully frozen in the gray morning sky like a slow parade of kites. They were mesmerizing and I nearly fell back to sleep watching them and the melancholy was only broken by the smell of burning plastic. Beneath the skillet, the table was burned and there was a great brown circle on the surface.

I could not think of anything else to do and so I left it there. Breath seemed very loud and I left through the side door. It was a screen door and it swung noisily open but I did not mind so much. I had made up my mind to leave and, once I had, the sound of a screen door groaning on its coils was very comforting because every screen door in the world made that sound.

It was a despicable thing to do. That much I know. It was a despicable thing to do but if I offered to pay for it she would refuse. And if she did not then I would rescind because I did not have the money to spare. So why not save everyone the breath. Better to let her down now than to make promises I could not keep and let her down a little down the road. Being let down by a stranger is not all that bad for the self and hatred is a better consolation prize than pity.

She would have been very adamant in refusing, I thought again as I walked down the quiet morning road. The pavement was littered with white sand, delivered on the early wind off the sea. Very adamant, I thought, she is just that kind of woman. I repeated it over again to convince myself, but in all the dark charisma of night I would not have dreamed of slighting her in any way, and I probably would not have known her very well in the morning.

CHAPTER 2
The Runner

Jacob Besalel had come to his family's home in Loch Arbour every summer since he was born. He was nineteen now and beginning to take his physical condition very seriously. Each morning, he ran four times around the eastern tip of Deal Lake, which separated Loch Arbour from Asbury Park. Every morning he ran the same route and every morning Julie Kowolski sat on the front porch of her home on Deal Lake Drive and watched him. It mattered to neither runner nor spectator whether there was rain.

What Julie liked to watch of the boy running was not his body but his face. She thought it was like the face of one of the mannequins in her shop, and she envied him for it. There was none of the usual pain of a runner in his face, but only a blankness that suggested his mind was elsewhere.

It was the third Sunday in June, and Jacob Besalel was completing the third of his four laps, when Lena Kowolski, wearing only a towel wrapped around her head and a bathrobe, came and joined her mother on the porch. It was raining lightly and Julie did not hear her daughter and so did not try to conceal the slow turn of her neck as she followed the runner's figure without shame.

"Who's that boy?" said Lena.

Julie jumped and brought the day's paper up before her face, and then dropped it again to appear as if she was only just noticing the runner now.

"How should I know?" she said. She flipped one page of the paper.

"He's attractive, isn't he?"

"He wouldn't talk to you."

Lena crossed her arms and smiled down at her mother. She had been away for her freshman year of college and now that she had returned she felt that her mother had changed. Lena had spent summers behind the cash register of her mother's store and she had watched the older woman make young girls twirl to show off clothing or talk about how men would react to certain bathing suits or loose dresses. Customers thought of "Madame K" as expressive and confident, bold and alive with a sort of sexual lucidity that defied her creeping age; Lena envied them their perception of her mother, but she could not share it. To her, the woman seemed always afraid.

"I thought you didn't know who he was."

"It takes real effort to not know who somebody is around here," she said. "The Besalels are Jews. Syrian Jews. They won't even talk to the other type of Jew."

"And what's the other type of Jew?"

"I don't know, but they won't even talk to them, so they won't talk to you."

Lena turned away from her mother and toward the runner. She put her palms against the banister and leaned her weight against it. "I've made people talk to me before who didn't want to."

Jacob Besalel was now perfectly before the Kowolski house, and he appeared before the two women in profile. Each watched him carefully, and they were silent as he passed. His jaw rose and fell with every step he took, and they could hear his footsteps slapping against the wet pavement. There was nothing graceful in his form, but something overwhelmingly mechanical; his body moved in defined cycles, as if powered by gears and not organs.

"Well," said Julie, "I think you'll find that people in the real world are a little more difficult to persuade than your college boys." When Julie said the word *persuade*, she looked her daughter up and down from head to toe. "And put some clothes on."

Lena looked once more at the running boy and then went into the house. She lived now above the garage, which was a small guesthouse that Julie Kowolski could not rent out for the summer and so allowed her daughter to occupy for a small fee; but by habit now, Lena did not cross the lawn to the garage but turned back into the house and climbed the stairs to her childhood room, where she stood before the full-length mirror. Keeping the towel wrapped around her hair, Lena undid her bathrobe and let it fall and tilted her head to one side as she studied her own reflection.

She had been so concerned with gaining weight in college that she had lost it instead. She was too thin and her ribs made faint stripes of shadow where they protruded against her skin—not severe lines like she saw on some girls, but definite and sharp. People, especially her mother, had told her that she needed to gain weight, but she liked the way she looked and so did men. There was nowhere that she loved her new thinness more than in her face, where it had pulled her skin tight against her cheekbones and made her eyes seem wide and catlike. A boy had told her once that her eyes had swallowed him whole, and afterward she opened them wider, as if they were twin black holes whose gravity increased with the mass of each star they consumed. It was all new to her and she enjoyed it; she enjoyed the feeling of coming back to the town she'd grown up in and swallowing whole the men who wouldn't look at her in high school. Hardly anybody recognized her, and at times she did not recognize herself.

Lena turned to view her own body in profile, the way she had seen Jacob Besalel's running figure, and then faced the mirror fully and made her face very stern. Sternness was a quality she found attractive in people and it was what she found attractive in the running boy. Still naked, Lena moved to the large, front-facing windows of the childhood room in which she no longer lived, where the light droplets of rain drummed and moved almost horizontally across the panes of glass, gathering in long clusters of water as the wind swept them along. The wind slowed as Jacob Besalel ran by the house for his fourth and final time, and it seemed to Lena that some of the water slowed to match his cadence. She tapped against the window, willing his mechanical face to turn up and see her.

After that, she watched him each day from her own window above the veranda while her mother watched him from the porch below, and for a long time, Jacob Besalel did not see either woman.

* * *

Jacob's younger sister had already met Julie Kowolski, though she had not known that the older woman liked to watch her brother run. Sophia Besalel knew hardly anything about the older woman, except that she owned a clothing store on the boardwalk, one of whose mannequins wore a pale-yellow dress.

The store was called Madame K's, and Sophia passed by it with almost the same regularity that her brother ran around Deal Lake. The boardwalk followed the sand from the northern tip of Asbury Park all the way south to Belmar and beyond—a stretch of more than three miles before the Shark River bridge interrupted it—but Sophia only cared for the half-mile commercial strip between Convention Hall and the Casino, which was not really a casino but only the burnt-out shell of one. She walked without shoes and knew the sections of the boardwalk by the way they felt against the soles of her bare feet. There was the cool stone floor of Convention Hall with inset brass lines that separated black stone from white; the warm and weathered wood of the boardwalk just beyond; the new, artificial wood of the boardwalk that faced the Stone Pony, which had been replaced after Sandy had torn up the original section, where the people who could not afford tickets to the summer stage shows would stand and listen, sometimes with their children sitting on their shoulders for a chance to see above the barricade; and finally, the hot stone floor beneath the shell roof of the Casino, eroded to a coarse, uneven surface that was always covered with grains of sand and puddles of brown water. There were restaurants and bars all down the strip of boardwalk and it was always busy in the summer. There was an antique arcade beside Madame K's that displayed refurbished pinball and skeeball machines and there was an old Atari Pong game in the storefront whose white pixel ball bounced from side to side the way that Sophia moved tirelessly between Convention Hall and the Casino.

She considered the boardwalk to be less a main street than a zoo. Outside of summer, the people she knew wore ankle-length skirts and covered their heads. They were civilized and rich, scholarly and well-spoken, argumentative but never violent. Here, she had watched the tattooed Dominicans haul their weight across the sand and slap their children for misbehaving. She had watched the gay men in tight bathing suits pouring out of the Empress Hotel, hand in hand or sometimes with their tongues in one another's ears. She had watched the young girls with pierced eyebrows and bars through their nipples that stuck out against the thin fabric of their bikinis straddle blond boys in broad daylight. She had watched an amputee go down the boardwalk in army fatigues holding out his veteran's cap for change. She had watched fists swing at a fight that had broken out between two skateboarders in the hollowed out carousel, and when it was done she had gone and dragged her toe through the gray concrete that was dark with splattered blood. Her heart had fluttered with the warm wetness of it.

She walked with a Dodger's cap that cast a shadow on her face and Wayfarers that let her look wherever she wanted. Also, she was not supposed to wander here alone, and any Syrian who saw her was likely to be a spy for her mother; the community was like that. And so she walked with her eyes and her face hidden, interested only in people and never in things.

Except for the dress. Or perhaps it was the mannequin who wore it. Sophia could not be sure which tantalized her more. It was a yellow dress that was either pastel or else partially transparent and stealing its paleness from the white surface of the mannequin beneath. The mannequin stood just outside the store with its shoulders back and its white hands on its hips and its cold, angular face turned slightly up so that it glared with the reflected midday sun. One of its feet was planted firmly on the boardwalk, while the other stepped on a raised platform. The raised leg emerged white and glowing through a long slit in the dress that ran from the waist down to the floor.

Julie watched Sophia through the front windows of her shop. At first, she did not recognize Sophia as the lanky girl who lived in the mansion across Deal Lake, as the girl who was the runner's sister. Even if she had not been intentionally obscuring her face, Sophia had grown four inches since the previous summer, from a twig-thin girl with a nose that was too big for her face into a seventeen-year-old of remarkable beauty, with olive-dark skin and a nose that had become noticeably smaller.

"Gabrielle," Julie Kowolski said to her assistant, "I think you ought to bring that girl in."

CHAPTER 3
The Names

Gabrielle checked the clock on the wall. Her shift was over, but she was not allowed to leave while a customer was in the store; that was one of Madame K's rules. Madame K had many rules and most of them were ultimately concerned with making customers forget that there was going to be a simple exchange of goods for money, or that they were in a store at all.

"They can't do that with salesclerks clocking out, now can they?" she often said.

Only Madame K called her Gabrielle, and she had worked in the shop long enough that she had begun to think of herself as Gabrielle whenever she was working. As she watched the clock on the wall, she was not thinking only of when she could leave the store physically, but also when she could go back to being another version of herself.

The version that Madame K wanted was a Black girl to work her shop; she shouldn't be so Black that the white patrons would think that she was from the bad parts of Asbury and then feel embarrassed about spending so much money on clothing—but only a brown as soft and light as desert sand, something to suggest that her politeness and subservience came naturally. Madame K felt that a beautiful, half-Black girl in the shop would inspire the white buyers toward a purchase because when they saw that Gabrielle's natural complexion and figure and beauty were out of their reach, they would understand that if they wanted to compete, then it was going to have to be by means of a more expensive wardrobe. The only requirement for Gabrielle's uniform was that each component—from shoes to earrings and everything in between—had to be the best-looking item from the middle range of price that was available in the store. Whenever a customer came into the shop and looked at an item on the shelf that was comparable to what Gabrielle was wearing, she was to go over to them and remark at how similar their tastes were. Gabrielle knew the response—an embarrassed smile, a shuffle toward the slightly more expensive versions. Nearly without fail, a purchase.

The other place where middle-priced goods were displayed was the mannequin out back.

"Don't scare them off before they get into the shop," was another wisdom of Madame K's.

So, on the day that Sophia Besalel walked into Madame K's shop, Gabrielle was wearing the very yellow dress that had so enamored the girl on the mannequin. It enamored her also on Gabrielle, but in a different way. Whereas the display dress stood out against the white plastic skin of the mannequin beneath it, Gabrielle's dress seemed almost paler by contrast with her brown skin, like the goldmoss stonecrop flowers that sometimes grew along the sand dunes.

Madame K watched the two girls interact and thought to herself that they could not have been very far apart in age. Once Sophia removed her glasses, Madame K could see that she was the Besalel girl from across the lake; Gabrielle was off to college in the fall, which put her at around eighteen. Of the two of them, it was Sophia who had darker skin—the tanned olive that Syrians get after spending a week in the sun. They were a similar height and had a similar litheness. Gabrielle turned Sophia toward the better dresses, but Sophia would not look beyond Gabrielle.

"Well, we don't have any in the store," said Gabrielle. "But I can take the one down from the mannequin."

"No," said Madame K. Both the girls looked at her, and she felt imbued with a sort of unquestionable power, as if she were their mother. "The mannequin stays. Gabrielle, why don't you get out of that dress and give it to . . ."

"Sophia."

"Sophia. Unless Sophia minds . . . ?"

Sophia shook her head. Gabrielle walked toward the dressing room—a crimson velvet curtain on a circular brass rod that hung from the ceiling in the middle of the space like a chandelier. Gabrielle pushed open the folds with one slender brown arm and stepped into the folds, but before allowing herself to be swallowed by the velvet, turned back toward Sophia.

"Aren't you coming?" she said.

Sophia looked at Madame K, and then back to Gabrielle. She paused, as if counting seconds in her head, and then followed Gabrielle inside. Madame K listened intently to the quiet rustling of fabric, to the sounds of her two young playthings undressing and dressing and watching one another's naked bodies in the space confined by crimson velvet. The curtain did not come all the way to the floor, and she watched their brown feet, flooding with a pool of yellow fabric as the dress was slipped off and then drinking up the yellow fabric until it was no longer on the floor, and there were only naked feet again.

Sophia stepped out, although nobody had told her to. She looked up at Madame K and smiled with nervous eyes and a body that was not used to being on display. She twirled around, and the hem of pale-yellow fabric spread out and then settled once more against the young girl's legs.

"Well," said Madame K, "it looks like Gabrielle will need to find something else to wear."

Gabrielle stuck her head out from the slit in the velvet ring and smiled up at Madame K, and then at the girl.

"Why don't you pick something out for me," she said to Sophia. "And you can wear that one out."

Sophia's lips began to turn up in a smile, but then they stopped. She brought her hand to her chest and then looked out the glass front that faced the ocean.

"What is it?" asked Madame K. Her face was pained. The dreamlike dance of the yellow dress had accelerated to such a velocity that its sudden halt carried consequences that were almost violent. All three women felt it. "What's wrong?"

"I—I don't have money," said the girl. She suddenly seemed like a child.

"Oh, don't worry about that!" said Madame K. "You can bring some later, can't you? You can wear it out now, and then bring some later. I'll hold your own clothes hostage."

"It shows too much skin," she said. "The congregation, I—I couldn't be seen in this. I'm sorry. I should go."

She began moving toward the door.

"But you're still wearing the dress," said Madame K, lingering on the word *dress*, as if by singing it she could somehow convince the girl of its necessity.

The girl looked down, as if surprised not only at her dress, but also at her body. She turned back toward the velvet curtain and was so desperate to be out of the dress that she ran back toward it and inside, and as Sophia ran, Madame K watched her face in profile, watched the jaw rise and fall and stretch the olive skin against her cheekbones. Madame K looked at the young girl and saw the runner's face. She turned away from the curtain, breathing hard, and when Sophia came out again, rushing to the door, Madame K called out to her.

"Wait," she said. Sophia's hand froze flat against the door. "It isn't in me to deprive such a pretty girl of such a pretty thing. Why don't you take it anyway. Think of it as a gift."

Gabrielle had come out from the curtain, once again wearing the yellow dress. She looked strangely up at Madame K, for she had known the woman to do many things, but to give a gift was never one of them.

"I couldn't," said Sophia from the door. "I could never wear it around my parents."

"There are plenty of places for a pretty girl to wear a pretty dress that are not around her parents."

"I couldn't go home with it."

"So don't go home with it. I'll have Gabrielle here leave it for you under the boardwalk. Would that be alright?"

Sophia looked down at her feet. "Where under the boardwalk?"

"Where Convention Hall juts out. Beneath the Anchor's Bend. You know it, don't you?"

Sophia nodded and went out.

* * *

"Gabby!" called Liam. He had been waiting on the street side of the store for her shift to end, and now came running around the back as she walked out onto the beach side. She did not slow down or even turn in his direction. She did not stop for the old lady who sold passes for beach access but marched passed her outstretched hand and down the stairs, onto the sand, stopping only to pull off her shoes when one short heel sunk low into the sand.

"Hey, Gabby!"

Gabby continued on in a straight line for the wooden pillars that held up Convention Hall. A paper bag with the yellow dress inside was in her one hand, and she held her shoes by their straps in the other. Both were clenched hard into fists and she muttered curses under her breath.

"Gabby!" said Liam. He caught up to her and grabbed one of her wrists, and as she spun around she raised her other hand as if to hit him. They looked at each other for some time, saying nothing, and eventually her shoulders sagged and her eyes softened.

"Come on," she said. They walked together in silence until they were underneath the Anchor's Bend. Gabrielle put the paper bag beside the northeast pillar, where Madame K had told Sophia it would be, and she paced back and forth as she spoke. When she was finished, Liam shook his head and laughed.

"Those Jew-girls just get anything they want. I bet she's got one of those houses over in Deal. You know the ones I mean."

"That isn't the point. It wasn't even her."

"I'll bet she's got one of those houses." He turned to look at the ocean and spat into the sand. "You know the ones."

"I'm talking about Miss K. I'm alright making the sales, but for a commission. I'm not there to give her gifts away. I've never felt like a servant before."

"You've never felt like a nigger before."

Liam spat again into the sand, and Gabby watched the spit fall and then collect sand into a darkened form that gathered and sat hovering the way that oil will in water. Liam kicked dry sand to cover it.

"I don't like it when you use that word," she said.

"Neither do most white people."

"Go to hell." She began to walk away and he walked after her.

"Me go to hell? You want to talk to me about how you get walked all over? What kind of job did you think it was, where you got to call your boss *Madame* and she makes you go by Gabri*elle* and flash your bracelets so that they think—'If she can afford it, so can I!' I mean, if they only knew!"

Gabby stopped and turned to face him. She pointed her shoes like a weapon in his direction.

"Knew what?" she said. "If they only knew what?"

Liam watched her, deciding whether or not to proceed.

"Knew what?" she said again. "Go on, knew what? You want to be a man and talk tough, don't quit now. Knew what?"

"Knew that your Daddy is richer than any of them! If they knew the things you could afford . . . And that's why you get so beat up when *Madame* makes you feel like that. Ask your Ma if she knows what it feels like. Cleaned floors for twenty years before your Daddy came along—you think she forgets? You go on and ask her about your day with *Madame K.* She won't blink twice before laughing your ass out of the house."

Gabby's eyes went flat and she looked at Liam now as if he were litter that had washed up before her.

"Don't you ever talk about my father, you understand?"

"Fine," he said. He laughed and shook his head. "That's fine. I won't talk about him at all. But if I'm allowed to talk about your job," he looked, looking for permission and getting it, "then I think you should quit. You don't need that money. I could sure as hell use the money, but I won't take a job like that. I can't figure why you take it."

"Maybe it's time you took a job like that."

"I make do just fine without it."

"Selling drugs isn't exactly a career."

"Only weed."

She squeezed his jaw between her fingers, and between her fingers his face became that of a child.

"Don't lie to me," she said. "It isn't only weed. I saw myself."

"That was one time. It's only weed, now. You can't even go to jail for that."

"Even if that was true, I think you could find a way."

She patted his cheek gently and then let go and began to walk away. Liam watched her hips sway as she walked. Her feet were light over the sand and left hardly any prints, and as he chased her he was aware of his own weight, and how deep were the impressions left by his own feet.

"And besides," he said. His tone was different now. "If you could sing a little better, then maybe our band—"

"My band," she said, unable to keep a smile from her face. "Bad drummers are a dime a dozen."

"And bad singers don't make a dime. If they did, maybe I wouldn't have to sell nothing at all."

"You find someone better to play with, you're free to go."

Liam walked backward just in front of Gabby and kept pace with her, so that they faced each other the whole time.

"When are you going to go out with me, anyway?"

"When are you going to stop asking me?"

"Never," said Liam, and smiled wide. They had come to the wooden steps which leaned up to the boardwalk. Liam spread his body wide to block her path for a moment, but seeing her eyebrows raised, he stepped politely aside and offered a mocking, low bow as she passed.

"Well then," she said. "At least we've got the same answer for one another's questions. Never."

"Well, as a loser's prize then—can I borrow your car? I need to get my kit down to the Saint before the show tomorrow."

"Don't lie to me. You need it to go sell something to someone." Gabby looked at Liam, and he confirmed her suspicion by inspecting his fingernails. She took her keys from her pocket but kept walking, and Liam followed behind and she spoke to him over her shoulder. "So who is it?"

"Some kid up in Long Branch," he said. "David Larkin."

Gabby came to a slow stop and turned to face Liam.

"What are you selling to David Larkin?"

"Just some weed," said Liam. He stuffed his hands in his pockets. "What—you know him?"

"Everybody knows him."

"Then you know he's got a whole lot of money. Why shouldn't I get in on that?"

Gabby crossed her arms over her chest and looked out toward the ocean.

"Long Branch isn't so far," she said. "Why don't you just walk?"

"Shit, it isn't so close either. And beside—you've got to walk through Allenhurst to get there. You ever see a nigger try to walk through Allenhurst?" Liam clapped his wrists together and took two heavy steps, as if being led away in cuffs.

"Is it any better driving?" she said.

"If I'm in a nice, clean car like you've got. If I wear a hat low over my eyes."

"Maybe you should get a ski mask as well."

"Trust me," he said. "I know what I'm doing."

"I hope you do," she said. She handed him the keys. "Better be only weed. I mean it. And don't be late tonight. And put down towels in the back so your cymbals don't cut into the leather."

"Anything else?"

"Did I say don't be late?"

"Sure did."

"Well, don't be late."

"Alright," he said. "I'll drive you home."

"No. I want to walk."

She walked away from Liam and could feel his eyes on her back. She knew he had stopped looking after her because she stopped thinking of herself as "Gabby." She walked past Madame K's, but did not look inside, and did not think of herself then as Gabrielle; she had to be inside the shop and on the clock for that. Nobody called her by her full name, which was Gabriella; to her mother she was Elle, to her friends she was

Gabby. Onstage and to herself, she was Ella, which is what her father had called her on the rare occasion that he had called her anything. She tried not to think of him, and that she thought of herself as Ella had nothing to do with her father. It was not even the name she liked best; it lacked the elegance of Gabrielle, the friendliness of Gabby, the exotic syllable of Gabriella, the simple grace of Elle. Ella was simply the name that she felt could best describe her, and as she turned off the boardwalk with her shoes still clutched in her hand, she thought of herself that way, and thought of her father, and walked home.

CHAPTER 4
Everything Else

I went down to the ocean and splashed some water on my face and found my half-drunk bottle of wine from the night before. It was still lodged where we had left it and there was something like the experience of déjà vu. I thought of drinking it for a moment but instead turned it out into the white wake. It stained the retreating tide purple for a moment and then it was gone and I felt that the night had passed from distant memory to dream. I got off the beach and walked down Allen Avenue. The houses here were small but well-kept and it seemed that everyone was growing rhododendrons.

"Well, well. If it isn't Casey Larkin."

I recognized the voice before I recognized the house or the person. Meredith Hawthorne had been a year above me in middle school but we'd been very close. She had been the closest thing I had to a sibling back then, including Davey. It had been before Davey and I were alright with one another.

In those days, Davey had lived with his mother and Joseph at their oceanside mansion in Long Branch, while I lived with my mother in a house that Joseph had bought for her in Allenhurst. Davey's mother was Joseph's wife, and Allenhurst was as close as she would allow him to keep his mistress. There was only the mile-long town of Deal to separate the two houses, but it did a fairly good job; I did not even meet Davey until I was eight years old, and did not go to live with them until three years later, when my mother decided that she'd had enough of being a mistress and headed to New York with the money she'd squeezed out of Joseph in order to try her hand at life as a single woman.

Meredith had grown up in the house next door to mine, and she lived there still with her mother. A large sun hat cast a shadow over Meredith's face but I could tell that she was smiling. She dropped a spade so that it stuck straight into the soft brown earth, and then stood there without moving for several seconds. I thought that probably she was counting seconds until the surprise of seeing me had gone away for her.

Meredith hated to be surprised. It was a repulsion that often got in the way of her being honest. If you said something that surprised her, she would respond with a phrase that at first seemed to be quick wit but was really only a cover, a tendency which had given her an unfair reputation in high school for having had a bad temper and a volatile character. I had once walked by her window in the evening and seen her looking in the mirror and speaking to herself; I had the impression then that she was repeating all the conversations that had surprised her and responding the way she would have liked to if she hadn't been so averse to appearing taken off guard. It was a sad way to be and it made Meredith sad to be that way, but it was more palatable to her than the alternative.

Meredith slipped between two hedges and out onto the sidewalk behind me. She held a garden hose in her right hand and she held it kinked so that not a drop of water came out. You got the sense that she was an expert at holding hoses in such a way. It was strange to see someone you grew up with doing such a domestic thing as gardening, and I felt a pang of guilt about where and how I'd woken up.

"Back from the dead," she said. She had a wonderful smile and I smelled soil when she kissed me on the cheek. "Or not quite, from the looks of it."

"I've gone the other way," I said, trying to be clever. "Only back to visit the dead."

"That's right. I was sorry to hear it."

"You lived too close to him to be sorry to hear it."

"Alright. I wasn't happy either, though, and that's more than you can say for a lot of people around these parts."

"Hardly the thing to say to a son of the dearly departed."

"Are you a son? I remember he had one son named David and then a bastard with some woman he brought down from the city . . . but I can't seem to remember this bastard's name."

"Good to see you haven't changed a bit."

If Meredith was saying things like that she hadn't heard about my mother. I had wondered before if anyone back here had kept tabs on her and I was happy to know they had not.

"Good to see you too. Second Larkin man I've seen today and it isn't even nine."

"Did Dave come around this morning?"

"He did."

"See him often?"

"Never, actually. But he thought you might have stopped by to visit while you were in town. If only a girl were so lucky. Said you were going to be late."

I had forgotten about the reading of the will but now I remembered. Or maybe I had not forgotten at all. It would not matter much whether or not I was there, and I would not have gone at all but if Davey was looking for me then it meant something to him.

"Do you have a car?" I asked.

* * *

Meredith's mother, Evelyn Hawthorne, had been something of a local celebrity once. She had run away from a convent in Ireland as a young girl and found her way to the United States. To hear her tell it, she had married Peter Hawthorne to get herself a citizenship but truly she had loved him and when he died she kept his name but gave away most of his money. When Meredith and I were in elementary school Evelyn established herself as the primary gardener in all of Monmouth County. She would walk us home from school sometimes and you got the sense that she had shaped the streets specifically so that she and Meredith would be happy walking through them. It was as if she were attempting to replicate the setting of a dream that she remembered and the town became an extension of her mind.

In the few years after Evelyn had gotten sick, the colors became brighter, as if she were combating the darkness of her condition with the vibrancy of flowers. They did not begin to fade until she was no longer well enough to do the work. For a long while she would go along the sidewalks in her electric wheelchair and give free advice toward gardens that had begun to abandon her fantasy, but it proved impossible for people with lawns in reality to maintain them in accordance with the specifications of a dream. Evelyn was seen less and less and eventually she was not seen at all. It seemed that over the past few years, Meredith had begun to take responsibility for reinstating her mother's old vision. As we drove, she pointed out certain houses and the patterns of ivy on their walls or the arrangements of flowerbeds on their lawn.

She was still parked outside when the executor left Joseph Larkin's—now David Larkin's—beachfront estate in Long Branch. Her car was blocked into the long circular drive by the group of hopeful cars before it. They all had the bright yellow plates of New York and they all left quickly. Nobody was pretending to mourn any longer. Only two names had been mentioned in the will; David's and mine.

Davey's lot had been straightforward. He was heir to the late Joseph Larkin's real estate endeavors, his various equity holdings, a large sum of cash and government bonds and, of course, the oceanfront mansion. They called it a mansion although it really was not so big; I suspected this had very little to do with the late owner's modesty and everything to do with the fact that he never considered it necessary to provide living space for anyone but himself.

Everything else he had left to me. I had not expected to inherit a dime, and so the fifty-thousand in accounts that were included in "everything else" made me feel as if he were still playing games, watching from beyond the grave to see if I would take the money. I would. There was no question about that. I needed it badly. I decided immediately that I would take the money so that there would be no illusion of a battle that I'd eventually lose. It was the rest of it that I did not know what to make of.

"Did you know about any house in Asbury?" Davey asked, once everyone except Meredith had left. David was eager to invite people into his new home and Meredith and I were the only ones present. The three of us walked through the empty house and through the yard and went past where it broke onto the sand. We walked out halfway toward the water.

Davey turned around and looked at his new house. It was dominating and cruel in the way it forced its presence on the land. It was everything Davey was not but maybe many of the things that he wanted to be. I got the sense that he would be living in its shadow for a long time.

"I don't know," I said. "He never talked to you about it?"

Davey shook his head. "Who knew he ever stepped foot in Asbury? He wasn't exactly a man of the people."

"What's that about Asbury?" said Meredith. Her house in Allenhurst was one town over, two if you counted the three streets that made up Loch Arbour.

"Casey's a proud new homeowner," said Davey. Meredith was appropriately stunned. I wondered what I looked like. "Will he keep it is the question."

So then it was plain on my face. I did not want any part of my father's house in Asbury Park. I'd had it to the brim with Joseph Larkin when he'd been alive and it was not a very tall glass. I did not want anything to do with him now that he was dead. There is nothing to the wisdom that the dead are absolved of everything. Fuck absolution. In dying, he had done the only thing he could have to get forgiveness out of anyone. He would not get it out of me.

"I don't know," I said. "He probably made the investment when they began to develop the boardwalk and forgot all about it. It's a shit part of town, anyway. Off the waterfront, the property probably isn't worth the taxes you pay on it."

Davey laughed. "You'll keep it."

"Will you keep this?"

"Yes. You'll keep yours too."

"Probably. The son of a bitch."

"Father of one too."

"Yes," I said, pointing. "One, two."

Davey laughed and he slapped me hard across the face. "Just one, Case."

I tasted blood in my mouth and raised my hand to my lip. I smiled and felt the sand give way beneath the weight of my feet as I hopped right to left. Davey played along. We bounced and weaved and kept our fists up like boxers. Suddenly we were children again. I jabbed with my left and caught Davey in the chin and his head shot back. He balled his fists tight and swung high at me with his right hand but I easily ducked under and hit his gut with my right and then his rib with my left. Meredith screamed for us to stop. It must have looked very serious.

We did not stop but maybe I should have. I was faster than Davey but my fists could barely move him and I got the sense that each bit of contact hurt his pride more than his body. He was guessing with his slow, lumbering fists, but eventually he guessed correctly and I moved into the path of a right cross which knocked me to the ground and blurred my vision.

Now I really tasted blood. I spat it out into the sand. Davey was laughing and I was laughing too. A string of crimson saliva fell out with the laughter and for a moment it spanned the gap between my lips and the sand and then it broke and fell into the sand and I covered it and rolled onto my back and laughed.

"What the fuck are you two doing?" Meredith rushed to me and held my eyelids open with her fingers. "Are you alright? Casey?"

"I'm alright," I said. "Just a strong morning wind."

"What the hell is going on?"

"A breeze," I said, panting, "a breeze off the sea. Or maybe from the west. It was too light to tell."

"Do you think he's concussed?" said Meredith. "What the fuck, Dave?"

"Don't you know Meredith?" said Davey. He was breathing hard and all laughter. He had won and he knew it. "Your boy there just closed on a beautiful new home in historic Asbury Park."

Meredith looked at me. I nodded. I had lost fairly and in the morning I would go.

CHAPTER 5

A House on Roseland Lane

Within a year of Joseph Larkin's first stroke, it was generally agreed upon that the thing had improved him. As notorious for his depravity as he was for his fabulous wealth, his arrival at Monmouth Medical Center had rippled through the hospital. By the end of his second day there, the nurses and even some of the doctors were finding excuses to pass through his room. They went in with their uniforms slightly undone or more rouge on their cheeks than usual in the hopes of drawing out of him the sort of things that they expected. He had been placed in a bad, semiprivate room because he had never bothered with health insurance and had been unconscious since the stroke. In the hospital cafeteria, it was said that the man considered himself to be immortal.

Joseph had only been to the hospital one other time—nearly twenty years before, for tetanus. He had not been vaccinated since childhood. Walking on the beach one day, the rusted edge of an iron nail had gone through his foot and he had thought nothing of it. All he had done was run water over the deep puncture in the sole of his foot and then dress it with a band aid. His maid had found him on the floor a week later in the throes of a spasm.

"Didn't you think about tetanus when you stepped on the nail?" the doctor had asked him. Joseph had described the rust vividly. He had understood what he had stepped on.

"It's 1996," Joseph had told the doctor. "People in America do not get tetanus."

"That's true, but it's because they keep up vaccinations."

Joseph Larkin could not believe that an ailment would have the audacity to affect him if it had no statistical basis upon which to do so. On waking three days after his stroke to the news that he had had one, he wanted to say that it could not be so, for his father's circulation had been good and he understood these things to be hereditary.

But it was an incredulity that he could not voice, because upon waking he could not speak. The severity of anoxia in the wrong area of his brain had killed off the pathways that linked his mind to his tongue. He sat there for one week in utter silence, and eventually agreed—by moving his eyes up and down—to have a special therapist called in from New York. When she came, she did not ask him to try to speak, as the others had, but instead asked him to read aloud from a board. He could not do it, but something must have stirred in him because his face, for the first time since the stroke, showed signs of hope, and when the therapist asked if she should come again the next day, he nodded his head. She returned without cards or written words, carrying only a stereo. She played him what songs she had, but he did not know them, and he could not speak; still, in his eyes there was something like hope.

When the older of Joseph's two sons—David Larkin—had met the therapist, and understood what it was that she was trying to do, he became angry, as if she should have understood his father better. The problem, he told her, was that Joseph Larkin hated music, especially popular music. The only thing he'd ever listened to was jazz.

The therapist came back with Thelonious Monk and Duke Ellington and Billie Holiday, and Joseph Larkin kept his eyes shut throughout the instrumentals and as the vocals on any piece began he opened his mouth and sang along with it. For hours he sang and his son watched him and smiled.

"The brain has a way of getting around its broken places," the therapist said. "Speech might be slow in returning, if it ever does. But if you can sing words, what's the difference?"

"Leave," Joseph had said to her, in such a brief and quiet voice that she could not tell if he had sung it or said it, though she knew in her heart that he had sung it. It was the only way for him to get out his words.

For several days, his singing was tied to his jazz. If a record played, he could sing a sentence to the melody. In a way, he mimicked his surroundings, became something as transparent as glass. Amidst song, he sang; in silence, he was silent. Most of the things he had ever spoken were bitter, and he felt that he could not sing bitter things. Eventually, it meant more to Joseph that he should communicate than that he should be serious, and he sang to anybody who would listen.

The necessity to sing had softened Joseph Larkin. First it softened his words, and then it softened his intention. His bitterness and anger had melted away, and anybody who had known him both before and after the stroke began to think of it less as a stroke and more as an exorcism. Had he had more time to live after the stroke, he might have changed the world's opinion of him, but his meanness before had been such that few were willing to stop in and hear him sing. He only ever had one visitor at a time, and mostly his bedside was empty. Before dying of a second stroke two years after the first, his only constant visitors were the older of his two sons and the maid who had found him writhing in pain during his spell of tetanus twenty years before. Her name was Tamera Walker.

* * *

Not a week after Joseph Larkin's death, Tamera Walker sat at the kitchen table of a house on Roseland Lane. It was a small, comfortable house that Joseph Larkin had bought for her to live in, and she sat at the kitchen table now and listened to his jazz music and thought of his voice. Her fingers traced patterns through grains of salt that were scattered on the table. Her eyes were closed, but she was not sleeping. A strange hum welled up from her throat and merged with the soundwaves of jazz on the air. She drank her mourner's cup of rum, and rings on its surface jumped and danced each time the bass drum came. In her fingers was a large brown cigar—a Cuban. One of his. She watched its embers climb up toward her lips each time she sucked the smoke in, and then she blew out shapes or rings like an artist or a witch, as if the embers had sent a message to the air by way of cigar, and lips, and smoke. She watched the shapes rise up and scatter on the air and drift toward the ceiling, where a yellow condom was stretched over the smoke alarm to keep it from detecting. Through the yellow latex, she watched the red light of the alarm blink and pulse and illuminate and die.

It was a hot day in June, but she would not turn on the air, and so the space of the kitchen was thick and hot, and the sound fell across it like ripples in tropical water.

She almost did not hear the doorbell.

When she finally heard it, it was like a remembered sound, from memory or dream. It shook her from her trance. She watched the red light blink twice. Off and on. Off and on and off. She rose and went to the door, and the smoke followed her from the room, drawn by her gravity. She knew that it came with her, and she was glad for it; she was not an easy woman to anger, but she was angry now. Seven days had not yet passed. She constructed in her mind the things she would yell to make this person go away. She constructed them in her mind and she swished the rum across her lips and tongue to warm them up for speech, but as soon as she opened the door, the words and anger all left her.

"Oh," she said. And then: "You look just like him." She looked past him, toward the street, and smiled. "You even drive his car."

Casey Larkin stood there, trying to decide if he had the correct house. He looked back at the car parked before the mailbox, and then down at the paper in his hand, and then up at Tamera Walker, and then leaned back and checked the number above the door. Tamera Walker stepped out and did not close the door behind her. Through it, the faint echo of Chet Baker met them on the porch.

"You look just like him," she repeated.

She reached out her hand, as if to touch his face, but then something stopped her.

"You're not David," she said. She had been at the funeral. She had watched David speak. "He didn't tell me there was another."

"No," said Casey. "He wouldn't have told you."

"Well, you'd better come in."

"Is this 31 Roseland Lane?"

Tamera looked back at Casey and then turned into the house. Casey followed and closed the door behind him. The temperature was higher in the house—the smoke and heaviness of air outweighed the sunlight. They sat together at the kitchen table.

"Drink?" Tamera asked him.

"There's probably no better way to honor the man's memory," said Casey. He looked down at his knuckles, embarrassed.

"He never drank around me," said Tamera. She put an empty glass in front of Casey and poured in two inches of rum.

"You must not have been around him much," said Casey. He took a drink as Tamera sat down. She sank into her chair, and never took her eyes from his face. It was like she was watching a ghost.

"What are you here about?"

"Well, you know Joseph Larkin died," he said. He fumbled for his words and put the deed to 31 Roseland Lane on the table. He adjusted it to face Tamera. She did not look down but brought the rum to her lips. Casey spoke again. "This house is 31 Roseland Lane. He left it to me."

Tamera stopped. She did not jerk, or offer any indication that she was surprised, but only froze, as if she had come face to face with the great Medusa. And then the stillness passed her.

"Oh," she said. "I hadn't thought about that."

"Well, you see—"

"Mr. Larkin?"

"Casey."

"Casey. Your father has not been in the ground yet seven days. There will be time to speak of business later. The house is going nowhere."

Casey turned the deed back toward himself and fingered the outlines of the paper. He tapped the top page twice and then slid his hand across the surface and off the surface and toward his drink. He finished it. "My Funny Valentine" had begun on the record, and it felt that there was a third person in the room.

"Alright," he said. "Should I come back then?"

"If you like."

He looked around as if he would not at all like to come back. He did not understand this place or its connection to his father or the dark woman who sat there filled with smoke and rum.

"Nobody's going to keep you here," said Tamera. She picked up the bottle of rum from the table and poured another two inches into Casey's glass. She watched his face. "Nobody's going to kick you out neither."

As if on cue, a loud stomp came from upstairs. The whole ceiling shook and pressed a wave of smoke to fall down off the ceiling, toward the table. Tamera took a long puff of her cigar.

"Might be I speak too soon," she said. A smile came to her lips and her teeth flashed white against the darkness of her skin.

There was a patter on the stair—a delicate noise that did not seem to match the weight of whatever had caused the sound. It sounded like a dog's footsteps, quickly descending. It grew louder and then there was a girl standing in the kitchen. Tamera looked between her daughter and her visitor, and for the first time, Casey saw her looking truly surprised.

"Oh," Tamera said again. "I didn't think of that."

"Think of what?" Casey began to say, but he did not get to

finish. There was no need to finish. He watched the girl and the girl watched him, and he thought that there was nothing more accurate to say about the appearance of her than she was beautiful in the way that you would want your daughter or your sister to be beautiful; that there was nothing inviting about the way she looked at you—in fact, a certain coldness seemed to radiate from her—but it was a fierce look and it was beautiful. He did not take his eyes from the girl and the girl did not take her eyes from him. He thought for a moment that she looked like his own mother. But his mother's eyes had been warm and brown and this girl's eyes were a pale blue that stood out like a single spot of color in a black-and-white film. Casey knew those eyes well. They were his eyes. They were his father's eyes. He recoiled from them and when he did, he understood. It was not his mother that she looked like. It was his father—her father too. She had worked it out as well.

"You aren't David," she said. Only her lips moved when she spoke. "I had half-expected David."

"I'm Casey."

"Who's your mother?" she said.

Tamera stood up and turned to look at her daughter. "I don't know how she gets to be so rude, Mr. Larkin."

"It's Casey," he said.

"Who's your mother?" the girl asked again. "He was only married once."

"Not a woman he was married to."

Tamera looked down, but the girl acted as if her mother did not exist. She nodded and stepped forward. There was nothing delicate about the way she held her hand out for him to shake—her palm arched back and her veins jumped.

"Ella," she said, once Casey had given her his hand. She

squeezed it as if she was trying to hurt him but they held one another's hands for a long time. Finally, Ella looked down at the table and saw the deed sitting there, and saw the address, and saw the name. She turned to her mother.

"Well, now it's happened. You old fool."

Tamera stared at her daughter and both their lips curled in the same way. Casey thought that one was going to hit the other. Tamera's eyes went down as she turned back to Casey.

"If you'll excuse me," she said. "A woman has the right to mourn."

"Don't bother," said Ella. "I'm going out."

She took two steps toward the door, and the smoke from the tip of Tamera's cigar followed her body. Suddenly, she stopped and turned to Casey.

"How did you get here?" she asked.

"I drove," he said. He raised his hand where the keyring was around his finger.

"That's good. You can drive me."

"Alright," he said.

"Goodbye, Casey," said Tamera. "It was nice to meet you. Come again."

By the time Casey reached the front door, Ella was already halfway to the car. They drove in a funny sort of silence, broken only by the low din of music; the car had belonged to their father, and his jazz still played from its stereo.

"Where am I taking you?" he asked.

"The Saint. You know it?"

"Sure, on Main," said Casey. "Anyone good playing to-night?"

"*I* think so, but I'm biased."

"Friend of yours?"

Chet Baker was coming on over the stereo and Ella reached forward and increased the volume.

"*My funny valentine . . .*" she sang. By the way her eyes were laughing, he understood her perfectly well.

"You're a singer, then?" he asked.

"That's right."

"Any good?"

"Would I have told you if I wasn't?"

Ella smiled and turned away from Casey. She raised the volume even higher and leaned her forehead against the window.

"*Your looks are laughable,*" she sang. "*Unphotographable . . .*"

"*Yet, you're my favorite work of art.*" Casey spoke quietly without truly singing. It was as if he was speaking to himself.

"So he got you hooked on this stuff as well?" said Ella.

"I wouldn't say he did. It was just around is all."

"It's alright. Like the way you learn in school that Robert Frost was a real asshole but you're supposed to read 'Birches' anyway. Isn't that right?"

"Something like that," said Casey. He hummed along for a measure. "That's giving the man more credit than he's due. It isn't as if he wrote it."

"Does David go for this sort of music?"

"Are we going to talk about David?"

Ella smiled and looked away from Casey again. "*Is your mouth a little weak . . .*" She shook her head slightly. "Don't you like talking about your brother?"

"Half brother," said Casey. He adjusted his grip on the steering wheel and looked at her briefly out of the corner of his eye.

"Half," she said. "Same as me."

"Same as you."

"Don't you like him?"

"I love him, in a way," he said. "If that's what you're asking. But when you're taken care of so often you start to get used to it."

"And was he taken care of so often?"

"Yes."

"And were you?"

"I'm not complaining," said Casey. "I lived with him for a while, you know. With him and Davey and Davey's mother."

"What's his mother like?"

"I've never met a person I liked less," he said. And then, in an almost apologetic way: "Which is not to say that I envied her position."

"And what's your mother like?"

They came to a red light and Casey slowed the car to a halt.

"Yours was the only one that came to the service," said Casey. "I wondered what she was doing there."

"You mean you wondered what a Black woman who looks like my mother was doing at a service for your father?"

"That's exactly what I mean," he said. "And I don't remember seeing you there."

Ella tapped her fingers against the window and nodded.

"I'm happy that you exist," she said.

"That's awfully nice of you."

"I always knew about David, but that was different. He isn't the same as us."

She curled toward him and watched his face as he watched the road.

"I'm looking at you more than you're looking at me," she said. "Aren't you happy that I exist too?"

"I'm driving," said Casey.

They were quiet for some time and she did not take her eyes from him. She watched the veins jump in his hands.

"What are you going to do about the house?" she asked him.

"I don't know. I haven't figured anything out."

When they came to another stoplight, he turned to her.

"I'm not asking you to leave," he said.

Ella smiled but looked straight ahead, out from the windshield.

"Don't tell my mother that just yet," she said. "If you tell her now, she'll be worried that you'll change your mind. Someone who can decide to give up a house in the course of twenty minutes is liable to want it again in the course of a day. You should decide before telling her anything. Maybe you'll keep it and let her live there. Maybe you'll keep it and kick her out."

"You don't live there?"

"I do, for now. I'm off to college in the fall. Your timing isn't bad."

"It wasn't my timing," said Casey.

"That's right. It's funny. I don't really believe he's dead. Nothing feels any different. Someone spends so much time away and it's difficult to attach any sort of significance to their being gone."

"Did you like him very much? Your mother seems to have known a different Joseph than I did."

"She wanted to know a different Joseph than was there. He wanted her to also, at the end. He almost wanted to be really different."

"Well," said Casey. "At least now she'll understand. He's the kind to leave the house she lived in to me."

Ella looked at him.

"She won't think twice about that," she said. "She was offered that house plenty. He drew up the papers the minute he bought it. It was hers to take, and she didn't."

"Why not?"

"Oh, I can only guess. I think it would've made her feel like a whore to take his money. I guess a lot of people assumed it anyway. He offered her cars and jewelry and a better house—anything she wanted. I think she only took this one because of me. And afterward, she was there any time he needed anything. It was like she was working off a debt."

"You would've taken the house?" Casey asked.

"Yes," she said. She seemed suddenly angry. "And a better one too. I took the car. I took the jewelry. Why not?" Her eyes thinned as she stared out the windshield, and repeated: "Why not? And I'll tell you another thing. He promised to pay for my tuition. I'll expect that money still."

"I'll talk to David about it."

"Well don't look so disgusted. If he promised you money and never gave it, wouldn't you take it? Wouldn't you?"

"Yes," said Casey. "He left me some money in the will. I thought of not taking it for a minute. It seemed like a good 'fuck you.'"

"But?"

"But that isn't the way to say 'fuck you.' You take the money and you do what you want with it and you don't think about where it came from."

"That's right," said Ella. "That's right. We're the same. Now I half believe that you really might not keep the house. We're the same."

They had arrived at the Saint. It was a small theater on the ground floor of a run-down building on Main Street. Two large openings in the beige stucco wall were filled in with glass bricks, so that from the outside at night you could see only the red and blue stage lights glowing through the walls.

"I told you I wouldn't keep it," said Casey.

"Yes, you did. But now I half believe you."

Casey was slow in bringing the car to a halt.

"Aren't family members supposed to trust one another?" he said.

Ella's tan fingers ran along the door's leather toward the latch. She turned to him as she opened the door.

"The entire basis of our relationship presents strong evidence to the contrary."

"And what is the basis of our relationship?" asked Casey.

"Well," said Ella, her eyes out the window on the beige stucco of the Saint. "We can drop the 'half' if you like and simply say that you're my brother."

She froze with one foot out the door and half-turned her face toward Casey, waiting for him to respond.

"No," he said quietly. "I don't think we should drop the 'half.'"

"I don't think so either."

She stepped out of the car and closed the door, but then turned back and leaned down into the open window.

"We go on tonight at nine thirty," she said. "You should come. Bring that brother of yours too."

"He's busy," said Casey.

"You don't need to hide me away. I'd like to meet him."

"It isn't that," said Casey. "As a matter of fact, I'm busy too."

"You're lying." Ella's voice had changed and her whole upper body leaned into the car with the force of her words and it was as if she were spitting. "I can always tell when somebody's lying. Don't laugh."

"Sorry. Only, you sounded like him just then."

Ella's eyes went flat and a thin smile spread across her lips. "I don't take that as a compliment."

"I didn't offer it as one," he said. They looked at each other for a while and then Casey stared down at his knuckles on the steering wheel. "When's the next show?"

"July fifteenth," she said. "They cut all the small shows around the fourth. Too much money at stake. It'll all be E Street cover bands for the next two weeks."

"Well, maybe you'll meet Davey before that."

Ella shrugged and tapped the hood of the car twice.

"I thought we weren't going to talk about David," she said.

As she walked away from the car, Casey watched the movement of her hips and the way her hair swung. The walls of the Saint were beige stucco and the door was covered in stickers and as soon as Ella opened it, the sound of music rushed out.

"Let's not pretend you're thinking about acoustics," said Casey aloud. "This is the sort of turmoil he'd counted on when he left you the house. And you're falling for it." He took the car out of park and headed for the exit.

"No," he thought, no longer speaking aloud. "There are a great many things you can accuse the man of but this is not one of them."

CHAPTER 6
Meredith

"Well," said Meredith. She looked down at her phone. "I don't think Casey's coming."

She sat with Davey at Pop's Garage Bar on the boardwalk. It was called "the garage" because the back wall came up in the summer so that the bar spilled onto the boardwalk. It was long past sunset now but the air of mid-July stayed hot even through the night. The only cool wind came off the ocean, and even then, in flowing over the beach it picked up all the heat that the sun had left in the sand and by the time it reached the boardwalk and the bar it was like a breath of warm dry air.

"No," said Davey. His words were slurred. "I don't think so either."

Davey sat in the stool that had by now become his own, with his elbows on the bar and his fingers curled around a tumbler of whiskey. The wooden bar was covered with a thick sheet of tin and Davey looked down into the half shadow, half reflection that he cast in its surface. Davey reached into the breast pocket of his shirt and placed two pills in front of him on the bar. He stared down at them and then put one into his mouth, swallowed it, and crushed the other beneath the flat surface of the base of his tumbler, twisting the glass back and forth until the pill was a flat crust of powder against the tin. He ran his finger along the bottom side of his glass and licked it clean, and then held his glass just beyond the bar and swept all of the powder into it and used a mixing straw to stir it into his dark whiskey and went back to drinking it. It was as if he had decided that Pop's Garage was an imaginary place without any power of law, and so there was no need for discretion. He drank quickly, as if he was afraid that his drink might evaporate on the warm summer air.

The bartender had looked away when Davey took the pills out, but now he came back.

"Another one, Dave?" he said.

"You understand," said Meredith. "That he won't be able to keep spending money here if you kill him, don't you? He's had enough to tranquilize a small horse. I think we ought to call it a night."

"I've seen him drink enough to kill an elephant and walk out of here in a straight line," said the bartender. Davey was drunk enough that both Meredith and the bartender had the impression that they could speak about him as if he was not there. "A small horse is nothing to worry about."

"One more," said Davey. He tapped the bar twice with his finger.

The bartender smiled bitterly at Meredith. "Coming right up," he said.

She sighed. "I guess make it two," she said. With her finger, she poked Davey in the middle of his breast pocket. "What are those?"

Davey turned to her and suddenly did not seem to be so drunk any more.

"I'm honestly not sure," he said. "But I'll let you know in about five minutes."

"You're not sure?"

"Somebody left them at the house. A lot of people have been over at the house . . ."

"They're called freeloaders, Dave. You ought to kick them out some time."

The bartender came back with their drinks and Davey did not even let him put it on the bar, but took it directly from the bartender's hands, hurrying to get his own fingers wrapped around the glass.

"That's what Casey said. He'll probably get them out." He took a long drink. "Casey's like that."

"Well, it won't help much if he's in the city all the time."

"He'll be home for a few weeks. Didn't he tell you?"

"No," said Meredith. She took a sip of her whiskey. "No, he didn't."

"He talked to his boss and took some time off. Six weeks or something like that. And do you know what he said when I asked him how he swung it? He says: 'My boss's father is still alive. He can't argue. If his father was dead he'd understand that there isn't anything to mourning but a few bad hangovers.'"

"That's sentimental," she said, shaking her head. "That's what I love about Casey is that he's so sentimental."

Davey smiled and looked up at Meredith.

"I didn't know you still loved him at all."

"What do you mean, still?" she said. She took a drink of her whiskey and wished that it was cold. "Casey and I were never like that."

She checked the time on her phone again. Davey smiled into his drink.

"You think he still might come," he said. "You don't like me or drinking enough to sit here just the two of us if you thought Casey wasn't coming."

Meredith had lifted the glass to her lips but now set it down again.

"What makes you say that?"

Davey looked down into his drink and turned it so that the surface shifted with the light.

"That's just always how it was, wasn't it?" he said. "It was you and Casey together and then me. It was alright when you were neighbors, but even when he came to live with us, it was still you and him together and then me. Well, now it's Casey and Gabby and then us. I'm sorry you got thrown in on my side."

Meredith smiled, but she did not look at Davey. "That's alright," she said. "There isn't a better side to be on than yours."

Davey's voice was not so drunk, but Meredith did not think that he would remember their discussion in the morning.

"What did you think of her?" she asked, still not looking at him.

"Of Gabrielle? I liked her. I've only met her twice but I liked her. At the same time, I didn't. It's like they've formed a sort of team. Maybe it wasn't them that formed it. I don't know. Casey was always forming teams."

"You had plenty of teams of your own."

Davey leaned his head in her direction, as if he could pour his words from his skull into her lap instead of having to speak them. He tapped his breast pocket. "Freeloaders," he said.

"I didn't mean only that," she said. "I hear you've teamed up with every girl south of Sandy Hook."

"Yeah," said Davey. He nodded and spoke emphatically, as if he needed it to be true. "Yeah, maybe I have."

But his bravado was short-lived and he quickly deflated and stared back into his drink. Meredith gave him an encouraging elbow to the ribs, but felt ridiculous as she did. The bartender smiled down into the cash register—maybe mocking her, maybe not—and Meredith felt ashamed. She felt that she was trying to pry information out of Davey, but also felt powerless to stop it.

"I don't think he wants me to meet her," she said. She spoke quietly, so that the bartender could not hear her.

Davey's eyebrows came together, and she could not tell whether he was considering her words or simply making faces in his reflection on the surface of his drink.

"She looks like him," he said finally. "Like Dad."

"Well, that explains why Casey likes her. If she looks like Joseph, she looks like Casey. If ever a boy loved a mirror. Same goes for you, I guess. Hey, I'm talking to you."

She poked Davey in the ribs and he looked up from his drink.

"Are you listening to me?" she said. "Or are you too in love with the boy in your mirror?"

"What?" said Davey. He suddenly seemed sober. "What boy?"

"Never mind," said Meredith. She sighed and looked down at her phone. "I think we ought to call it a night. He isn't coming. Why don't we raincheck for tomorrow."

"I can't tomorrow," said Davey. He looked at her fully now and she had the impression that he was trying very hard to focus.

"Hot date?" she said.

"Just a friend visiting," he said. He finished his drink. "From college."

Meredith followed Davey's lead and finished her drink, too. She winced at the taste and shook her head.

"I sometimes forget that you went to college," she said.

"Everybody seems to forget it," he said. "Sometimes I forget it myself."

The bartender was not facing them, but Davey stretched his fingers out toward his back, as if they could somehow communicate through another medium entirely.

"Anyway," he continued. "It's only a friend from abroad. That wasn't really like college at all. More like a long vacation."

"I could use one of those," said Meredith. "Well, anyway, we can all go out if you want."

Davey did not say anything and the bartender came back.

"Come on," said Meredith. "No more for him."

"Oh, I'm fine," said Davey. His skin was shining with the red light of the bad neon bar signs, and Meredith could not tell if he was flushed or only reflecting.

The bartender took another glass and put it down on the side of Davey where it would be out of Meredith's reach. He poured it full of Jameson and left the bottle on the bar.

"They love me here, Mer," said Davey. His voice was deeper and sharper now, as if he were making a conscious effort to sound sober and untouchable. "They'll give me a drink any time."

"Yeah, well," said Meredith loudly enough that the bartender could hear. She felt that her conversation with Davey had come to an end; now the bartender was part of it too. "That's a perk of spending ten thousand dollars a week at the same shitty bar. The bartenders start to love you. Finish that and let's go, yes?"

"Yes," said Davey. And then: "No."

He had begun to stand up but then had stopped and sank back into his seat. An ugly smile had spread across his face and his eyes moved to the far side of Meredith, where a girl had just walked in and taken a seat at the bar.

"Oh, Jesus," said Meredith. "Really?"

But Davey had sat back down and so she sat back down beside him. She turned slightly to watch the girl the way that Davey watched her. A sudden urge came over her to understand the hunger in Davey's expression, the lust he could feel upon sight alone that was so exaggerated that it seemed nearly staged. Davey was always extravagant in his desire for girls and she longed to understand it. It was like a drug whose effects she wanted to know, and with the looseness that the drink of whiskey allowed her, she drank in the girl's figure without shame.

The girl was pretty—of that there was no question, but she looked too formal to be in this bar. She sat with her shoulders square and her legs crossed and she tapped the bar twice with her fingers. "Can I see a menu?" she asked the bartender. He went to get one, although it was not the sort of place where patrons requested the small, laminated menus that were sandwiched between two bottles, stuck together by a film of grime. The girl's voice was confident, but it was a practiced sort of confidence, as if the girl had practiced entering a bar and ordering a drink—as if the girl had taken notes on how one should act at a bar from an old movie. That's it, thought Meredith, she's never been to a bar before.

"How old are you?" Meredith asked her. The bartender pretended not to hear.

"I'm twenty-two," said the girl.

"That's right. You're twenty-two because everybody who fakes it says that they're twenty-one, so you figured you'd be clever and be twenty-two. Isn't that right?"

"No," said the girl, but she stammered now and her voice was quiet. "It's just my age."

"What year were you born?" said Meredith.

"Oh, leave her alone, Mer," said Davey. "Let her have some fun." Davey leaned forward so that he could look past Meredith and speak to the girl. "What are you drinking?"

"A—a sea breeze," she said.

"Tony," Davey called to the bartender. "A sea breeze. One sea breeze for the beauty in the yellow dress." He turned back to the girl in the pale-yellow dress. "One sea breeze coming right up."

"Don't you make that fucking drink," said Meredith. "I'll call the cops. I swear to god I will."

The bartender walked toward them without looking at Davey.

"Alright," he said, looking at the girl in the yellow dress. "I'm going to need to see some ID."

The girl pretended to sift through her purse, and then raised her hand to her mouth in mock surprise. "It must have fallen out."

"OK, well when it falls back in, come back. Until then, I'm going to have to ask you to leave."

She began to walk out, but Davey stuck his arm out to

intercept her, and he wrapped it around her waist and pulled her in toward himself.

"Oh, come on, Tony," said Davey. "Get the girl a drink. She can have one if I say so, can't she?"

"Not without an ID, she can't," he said, with a hint of regret. He did not like to see the young girl or her money turned down. The bartender looked up at Meredith. "I wouldn't want the cops called."

"Oh, I'm awfully sorry to be such a downer," she said with her hand over her heart. She turned to the girl. "I'm awfully sorry."

Davey held the girl close to him and she did nothing to resist the force exerted by his arm. She inspected him up close the way a child will put her face to the glass in an aquarium, as if protected by some separating plane. The whites of her eyes shone against her dark olive skin, and her breath was so deliberate that it seemed to Meredith that she was trying to commit the smell of Davey to memory.

"Davey," said Meredith. She forced her fingers into the space between Davey's forearm and the girl's body and pried his grip loose. "She's just a kid, Davey. Let her go."

Davey was slow in looking away from the girl in the yellow dress, and he was slower in releasing her. But slowest of all was her willingness to move away, and though there was nothing left to keep her there, her body remained pressed against his until Meredith put her fingers there, too, and gently separated them.

The girl looked at Meredith as if she was waking from a dream, and Meredith thought that her wide and dark eyes looked like a deer's caught in headlights.

"Go home," said Meredith quietly. "You'll have plenty of time for this sort of thing."

With one more look at Davey, the girl spun away. Meredith watched the hem of her yellow skirt spread into a wide arc as she turned and then flatten as the girl moved quickly out into the darkness.

"Meredith," said Davey in a slow drawl. "Why do you have to ruin everything."

"It's just my nature. Alright, let's get you home. Let's get you in a taxi."

They left the bar and walked out to the street. Meredith jogged ahead to catch a passing cab, and while it slowed down she turned to watch Davey catch up.

"Well, he wasn't lying," she said to him. "You can still walk straight."

"Yeah, well," said Davey. He was calm without the girl there. "Just don't get me started on the alphabet."

"You take this," she said, holding the door open.

"Why don't I drop you on the way?"

"That's alright. I want to walk. You're alright alone?"

"I'm alright. Night, Mer."

He kissed her on the cheek and ducked into the cab. Meredith watched its red taillights until it turned off Ocean Avenue and its yellow body was swallowed by the night. She went back to the boardwalk and walked along slowly, listening to the hollow sound of each footstep. A warm breeze blew out toward the ocean and even though she could see the white crests of waves crashing and breaking against the slick line of sand, the sound of it was muted, more like the echo of rushing blood that a seashell will make when held up to your ear than anything like a real ocean.

She thought about Casey and felt a certain tightness in her chest. It was a familiar feeling—the same one she'd had when he had told her that he was going all the way to North Carolina for college. She had not thought of that conversation for a long time, but she remembered it now as if it had happened yesterday. "Well," she had told him then, speaking in her instinctive rudeness that was meant to cover surprise, "you've always been one for loose blondes, and I'm sure you'll get your fill in the south," and then she had turned away and walked home, thinking *Yes, nobody could think that somebody with a joke about loose blondes on the tip of their tongue could be any sort of fragile*, but she had felt fragile and had gone back to his house that night, had gone tapping on his window the way they had when they were children. She had looked down at her hands while she spoke, because she had practiced reading her words from a notecard she had written them on, and she had tried them so many times that once her tongue got started on the dialogue, her body remembered a phantom notecard that wasn't there. "I understand why you're going, but I hate it. It makes me wonder if I should be going somewhere. There's something about your moving to a place that you'll need to fly to that makes me jealous. I don't know if it's exactly that I'll miss you or something else." Her sentences had come out like staccato, with short unnatural breaths between.

"I'll call all the time," Casey had told her. He had whispered it because his father had not liked that she'd visit in the night, not because he thought that they were having sex, but probably because he understood that they were not and had always considered it a weakness to have platonic relations with a girl. "All the time."

Meredith had turned away from Casey then and she turned away from the ocean now just thinking of it. It had been very dark in his room and they had not been touching and it was all she could do to keep her body from shaking.

"No," she had said, not trusting her voice at anything more than a whisper. "Don't. I wouldn't like that. I believe in really being in a place."

And then Casey had slid one hand toward her on the mattress and his fingers were shaking as they climbed across the small of her back, from hip to hip, until his arms were around her waist and he had sidled his body forward toward hers. Meredith had felt her body go rigid and wanted to move but could not, could hardly breathe. She could hear the pounding of her heart and the sound of her throat moving as she swallowed from the buildup of nervous saliva and she burned with how ugly the sound was but she could not stop it—it felt that she might drown in her own nervous saliva and it felt like the roof of her mouth was melting. And after the uncountable seconds-minutes-hours of lying there frozen and still, Casey had taken his arm away, and with it the spell of disanimation.

"What time is it?" she had asked him.

She felt the depression in the mattress shift as Casey turned his body to read the clock on his nightstand.

"Five thirty in the morning."

By how flat the mattress behind her had become, she knew that he had not turned his body back to face hers, but lay on his back, facing the ceiling, with his weight spread evenly across his shoulders and his spine. Now she could hear the sound of his swallowing.

"Why don't we watch the sunrise?" he had asked eventually.

Meredith had felt her eyes grow hot and she squeezed them together and felt the water collect and fall, but she could not raise a hand to wipe a tear away and there was only one, so it had not even been like crying. She had not been able to stand the politic in his voice, the gross indifference of his question to anything relevant, and how he had asked to watch the sunrise only because he'd felt that it was necessary to suggest an alternate activity as if to prove that he'd been interested in more than only what might have come from his hand around her waist. He had lightly tapped her in an attempt to reinstill the effortless but platonic physicality between them.

"No," Meredith had told him. "If we watch the sunrise, then it's all of a sudden romantic. That isn't the kind of thing we go for."

"Good old Meredith," Casey had said.

"Good old Meredith," she had repeated in a whisper, acutely aware of the cadence of Casey's breath. It had slowed down and fallen into its sleeping pattern. "Good old Meredith," she had said again, and alone in bed she had watched the light outside fall in through the open window and change the color of Casey's ceiling, so that by the time she had fallen asleep, it was painted gold with the coming sunrise.

CHAPTER 7
Ella

I did not like the idea of staying in our old house—in Joseph's old house—but I liked the idea of paying for a hotel room even less. When you don't have any money there's nothing to spending it. I never had enough money before to know whether or not I was a miser. Within a few weeks of achieving my inheritance I knew with certainty that I was. I hated to spend it. Davey did not mind so much to spend his. He had a whole mess of it and everybody knew. He had a personal stool at the bar of Pop's Garage in Asbury Park and bought a drink for anybody who approached him to offer condolences. It was funny to watch people come up and try to look dignified while begging for a drink. Mostly, they would not look Davey in the eye and even if I was sitting just beside him, I was never offered any condolences. It was not my tab at the bar. I knew that Davey was there now and that Meredith was there with him. I could have told them to come watch Ella at the Saint, but I did not really want them to come.

I did not like the way that Davey saw Gabrielle—for she introduced herself to him as Gabrielle; you could tell from the start that he saw her as nothing but a sister and it made me feel unclean. He could not for a moment see how beautiful she was or in any way other than as a relative. It seemed almost a relief to him that he could have an excuse for merely platonic relations with a girl. She thought it was funny, in a way, but you could tell that she was almost shocked by the genuineness of it.

Now she was on stage. From the inside, the Saint had the appearance of an old and smoky jazz bar. With the exception of a single incandescent bulb at the ticket booth along the back wall, the only lights they kept on inside the place at night were pointed at the stage. The traffic lights from the intersection of Main Street and Monroe fell distorted through the glass-brick wall. Something about the curvature of the glass made it seem as if it had slowed down the red, yellow or green lights as they passed through its medium, and you got the impression that the light you were seeing had been the traffic signal a minute ago, as if they were distant, dying stars whose shine took years to reach into the little bar.

Ella wore a long, black sequin dress and swayed to the smooth, round bass with her delicate fingers wrapped around the microphone in its stand. The band had been barely distinguishable in the blue-black darkness surrounding her, and now—aside from the bassist—the band had left the stage in order to let her finish the set as a soloist. Her fingernails were painted a deep, sincere crimson and it seemed that they were the only things of real color in the whole world. Her voice was soft and she did not seem to be singing into a microphone on stage, but instead whispering songs into your ear, just for you. I closed my eyes and half believed that. It was as if the whole room had shrunk so that I was standing just before the stage, just beneath her—so close that I could reach out and touch the sliver of her calf, exposed in the split of her long black dress. I watched her calf tense and relax with the burden of her wonderful slight weight as she swayed back and forth, naturally as drawing breath. She looked down at me for a moment and I wondered if she really saw me or if the stage lights were in her eyes and it was only by a matter of chance that she had looked in my direction.

"You're Gabby's friend?" someone said. "Gabby told me she had a friend coming."

As he sat down beside me, I recognized him as the drummer. He put two bottles of beer on the small, round high-top table and slid one in front of me. There were lines of sequins sewn into the lapels of his jacket, and now that he was no longer on stage they looked like something belonging to a costume. I did not know what she had told him and decided not to answer the question.

"Thanks," I said, taking the beer. "You were good."

"It doesn't matter if a drummer is good. All a drummer can be is good enough. Liam."

"Well," I said. He offered me his hand and I shook it. "You were good enough. Casey."

"Where are you from, Casey?"

"Here."

"Here?"

"I live in New York now, but I grew up here."

"On which side of the lake?"

I understood what he was getting at and laughed. "Alright then," I said. "I grew up in Allenhurst."

He wagged a thick finger at me and smiled. With the blue

glow of the stage lights, his teeth shone brilliantly against the darkness of his skin.

"I knew it," he said. He took a sip of beer and looked up at Ella on the stage. "I knew it."

"Knew what?"

Liam took another sip of beer and sucked the air in through his teeth, as if he was tasting expensive wine.

"All of a sudden, Asbury Park is the place to be again. Now all the white folk like to say that they're from here, even if they aren't really. Even if they really grew up in *Allenhurst*. Twenty years ago, any white people unlucky enough to be living here wouldn't be caught dead admitting it."

"You couldn't have been ten years old twenty years ago."

"What does that matter? It isn't me I'm talking about. It's just the way things were."

"Alright," I said. I did not like to be speaking while Ella was singing. "So that's the way things were. And I suppose you remember the race riots too. And when they finished the Paramount Theatre."

"You don't need to have been there for the riots to remember them. The whole town remembers them. It's only the winners who can forget."

"I'll try to remember that," I said. I spoke without looking at him but out of the corner of my eyes I could see the whites of his eyes glowing with the blue light from the stage.

Ella's song finished and everybody began to clap. I stood up from my stool and clapped very loudly, both because she had been terrific and to drown out Liam's presence. I did not have any interest in discussing race or politics with one of Ella's friends, if a friend is what Liam was.

"Alright," said Ella. The bassist left the stage and it was only her now. "I'm going to sing one more for you. Thank you all for coming."

"You'll like this one," said Liam. He wanted to prove to me that he knew her set. "She's trying it new. Listen."

"Is that what I'm here to do?"

Liam smiled and shook his head. Ella began singing and the bass was so faint now that it hardly seemed to be there.

She was as tender as a rose . . . she was as soft as snowy down . . .

"For instance," said Liam. "I bet you think it's alright for a Black girl to be with a white boy."

She was a dream that hung around . . .

"But it's only you that can think it. You all love to show off how equal-eyed you can be. It's like saying you grew up in Asbury Park. But you didn't grow up in Asbury Park any more than I grew up in Allenhurst. Now here in a bar like this, we can sit down across from one another and have a drink, but we go five blocks east and you'll get jumped. And we go the other way and cross the lake and I'll get arrested. That's just the way it is."

Her love to him was like a kick . . . His ego needed her a lot . . .

"So you can go and show her off and all your friends smile because that's all there is to being white. Just smiling. No difference in color between skin and teeth. So you can afford to smile. But for her? It's not so good. A girl goes off with a white boy and it's like she did something wrong. Like she wanted to forget who she was. You understand? It isn't so good for her when she comes back to all her friends."

We knew that everything had gone wrong . . .

"Is that what you are?" I said. "Her friend?"

"The real question is what are *you*?"

I looked at Liam, but he was not watching me. His eyes were on Ella. You could see her reflection flipped on the surface of his lenses and she was more of a color than a shape, a shimmer of midnight blue with sequin scales that moved like water. I figured that Liam was in love with her and I could not blame him a whole hell of a lot. Probably the whole bar was in love with her.

I was as tender as a rose . . . She was as tender as a rose . . .

Everybody stood to clap. I could not help but find it funny, in a way, that he thought the biggest barrier to my and Ella's being romantic would be the colors of our skin.

"It isn't like that," I said to Liam. Everything was less tense without her singing. In a way, her voice had wound tight the fabric of space, putting tension on the very air itself. "And if you're so interested why don't you ask her out yourself."

Liam clapped his hands together. He had delicate hands that were dark on the outside and white on the palms. I watched his hands and heard his claps distinctly.

"God knows I have," he said. "Have you?"

"It isn't like that," I said again.

He seemed to relax. Ella came over to where we were sitting.

"I hope my drummer has been polite to you," she said.

I raised my beer to Liam. "Very," I said.

"Well," she said to him. "I was nervous to try that out. How was it? Good?"

Liam's eyes shifted between the two of us and a smile spread across his lips.

"Good enough," he said. He tapped my bottle with his own and stood to let Ella sit and then walked off to speak to the rest of the band.

"You were better than good enough," I said. I tried to say more but everybody was leaving the bar now, and many of them stopped to shake Ella's hand. Within five minutes the place was empty, save for us and Liam and the rest of the band. They came up to us as ceiling lights went on.

"Well," said the pianist. He was thin and tall enough that his torso while playing hovered fully over the keys. Though he was older than the rest of them, there was a restless energy about him that suggested youth. He had a gold earring in either ear and wore a fedora low over his eyes and he would not look at me. "Let's go out. I can't go home just yet. Gabby, why don't you come out with me? You deserve a little something after how good you sang the encore."

He flickered his tongue at her and she turned away.

"I wonder how your wife would like you talking that way," said Liam. He crossed his arms over his chest and one of the blue sequins that was stitched into his lapel came out.

"Oh, she wouldn't mind," said the pianist. He winked at Ella. "It's only talk, after all. We're very trusting people."

"There aren't any trusting people," Ella said to him. She reached up and patted his cheek. "Only less intelligent."

It was Liam who answered, and in his voice there was something of a challenge.

"And I suppose there aren't any loyal people either?" he said. He looked very directly at Ella and she turned away and looked at me.

"No," she said. "Only better liars."

"Well, *I'm* just heading back to mine. *I* don't have a wife. Everybody is welcome to come. You too, Casey." He looked at me and winked. "It's just about five blocks that way."

"Thanks," said Ella. "But we've promised some friends that we'd meet them down on the boardwalk."

Liam looked as if he might protest, but instead stuffed his hands into his pockets and nodded. "Well, goodnight," he said.

"Goodnight."

They all went out. Ella and I were the last ones out of the bar and we did not say anything for a long time. We walked east down Monroe until it turned into Cookman and we could see the tower of the Casino up ahead and the flashing rainbow lights of the Empress Hotel.

We turned onto the boardwalk. The air was cool and pleasant and there was the dull pulsing of music in the air, muted but loud enough that you knew it was just on the other side of every wall. It seemed that the music was everywhere we were not. We did not care.

"Would David and Meredith mind us being a little later?" she said. "I never eat before a show. I could use a drink as well. I don't like being so far behind."

"Alright," I said. "Let's have dinner and catch you up quickly."

We sat on the roof of a boardwalk restaurant called Stella Marina. It was crisscrossed over with hanging strings of light and we sat at a small, two-top table at the balcony's edge. It was a clear night and out over the water there were bright clusters of stars hanging low against the dark horizon. We had a cocktail each and then shared two bottles of wine. I did most of the drinking while Ella ate, and afterward I paid the bill.

"I don't really want to go meet up with them," she said, once we were back on the boardwalk. We were walking north.

"No. Me either."

"I'd feel strange at a bar like that in sequins."

"You'd look strange too."

"Thanks," she said. She stopped walking and turned to the store on our left. "This is where I work, you know."

"Madame K's," I read. I had always been aware of the store but it had been invisible, in a way, until now. A few stores up ahead would be Pop's Garage, and Davey would be there with Meredith. I was about to suggest that we walk on the beach to avoid seeing them when Ella took me by the hand and pulled me that way herself.

"What is it?" I asked. We ducked under the railing and hopped down onto the sand.

"Nothing," she said. "Only I knew the girl walking toward us."

I looked back to the boardwalk. A girl in a yellow dress was walking quickly in our direction, away from Pop's Garage. When I turned back to Ella, she had taken off her shoes and was walking just beyond the line of shadow, where the lights from all the stores and restaurants and bars came over the edge of the boardwalk and faintly lit up the sand.

"What does it matter if you knew her?" I asked. Ella did not answer. As we passed by Pop's Garage, neither of us looked inside, and we moved farther away from the light, as if by instinct.

"That Liam seemed to like you," I said.

"He does. Lots of people like me. But him I like to rile up, if you want to know the truth. Do you think that's awful of me?"

"No," I said. "Nothing you could do is awful. If you don't give someone an invitation to be near you, they ought to stay away."

"That's practical until you're on the bad end of it."

"Everything is practical until you're on the bad end of it."

Ella slowed for a moment and turned toward Pop's Garage, stopping just short of fully looking at it. I was two steps ahead and turned around to face her. She had been dragging her toes as she walked, and behind her were two broken, swerving tracks of shadow where she'd left an indent in the sand, like marks left by ice skates.

"Do you think David likes me?" she asked.

"What do you care what Davey thinks."

"Oh, I don't know. He didn't seem to like me. Not in the way that most people do."

"Davey likes just about everyone. He thinks of you as a sister is all."

"And how do you think of me?"

"I don't."

"Do you know, I almost think of David as a brother. Maybe it's because I knew about him all along. Joseph would talk about David, you know. Mostly about how good he was at football, or how popular he was with women. I never met him, but he was built up in my mind, in a way. He was like the kind of brother it would be funny to have. The one who sleeps with all your friends. Maybe that's why I think of him like a brother. What do you think?"

"It doesn't matter what I think."

Far ahead, at Convention Hall, the lights were purple and white against the red brick wall and you could see the shadows of people moving. The far-off music filled the silence between the sets of waves, and the closer we came to Convention Hall, the more equally the two sounds competed for airspace.

"Does it bother you that he never talked about you?" she asked me.

"No," I said. "I wouldn't have wanted him to. People prefer being in a unique position to being in a truly good one. A wife and a mistress are two different things. One does not always need to compete so directly with the other. It's different between two mistresses."

"Or between their children."

"Yes," I said. "Or that."

We were quiet as we passed underneath Convention Hall. When we came out on the other side it was as if all the music had only been a dream and there was only the sound of the waves and the empty boardwalk now with nothing on it but a single wall of murals. We climbed back from the sand onto the boardwalk and Ella put her shoes back on.

"I think you would have won that competition," I said finally. "For everything else that was the matter with him, he had good taste in music. He would have thought you were good."

"Maybe. But not as good as David at his football."

"No," I said. "Maybe not as good as that. But David wasn't always good."

I began to laugh.

"What is it?"

"Nothing. I'm only remembering a story. About a week before the first junior-high game that he ever played in, Davey hadn't studied for a test and he pretended to have a wheezing fit during recess. The wheezing fit had been my idea. It was just after we met and I thought that those sort of ideas would get him to like me. It's funny how much you want to be liked when you're at that age. Anyway, his mother had to come pick him up and take him out of school. Only, Davey isn't any good at secrets. After she had spent the whole day with him at the doctor and picking up prescriptions, he finally tells her before Joseph came home that he'd been making it up. It was easier for him to admit to her that he'd been lying than it would have been to admit to Joseph that he had a physical weakness."

Ella stopped and turned to me. I hadn't noticed before the sound that her shoes had made against the boardwalk, but now that they had stopped I noticed it by the void they'd left behind. They sounded and stopped again as she moved toward the ocean and put her hand against the railings that separated the boardwalk from the sand below. Her figure was like a dark shadow against the white surface of the night ocean beyond. She turned to me and hoisted herself up to sit on the railing with her back to the ocean. If it were not for the small amount of light that touched her face, I would not have been able to tell which way she was facing.

"And what did she do—his mother?"

"I don't think anyone has ever been so sensitive about having her time wasted as Davey's mother," I said. "She didn't care so much that Davey lied, but she cared about having her time wasted, and when she found out that the idea had come from me, I think it gave her the notion that we'd teamed up to fool her. She hated being fooled."

"So she told Joseph?"

"No. Not immediately. She just went along with it until the first junior-high football game of the year. At halftime she ran down onto the field and made him take the inhaler with the whole crowd watching. He wasn't so big back then and was anything but the star of the team. Well, the Trojan uniforms were crimson and Davey's face turned so red that it almost matched the fabric. The coach kept him on the bench for the rest of the game. I remember watching and thinking it was very funny at the time. It doesn't seem so funny now."

"No," she said. "It doesn't seem very funny at all."

"She didn't get off easy herself," I said. "If there was anything Joseph cared about in Davey it was that he shouldn't be weak. It was a weakness for Joseph himself to have a weak son. When he found out about it. Well," I said, "she looked so bad that she couldn't leave the house for two weeks. It was the only time I remember him really being violent."

We were quiet for a while and listened to the waves breaking against the sand. They were always gentle at this hour and the ocean was less like a drum than it was like a snake, throwing itself up onto the sand and then slithering back down it again. The small waves glowed when they formed and reflected the moon and then when they broke the brightness dissipated into wake, shimmering like broken glass. I was a little drunk and it seemed for a moment that I was conversing with the shadow of the ocean. Ella slid down off the railing and kept walking north.

"Was his mother really awful?" she asked.

"Worse than that."

"And yours?"

"What about mine?"

"I don't know. What was she like?"

"To tell you the truth," I said. "I'm not so sure that I know. We were never so interested in one another. After I moved in with David and his parents, her very existence was a shameful topic, and that's a little bit how I see her now. On the rare occasions that she came up out of necessity, David's mother would have a sort of meltdown. Eventually, there wasn't any necessity and so it never came up. I never thought about her much."

We walked quietly for a while and I felt that the entire night was set to the cadence of Ella's footsteps.

"And your mother," I said. "Will she worry now if you're not home?"

Ella checked the time on her phone and looked out over the ocean but did not stop walking. We had finished dinner nearly two hours ago and it was half past midnight.

"At this hour, it would be better if I didn't go home at all," she said. "I could tell her I stayed with a friend."

I became very aware of the saliva in my throat and swallowed.

"And do you have a friend's to stay at?"

Ella did not answer me.

"You could always stay at ours," I said. "Davey's there, of course."

"Do you think he'd mind?"

"No. He doesn't mind anything."

"And there's enough room?"

"There are plenty of beds."

"I've never been there, you know. I've always been curious, but I've never been there."

I called a taxi and we drove the whole way home in a sort of silence. I leaned my head against the window so that I could look up at the streetlights. I dragged my eyes from one streetlight to the next and tried to make a long, continuous streak of yellow light that floated and ran just above the periodic rise and fall of the telephone wires. It was only a ten-minute car ride back to Davey's house, and it felt like the better part of a day.

When we pulled up, I became aware that the back of my

hand was against the back of Ella's, and one finger of mine was extended so that my fingernail was prodding one of her sequins. I quickly took my hand away and did not catch her eye. The front door was unlocked and we went into the house.

"Casey?" said a voice from the kitchen. Ella shut the front door behind her. I looked back at her and her face had gone a little white.

"It's me, Dave," I said. He walked out from the kitchen into the entryway. "I brought a guest. She wanted to see the house."

Dave smiled when he saw Gabrielle. He spread his arms wide. "Of course, why shouldn't she? Welcome," he said. He spread his hands wide and staggered slightly. There was a whiskey in his one hand and the sound of ice against the glass. You got the impression that he was trying to convince himself that the house was really his.

"I just wanted to see the house," she said.

"Of course," Davey repeated. "I'll give you a tour. Can I make you a drink?"

"I'm tired," she said. "Do you mind if I sleep here?"

"Of course. You'll have the . . . master bedroom."

He had wanted to avoid saying directly that the room had been our father's. Our. The word had become suddenly funny. I watched them move up the stairs, Davey first and Gabrielle in tow. It was a long, curved staircase and she looked back at me. Her face was stern and barely lit in the darkness of the house. It showed nothing. I went into the kitchen and poured myself a glass of whiskey. I stared at it for a while and eventually Davey came into the kitchen.

"She seems like a good kid," he said.

"She isn't a kid." I took a drink. "Do you want another?"

"Sure."

Davey put his glass down and I poured it halfway full with whiskey. We clinked glasses.

"It's kind of funny," he said. "Our having a sister."

"She isn't our sister," I said. I took another drink. Davey's glass was halfway to his lips and he stopped and then put it down. I had not meant to say it so brashly and I felt my face become hot.

"You're not taking this all badly, are you?" he asked. He took a long drink but watched me over the rim of his glass.

"I don't know. What other way is there to take it?"

"Well it isn't wonderful, but it's not all that surprising, when you consider everything."

"Yes, well. Who considers everything?" I said. He didn't answer and we both drank. "You've gotten used to your position. It dilutes mine a bit. Being one of two."

"I didn't think of it like that."

"Maybe I didn't either until just now," I said. "I don't know. Were you with Meredith tonight?"

"Oh," he said. He ran one hand through his hair. "Yes, I was."

"Was everything alright? You seem on edge. Like you used to get the night before a game. I'm sorry we didn't make it over to the Garage."

"No, it wasn't that. I'm tired, is all. I'm sure you're tired, too. We should get some sleep."

He finished his whiskey and something in his face made me want to speak. He seemed to be waiting for me to say something.

"I don't think he would ever have expected all three of us under one roof," I said.

"No," said Davey. He looked around at the walls and then brought his glass over to the sink. I could see that there was a film of powder on the bottom, and as he saw me watching him, he rinsed it out with water and then quickly turned away. "Goodnight."

I poured myself another glass and sat on the living room couch for a while in the darkness and listened to the sounds of the house. Everything was still. Everything was silent. Outside the sand was white and because of the slope of the beach, I could not see the place where the waves were breaking. I could hear the subtle roar, but all I could see was the white sand and then above it was the sky. There were gray clouds that covered all the stars. Eventually the sound of waves went away and the house seemed really to be silent. It was as if we were inside a coffin.

And then a slow, bright sound came whining up, as if it were morning fog that comes from nowhere, or cockroaches that wait inside the walls for total darkness before they emerge. I closed my eyes and listened for it to be sure that it was really there. It was. I felt that the house was whispering. I got up and went out toward the foyer and stood at the bottom of the stairs. Everything was very dark but on the ceiling of the floor above the second floor landing, there was a trace of yellow light. I put one foot on the first step to see if it would creak. I climbed the stairs and turned toward my father's room. The door was open a crack and there was a vertical yellow line where the light came through. Everything was a pulsing sort of silent and between the waves of sound, between the muted drum of blood rushing in my ears, there was another sound. It came from the vertical streak of light, as if it were a quiet siren.

Gabrielle was standing with her back to a record player and

the speakers were turned off so that all you could hear was the needle scratching against the black vinyl grooves. It was too quiet to hear what music was playing but she could hear it just fine or at least her body could and it swayed left to right as if she were a reed compelled into motion by the frequency of air-waves as they came flying from the turning black surface. She moved like a shadow or like those illusions of ballerinas where you are meant to be confused as to which way they are spinning. It was too quiet to hear and it asked you to move closer and if, once you were closer, the sound could still not reach you, you could wrap your arms around her and since she was a receiver for the vibrations of air, she would tremble with that motion and it would be present on her flesh and so by pressing your palms against it you could understand the sounds. It traveled through my fingers and up into my ribs.

The world seemed to slow in its turning, as if a spell had been cast over the night. The song had changed and I could understand it now. It was an old Dinah Washington record, a first edition that Joseph would never have played because he was afraid of the vinyl getting worn. That didn't matter now. Gabrielle hummed the instrumental and when she sang, her voice trembled in all the right ways. The words were sharp and nothing was ignored. She paused and allowed the stillness of the room to orchestrate its silence, broken by the waves of sound whispering from the record.

I felt her fingers brush against my temples *oh, this bitter earth* across my cheek *may be so cold* her palm came upon the underside of my jaw and there was not a bead of moisture on it, *today you're young* only the cool tremble with which her body resonated *too soon, you're old* I felt her breath on my face with each syllable advanced, *but while a voice* felt her there before I opened my eyes and was not surprised at her proximity *within me cries,* her lips came down on mine and I pushed her away because I did not want her to stop singing *I'm sure someone may answer my call* but wishing there was a way to do both I leaned forward and kissed her neck and in my teeth I felt the echoing of her lungs and of her vocal chords *and this bitter earth* I was gentle in laying her down on the bed so as not to disturb that fragile pitch and then her head was back and her throat exposed *oh, may not* and echoing through me and then I brought my lips back to hers because I did not care anymore.

CHAPTER 8
Empress

There was the hollow sound of footsteps on the boardwalk and the rolling crash of waves against the sand and the voices of children or adults like music in an echo chamber and they all blended together on the pink evening sky and seeped into David's mind like sound or wind or temperature. He pulled a hat low over his eyes and felt that it was trapping all the heat that was let off by his body. His feet moved, but they felt to him like balloons, or like the long dragging tentacles of jellyfish that never touch the floor of the ocean. It seemed to David that the only part of his body that was real was his head. It floated up and down, oscillating on a sinusoidal path like a particle of light. His mouth hung slightly open and he did not feel himself breathing so much as the air seemed to flow in and out of his body, filling his lungs—wherever they were—and then leaving them empty again.

He nearly walked straight into Eli Trask. Or maybe Eli had

intercepted David's path. Or maybe David had steered himself toward Eli, as if pulled in by his old friend's gravity. David did not think that he had noticed Eli standing there, but now that they stood face to face, he could not be sure.

"Eli," he said, and he felt the words escape his lips in slow, drawled syllables.

Eli smiled. "Attaboy, Dave," he said. "Miss me?"

David looked down at the boardwalk. His toes and Eli's were almost touching—he in his gray sneakers and Eli's in red Converse with a white rubber cap.

"When did you arrive?" David asked.

"Just an hour ago. This is a David Larkin special visit."

"Oh," said David. He raised and dropped his toes and watched the material of his sneaker move. "Where are you staying?"

"A king suite at the Empress. On the top floor too. You can see all the way to Portugal from the balcony. Have you been back to Portugal?"

"No. Not since I was abroad."

"Since *we* were abroad. Don't be selfish. I hate it when you're selfish. Well *I* have been back. I went last year. I wanted to get away. All the buildings are different colors, you remember? Blues and yellows. And all the roofs are red."

David looked up from their feet and looked at Eli. His eyes were bright green and the whites of them shone red with the neon lights of the boardwalk restaurants. David looked away, over Eli's shoulders, above the canopy of the restaurants and toward the balconies of the Empress Hotel. They were painted white, but bathed in the rainbow-colored spotlights that shifted and moved along the walls and balconies and railings, making them glow pink and orange and purple. Above the lightshow, the hotel sign—The Empress—glowed green against the sky, with a yellow crown that straddled the space above the letters.

"Why are you staying *there*?" asked David, his eyes still on the crown. He pulled his hat low over his eyes. "Don't you know what kind of hotel it is?"

"Sure," said Eli. "The kind of hotel where you can see Portugal from your balcony. Come on. I'll show you. It's past midnight in Lisbon, but I bet all the lights are still going. They never sleep. Come on. I'll show you."

"Let's go get a drink somewhere."

"There's a bar at the hotel. It's a wonderful bar."

"No," said David. He swayed side to side. "Not the Paradise. I know all about the Paradise. Let's go somewhere normal."

"What do you mean, normal?"

David spun around, first toward the ocean—as if the normal bars might be resting on the dark horizon—and then to the long boardwalk strip.

"Would one of these bars be alright?" said Eli, waving his hand down the row of boardwalk lights.

"No," said David. "These are all local bars."

"Well, we wouldn't want to go to any local bars, would we?"

"Let's go to Porta."

Eli laughed. "That pizza place?"

"It's a bar at night. It's where all the New York girls go."

Eli sighed and rocked forward onto the balls of his feet, bringing his face closer to David's, and then swung back onto his heels.

"Well," he said. "If it's where the girls go."

They walked in silence and when they arrived at Porta they

waited together in the short line. It was early in the night and the line was only a few people. By midnight, it would wrap around the block. When they came up to the bouncer, Eli handed over his ID first, and the bouncer looked him up and down and then flipped it over and ran it through a scanner and handed it back. David fumbled with his wallet and then handed the bouncer his ID.

"It's a fake," said Eli. "He jumped some pretty boy on the boardwalk and took his wallet. Beat him to a pulp. His real name is Crazy Craig Rodwell, and he's a criminal if I've ever seen one."

The bouncer shook his head but did not even look at Eli. He looked David up and down and then scanned his ID and was about to hand it back but then he looked at the name and at the face. He held it up so that he could see David's real face beside his photograph.

"David Larkin," said the bouncer. "That you? David Larkin."

"Yes," said Eli. "This is David Larkin. He's twenty-five years old. Crazy Craig is the one in the gutter."

"Weren't you here just the other night?" said the bouncer. "Wasn't there trouble."

"You're thinking of someone else," said Davey. He pulled his hat down so that it cast a shadow on his face.

"Alright, David Larkin," said the bouncer. "Go on in."

They went in. It was still early but already the lights were pulsing and the music was loud, its heavy bass made David's chest feel as if it were confused as to what should be the cadence of his heartbeat.

"I think that guy knew me," said David. He had to speak loudly to make his voice heard over the music.

"Who—the *door* guy? God, they really piss me off. I mean,

if he's going to scan an ID anyway, why does he need to act like he doesn't believe you?"

"He knew who I was."

"Let him pick only one method of being an asshole."

"We should go," said David. "He knew who I was."

"Oh, poor baby, you're just coming down. Let's go to where it's quiet. I've got a present for you."

Eli started to move away and, as he did, his hand slid down David's arm and then grabbed David's own hand and pulled him along. David took two steps and then pulled his arm back, almost violently.

"Stop it," he said.

"Oh, I was only leading you along. Come on. I've got a present for you."

"Where are we going?"

"Just to a quieter corner of the bar. Somewhere we can hear each other talk."

David looked at him, and then back to the door, where the bouncer had caught his eye again.

"Oh, alright," said Eli. "We're going to where all the girls are. Is that what you want to hear?"

They stood facing each other and the music of the room was the only sound between them.

"Alright," said David. He adjusted his hat. "Let's get a drink."

They went over to a quiet corner of the bar.

"Vodka soda," Eli told the bartender. "With a lime."

He turned to David and stuck up two fingers.

"Two of them?"

David looked at Eli's fingers and shook his head.

"Jameson for me," he said.

"Straight up? Ice?"

"Straight up," said David. "A double."

"Make mine a double too, then," said Eli. He spread his hands wide on the bar and raised and dropped his fingers in quick succession, from pinky to thumb and then back again, as if he were rolling a coin across his knuckles.

"Wow," he said finally, "a Jameson guy. And to drink it all on its own."

"I always drink Jameson."

David turned his back to the bar and watched the door and the bouncer. The bartender came back with the drinks and Eli took both of them and put David's whiskey in David's hand.

"Here you are," he said. "A big tough whiskey neat for a big tough guy. You can drink it fast and then go fuck a girl in the bathroom and then go get into a fight with that bouncer."

"He's looking at me."

"So drink your whiskey and then go punch him in the mouth. That'll show them."

"Show who?" asked David.

"Indeed."

David turned away from the door and looked at Eli. He opened his mouth to speak.

"Nobody's watching you," said Eli. His voice was only just audible above the sound of the music. "We're at a bar for out-of-towners and nobody is watching you. Just be here for a minute. Look at me."

But David would not look at him. He turned sideways back toward the door.

"He's looking at me," he said again.

"God I wonder what that feels like," said Eli. "It must be

nice, being looked at. I think you just need to calm down. Here, I got you a present."

Eli's hand slid into his pocket and when it came out again it held two little white pills. He stuck out his own tongue and put one of the pills on it. With the other pill pinched between his thumb and forefinger, he looked at David's lips. David stared at the pill and opened his palm.

"Ah-ah," said Eli. "Open up."

David looked to the door once more, but only with his eyes. He swallowed nervously as he looked back to Eli, and then he opened his mouth and stuck out his tongue.

"Attaboy, Dave," said Eli. He put the pill on David's tongue, and his fingers came away wet with saliva and he wiped them against his own shirt. David pulled his tongue back inside his mouth and took a drink of whiskey to swallow the pill. " Attaboy. Now, do you want to dance or should we just stare at all the girls?"

David looked down into his cup and swirled the whiskey around. He took another sip and winced at the taste and then took out his phone and looked at the time.

"Take it easy," said Eli. "It'll kick in soon enough. Dance until it does?"

"I want another drink," said David.

"That's good. Let's get you another drink. Only, I feel like such a pussy drinking vodka while you're having a whiskey neat. Will you have a vodka with me. With soda and lime?"

"Alright, Eli."

They had a vodka soda each. It was easy to drink and they drank it quickly, and once it was done they ordered another. David was smiling more now. His body began to move side to side. The crowd blurred. The lights above him seemed to dance. The music no longer felt like music, but like a separate, common heart that kept time like a metronome. They stayed beside the bar, but moved now together. Their fingers and their skin did not touch, but something in each of them intertwined with that same something in the other.

"You remember this song?" said Eli.

"Yes."

"It's different now. They always make them different a year later by adding extra noise. I liked the way it was."

"I liked it too," said David. He looked down into his glass. "I need another drink."

"Attaboy, Dave. You get another drink. I'm going to the little girls' room."

David went back to the bar and leaned his weight against it. He felt the warm wood underneath his palms, and as he exhaled he seemed to push the bar farther away, as if his arms were stretching. When he breathed in, they contracted again. The room was spinning and he opened his mouth wide and rolled his head back to stretch his neck and his jaw, which had been working hard and moving side to side.

"Hey," said someone beside him. There was a rough hand on Davey's shoulder. "Aren't you Dave Larkin?"

Dave looked in the direction of the voice but could only half make out the face amidst the pulsing, spinning lights. He felt his eyelids droop and strained to hold them open and to hold his head steady. He nodded slowly, but at the same time pulled his hat down low over his eyes.

"Thought so. Remember me? Scotty Brent, class of '13. You were a senior when we were freshman," he gestured to three friends behind him. "Mike and I played varsity with you. What's the matter, don't you remember us?"

"Sure," said David. "Sure I do. Scotty . . . Scotty Brent. How are things."

Scotty shrugged and David noticed how large he was in the shoulders, how sharp he was in the jaw. David turned toward the bar.

"Have a drink," he said.

"Thanks, I will."

Davey ran his palms over the smooth warm wood of the counter while he waited for the bartender's attention. Twice the bartender came around, but Davey was so distracted by the sensation of the wood that both times the bartender went by. "You've got to get in there," said Scotty beside him, but Davey did not look at him, and on the third time that the bartender went by, Scott leaned forward over the bar and grabbed him by the arm.

"We're trying to order drinks," he said.

The bartender looked at Scotty's hand on his arm as if a pigeon had shit on his sleeve, and eventually Scotty removed it and retreated his torso back over the bar.

"I see you," said the bartender to Dave. "I'll be with you in a second."

But it was a second that never came, for just as Scotty—embarrassed at having been rejected at the bar—turned back to his friends, Eli returned from the bathroom and tried to squeeze through them to make his way back to David, who had not yet noticed his friend's return. The others formed a wall and, as Eli tried to pass through it, they began to toy with him.

"That's a nice shirt," said the one called Mike, "but you've got something on it."

And even though Eli did not look down to where Mike's finger was prodding into the clean fabric over his chest, Mike moved his hand up and slapped Eli in the face anyway. Eli stumbled forward while they formed a sort of circle around him. They took turns pushing him from side to side. *Minnow, minnow,* they chanted—and finally David turned, recognizing the old hazing song from his high school football days. *Minnow, minnow.*

"Hey," he said. "Leave him alone."

But his voice was quiet, far too quiet to be heard above the rising chant—*minnow, minnow*—with a cadence like an African drum and Eli's body being pushed between them like light caught in a hall of mirrors.

"Cute jeans, minnow minnow."

"What a toss, minnow minnow."

"That's enough," said David, but he did not say it very loud. He watched Eli's body bend and flex like a rubber toy against the strength of their hands, and knew that his friend was somewhat protected by not attempting to fight back; they would push you around if you did nothing, but they would only really hurt you if you fought back.

"Skinny legs, minnow minnow."

"Four eyes, minnow minnow."

They were repeating the insults by memory, and many of them were not even reasonable to apply to Eli, but they were beyond the realm of reason now, and through the chaos of his forced, erratic motion, Eli caught David's eye, and he looked like a fish on a reel.

"That's enough," said David again. His voice was louder now, and he wedged his way between Scotty and Mike.

"Don't tell me he's with you," said Scotty. He looked to his friends for validation. The two smaller of them, whose names David did not know, still pushed Eli, but the chant had died away.

"Just let him be," said David. "He's a friend."

"That's good," said Mike. "Davey Larkin's got a friend."

As he said it, he reached out and pinched David's cheek. Scotty's face fell as he watched it, and he saw the drunkenness leave Davey's face before Mike noticed, saw it leave and then saw it be replaced by a laughing sort of violence. Mike was still speaking when Davey turned and, with his own left hand, took a grip on Mike's right shoulder. It was always Davey's first move in a serious fight and it was not only effective, but recognizable too. By the time Mike understood what was happening, it was too late; the first problem for him was that he could not swing his right fist because the shoulder was being held down by Davey's weight; the second problem was that as Davey drove his own right fist toward Mike's jaw, he pulled in with his left hand—still gripping Mike's shoulder—so that Mike's body and head came to meet it. There was the sound of flesh meeting flesh and of cartilage snapping. Mike's mouth had been open and now his head shot back and he made a sound as if he were choking—on saliva or on blood or on teeth. When Davey pushed him away and released his shoulder, Mike's muscles offered no resistance and he fell in a slump on the floor.

The others had let go of Eli now and their chanting had stopped entirely. One of them swung and caught David in the chin. It was not a very hard swing but it was well placed and it stunned David to be hit. He staggered but caught himself in a kind of half lunge, bent at the knees with his torso low to the ground, and as he pressed his weight up he drove the side of his fist into the throat of the smaller one on his right and used the momentum of his thrust to hurl his body into Scott's. They fell together into the wooden bar and stayed there, each trying to lock a grip around the other's body, until the last of the friends punched David twice in the back of the skull. David turned around, but much of the light had gone out of his eyes from the blows, and he could not shoot his fist out to strike but instead grabbed his assailant by the throat and squeezed. Scotty, now freed of David's attention, drove his elbow into David's face, but still David held onto the last one's throat until Scotty grabbed David's head and with all his weight drove it down into the bar and then threw him to the floor. David landed on his forearms and he felt his elbows crash hard against the polished cement. His head was bleeding and three dark drops of blood were on the ground before him. Time stopped being continuous for him, and he felt that each moment of his experience followed from one that was multiple seconds before, as if his life were being played out with a strobe light and anything that occurred in the dark channels between bursts of light would be unknowable to his conscious mind. He tasted blood; it fell from his nose down into his throat like a cocaine drip and he struggled to breathe as the room blurred and spun around him.

David lay there motionless, less from the blows than from the chemicals inside him. He could hear voices speaking as if they were echoes. The ceiling lights spun when he opened his eyes and so he closed them and breathed through his nose. The blood tasted metallic and there was the feeling that it was rushing toward the places where his skin was broken.

He was aware of hands beneath his armpits and then of his

weight being pulled up. There was the cool air of night, and through his eyelids he could make out the flashing red and blue of a siren.

"David, hey David."

There was a gentle slap of a hand against his cheek. Contact was barely made, but the nerves were tender and the skin swollen and a pain shot through David's face.

"David, it's me. It's Eli. You've got to wake up, otherwise they're going to take you into the hospital. You're alright now— aren't you? You don't want to go into the hospital now—do you?"

"I'm alright," said David slowly, feeling like an echo chamber himself. "I don't want to go into the hospital. I'm alright."

"Attaboy, Dave. Attaboy. A big boy like you doesn't need to go to the hospital. Can you open your eyes?"

David opened his eyes and everything looked clear, as if the adrenaline had burned off all the liquor and chemicals from his veins, or as if they had all been squeezed out of his wounds. He looked for his hat but could not find it. Eli's face was just in front of his, and behind Eli there were policemen watching him. He knew most of the policemen in town but these ones he did not. He breathed a sigh of relief. There was a long line to get into the bar now, and those in front were leaning out to see what they could of the blood.

"I'm alright," said David. He tried to make his voice deep and unbroken. "Just some water."

"Attaboy," said Eli. He held up a straw to David's lips and David drank in and then swished the water around his mouth and spat it on the ground.

"Drink up," said Eli. "Drink up."

David drank. He felt like a balloon, filling slowly with air. All the sound became sharp and clear. Over by the door, one of the policemen was half-heartedly questioning the bouncer. He came over to David when he was done.

"You alright?"

David looked at Eli and then at his hands.

"I'm alright. Can I go?"

The policeman nodded. "You can go."

"Wait," said Eli. "Can you give us a ride? It's a long walk and those guys might come back."

"Let's just go," said David.

"What guys?" asked the policeman.

"Dave knew them."

"I didn't know them," said David.

"It's no good to know something and not to tell us."

"Tell him, Dave. They'll go get them."

"Shut up," said David again. "I didn't know anyone. Was just a bar fight is all. Let's go."

The officer stood and sighed. "Alright," he said. "Where you going to?"

David opened his mouth to answer, but Eli spoke first:

"To the Empress Hotel."

The officer looked at Eli, and then down at David, and at the blood on his face, and then the officer began to laugh.

"Well, that's something new. To the Empress Hotel," he said, loud enough that even the front of the line could hear. David turned his face away from the door, away from the line. The other officers had heard and were trying not to laugh. "Oh, you'll be fine at the Empress. They'll clean you right up. Make your face look nice and pretty again."

"We could use a ride there," said Eli. He was kneeling beside David and his voice was loud but trembling.

"Well, how about you call a taxi. Last time I checked, this wasn't any taxi medallion."

The officer tapped his badge and then spit on the ground. He turned away from Eli and David and went to join the other officers. Eli stood from where he was kneeling beside David and began to move toward them.

"I'll call a taxi," said David. His voice was hardly more than a whisper but Eli heard it. "Just stop. I'll call a taxi."

The taxi came quickly and Eli and David walked quickly to get in.

"Wave goodbye to the queen!" called someone in line. David turned his face away from the light. "Goodbye to the Empress!"

"Goodnight moon! Goodnight Empress!"

"Goodnight and sleep tight at the faggot hotel!"

They ducked into their minivan taxi and slid the door shut. The window was tinted and threw a dark screen over the bar, and the line, and the officers. They drove down Kingsley and David leaned his head against the east-facing windows. There were lights all around but then faraway beyond them the sky was dark over the ocean.

"Isn't the Empress back the other way?" said Eli.

"Oh," said David. He looked down at his phone. "I put in my own address. I'll change it now."

The driver saw the new destination and his eyes flickered up in the rearview mirror.

"I'll turn around up here," he said. He did not care where they were going.

David looked out to the east and toward the ocean. They were on the flat plaza of grass before Convention Hall and facing them, in large block letters composed of strings of Christmas lights, hung the words of the town: "Greetings from Asbury Park." David read it over and was suddenly afraid. "Greetings from Asbury Park," he read, and amidst the pounding in his head, he heard, "Goodnight and sleep tight at the faggot hotel!" The two seemed to merge and fall into one another, and as his eyelids drooped, he could not tell which was a soft glow of white Christmas lights and which was a scream on the hot summer air.

"Do you want a drink at the bar?" asked Eli once they got out of the car. The Paradise was alive and its music spilled out into the night.

"No."

"Please," said Eli. "If we're in a quiet place now we'll only remember how it ended."

They went into the bar and sat at a small table in the corner. Nobody bothered them. It was the type of place where you were not supposed to be taken aback by anything, and it was out of vogue to stare, even if a thing begged to be stared at. Even if a boy came in with blood down one side of his face and his cheek swollen to the size of a golf ball.

"It's nice to be in a place where no one stares," said Eli.

"I don't know," David wanted to say. "It's where you draw the line that matters. Staring and not staring are the same if there isn't any decision behind it."

But he said nothing and they sat and shared a carafe of ice-cold, flavored vodka and nobody watched them. The fighting had sobered them both up, but all the chemicals had lingered in their blood, waiting to spring into action again. Under the weight of the pulsing, spinning, brightening, dimming, swirling rainbow lights they began to work again, like cicadas quitting hibernation.

"Do you have another of those pills," David asked. "I'm in an awful lot of pain."

Eli smiled and reached into his pocket. By the time he had fished out a pill, David's tongue was out like a snake's, tasting the air.

"Attaboy, Dave. Now, why don't we go get you cleaned up."

"Alright," said David.

"We'll see if the lights are still on in Portugal. Or maybe it'll be the sun. I've got no idea what time it is."

They laughed. And stood. And left the Paradise without inspiring a single look. The party kept going and did not take note of them. They took the elevator up to the sixth floor, and Eli sat David down on the balcony, looking out over the boardwalk and the sand and the shining silver surface where the ocean met the country and then the wake and the ocean itself and the dark sky above it with horizontal stripes of silver moonlit clouds. Somewhere in the distance the ocean blended with the sky. Each was so dark that it did not matter which was which.

"Let's not get your shirt all wet," said Eli. His fingers found the top button on David's shirt and undid it. David looked out over the water and listened for the sound of crashing waves but could not find it. Eli undid another button. And another. When the shirt was off he went in and hung it in the closet. He soaked a towel in warm water and brought it outside. He dabbed at David's face and the towel came away brown with blood, but David did not flinch, and his eyes did not leave the spine of moonlight reflected on the ocean like a long and silver road. Eli held the towel to David's eye with enough pressure that the warm water came out of it and mixed with blood and ran pink down David's face, and then his chest, and toward his waist.

"Let me get you out of these, too," Eli said as his fingers followed the trail of water. "Blood stains, you know?"

But if David knew he did not answer. He only moved his body to allow it and never looked at Eli. He let his eyes go dim with all the light. There was the green light of the Empress sign above. Yellow of the boardwalk lanterns. White of the moon. And far away, the sunrise over Portugal.

CHAPTER 9
Acacia Grove

"You used to be so much fun," said Sophia. "I can't understand what happened."

"And you used to listen," said Jacob. It was a Saturday afternoon and they walked home together from synagogue. Sophia quickened her pace and Jacob moved to keep up. The sun was as hot as it would be all day, but he would not remove his black jacket. There was no religious reason not to do so, but he would not do anything to diminish the formality. Spots of moisture showed through his white shirt beneath, and his forehead glistened with sweat. Ahead of him, his sister had pulled up the waist of her skirt so that more of her calves were showing than was proper, and she had undone the top two buttons of her dark but thin silk blouse so that when she turned around to face him, he could see a flash of her exposed and beige bra.

"Well," she said. "I guess we've both gotten worse with time."

Jacob lunged forward and Sophia backed away.

"Fix your shirt," he said.

"You fix yours. In this kind of weather, it's broken to be so buttoned up. You're sweating like a pig."

The sun beat down onto the pavement and rose up so that it hit them from both sides. Sophia stepped off of the street and onto the sidewalk, slipped off her shoes and then walked on the grass. Jacob stayed on the street and, as they walked, the yellow and gray trunks of the London Plane trees passed between them.

"That isn't your property," said Jacob. "Come back to the street. And put your shoes on."

Sophia looked at her brother and she understood his apprehension. That isn't *our* property is what he had meant—not the property of Jews. She was on the far side of the eruv, a border of white string that outlined the Syrian community. Technically, its only purpose was to establish lines within which community members could carry items on Shabbat or Yom Kippur without breaking the ban on physical labor, but really it was like a moat or a break in the fabric between them and the rest of the world.

"It's only a string," she said. "It won't zap you. I promise."

"We've got to turn here anyway," he said, still not looking at her. "Fix your shirt."

Sophia liked the feeling of the grass beneath her feet. She closed her eyes and tried to determine whether or not she was in shade or in sun by the temperature of the soil against her soles.

"Sophia," said Jacob. "Let's go."

"I'm going to keep walking. I'll be back in a little."

"They said I was to bring you home."

"So tell them you brought me home. You're not my father."

"No, but you do have one, and he wouldn't like you going off."

"I don't think he'd mind so much," she said. "And anyway, they're at kiddush for a few hours. I'll be back before they are."

"Sophia, I said—"

"I heard you, Jake!" she called out to him. She began to run. "You said 'be home before they are,' and I will!"

Sophia knew that her brother was not following, but she ran anyway. She ran over other people's lawns and other people's driveways, keeping the white string of the eruv on her left as she moved east toward the ocean. When finally she came to the house at the end of the street, she slipped between the fence posts and over the concrete landing which sloped down to the sand. Across the gray, eroded surface, was spray painted in large red letters that faced the ocean: NO TRESPASSING. Sophia ran her bare feet over the painted letters to see if they were hotter than the concrete in the sun. They were. She hopped down onto the sand and walked toward Asbury Park.

When the boardwalk began, just before Convention Hall, she pulled herself up onto it and slipped between the railings. She walked alongside the murals and then through the arcade and onto the stretch of boardwalk that she knew so well. It was a bright, busy Saturday afternoon and the restaurants were already filled with people. Rainbow-colored sun umbrellas dotted the beach like a line of shields prepared to take fire from enemy arrows. There was the uneven drum of skateboard wheels rolling across the uneven planks, and the sounds of children screaming, and of glasses touching and breaking, and of poor boardwalk musicians playing, and of Madame Marie urging throngs of tourists to come and hear their fortunes.

When she passed by Pop's Garage, Sophia could not help but look inside. He wasn't there—of course he wasn't there—but the stool he'd been in was not occupied. It made Sophia feel that maybe it was being saved, that he'd be back. She kept walking down the strip, past the magician and his crowd of children, past the mini golf and small waterpark, until she saw the mannequins before her.

They glittered white in the sun and Sophia stood still and watched them, as if she expected them to turn in greetings; there was something shared between she and them, something like a secret or a vow. She was about to keep moving when the door to the shop flew open, and two people came out. One of them she recognized as the girl who had given her the pale yellow dress, and the other looked familiar; he looked like the boy from the bar, and yet he did not look like him too. The girl also looked like him, and they looked like one another.

"Perhaps," she thought, "I am only seeing his face everywhere after expecting to see it somewhere it was not."

She knew that the boy she was following was not the boy from the bar, but she followed him anyway. He walked side by side with the girl from the shop, but it seemed to Sophia that there was a strictly measured space between them—almost enough for a third person to stand in—and that it grew smaller the farther they moved from the shop, as if their attraction followed inverse-square laws of distance, like gravity or magnetism. By the time they passed under the shadow of the Casino and came out on the other side, they were shoulder to shoulder; when they walked past the final strip of Asbury stores and were firmly within Ocean Grove, he took her by the hand.

They turned off Ocean Avenue onto Bath and followed the

street up through the colorful Victorian houses. Sophia followed behind. They walked on the south side of the street and she walked on the north, off of the sidewalk, barefoot on the grass. When they turned left onto the Pilgrim Pathway, Sophia waited behind and then followed. She had never been to Ocean Grove before, but she knew that it was a dry town owned almost entirely by the Methodist church, and that the worshippers—who called themselves Pilgrims—pitched tents in large cities all along the streets in May and stayed throughout the summer.

Ma tovu, she thought. *How lovely are your tents!*

It was the prayer for beginning all other prayers, a catalyst. The prophet Balaam had been sent by the king of Moab to curse the Jews. Only, upon seeing their tents he could not bring himself to do it.

How lovely are your tents, Jacob—your dwelling places, O Israel!

Sophia thought of her brother, of what he would say to her being here. She thought of the tents now as being his, as being Jacob's, and followed the couple through the rows of tents and onto the plaza of the Great Auditorium, the giant Methodist church that dominated the town. There were crosses all around, and she felt the strange exhilaration of one behind enemy lines.

"Do you want to buy an apple?" said a young boy. Sophia had nearly tripped over his table of goods, a plastic, foldable table with blue-and-white checkered tablecloth where small yellow apples were arranged in three stacked pyramids.

"Very much," said Sophia. The boy's eyes were nearly covered by straight brown hair which fell over his forehead in a bowl cut, and she could feel them drink her in. "I'd like to buy one very much, but I haven't got any money."

"Are you poor?"

"At the moment, yes. Very poor. Aren't you supposed to give to the poor?"

The boy looked around and leaned slightly forward in his chair.

"Are you really poor?" he said.

"No."

"But you'd like an apple anyway?"

"That's right."

"And you don't have any money?"

"No."

"But you aren't poor?"

"That's right," said Sophia again. "You wouldn't tell, would you?"

The boy shook his head, as if mesmerized by her words. Sophia took the apple and bit into it once before the boy, so that he could see what it was he had allowed, and then turned away.

She could not see the couple she'd been following, but she knew that they had gone into the Great Auditorium. It was the only place for them to have gone. Above its entrance was a white painted cross whose borders were lined with rows of incandescent bulbs, either turned off now or else simply outshone by the light of day. Beneath the cross, in brown paint against the beige-yellow exterior walls, read: Auditorium, and below it: 1894. Sophia tried both sets of front doors, although she knew that it was foolish. The front doors were bathed in sunlight and the couple had been sticking to the shade. They were like vampires, almost, or nocturnal creatures caught at daybreak. The third door she tried was a side door, an ugly brown rectangle painted into an ugly yellow wall. Its brass knob had been in the shade for so long that it was cool in her hand and the door pushed open easily. Sophia slipped inside and pulled the door shut behind her.

Her father had told her about the Auditorium, and she had read about it, too, but she had never been inside. She looked up now at the barrel-vaulted ceiling, which expanded out from the stage and made the room seem like the inside of a whale. The wooden surfaces glowed copper in the sunlight that poured in through the giant, vaulted windows and all through the air there were shining clouds of dust that drifted slowly, like clouds on a day without wind. Above the stage, there were three sections of brass organ piping, and the center one was covered over with a painted American flag, waving in an imagined wind, with lightbulbs standing in for stars and rows of them for stripes. It was funny, almost, this vulgar amalgamation of modernity, state, and god.

"Holiness to the Lord," said a voice toward the front of the room.

Sophia quickly ducked behind a row of benches, and the sound of her body coming down against the floor went through the hollow walls like thunder.

"Who's there?" said another voice up ahead.

Sophia recognized this second voice as belonging to the girl from the shop, but even as a whisper now within the vaulted skeleton of the Grand Auditorium, it echoed and rang with a strength and an authority.

"It's nobody," said the one with her. "Just some kid knocking on the outside. This place is like a drum."

Like a drum.

"Somebody's in here with us."

With us.

The echo of her whisper slithered out like a hiss from all the spaces in the walls.

"There's nobody in here. Watch—hello? Hello?"

The call echoed through space.

"Casey!"

Their echoes died down. Sophia crawled forward, under one row of benches and into the next, and then risked peeking out into the aisle until she could see all the way up to the stage. HOLINESS TO THE LORD read letters on the left side of the stage, and then jumped over the brass organ pipes and the painted flag to continue on the other side SO BE YE HOLY.

"Not here," said the shop girl. "No, not here."

"Not there. Not here. Where then?"

"Not here. Think of where we are."

"And also think of why we came."

"It's a church."

"So be ye holy."

"Casey."

The sound of her gasping filled the air like a storm and—as if by instinct—Sophia's eyes were drawn to the painted flag, whose painted fabric made waves along a flat and painted wind. Sophia crawled further one more row, beneath another bench. Her chest was pressed so firmly to the ground that she could feel her heartbeat going off like a mine beneath her. Down the long aisle between the center and right sections, she could see all the way to the front. She crawled under one more bench, and then another, and each time she felt the rough wooden edge of each bench's underside scrape along the back of her shoulders and the notches in her spine. She could hear the heavy breath of them ahead, and it seemed that the tall, barrel-vaulted beams were expanding and contracting, like a diaphragm or ribcage, growing and squeezing breath from the lungs of space, and on the glowing towers of sun-lit dust, she thought that she could understand the cadence of their motion by the pulsing out and in of particles or grains, as if the movements of her subjects had cast ripples in the air.

"That was someone," said the shop girl. Though afraid, her voice was not so quiet now. "I'm sure that was someone. I'm sure of it."

Sure of it.

"You're paranoid. Why do we come so far if it's only for you to be paranoid? You could be paranoid inside your car or underneath the boardwalk."

"There are people there who know us."

"And there aren't any here. That's the point. Isn't that the point?"

Sophia thought that the two of them were repeating their words because they felt that they should speak but could not think of anything to say besides what had been said already. In her own mind, she repeated their words over and over again. *That's the point. Isn't that the point. I'm sure of it. I'm sure of it. I'm sure.*

"That was someone. I'm sure that that was someone."

Someone.

Sophia could no longer tell whether or not she was responsible for sound. The beating of her chest against the floor was so heavy that she rolled onto her back and stared straight up at the underside of a bench. In the bottom of her vision, she watched the mounds of her breasts heaving and tried to make their motion shallow by restricting her breath to short, sharp breaths, as if reducing the volume of air moving in and out of her lungs would be critical in avoiding detection. She put one hand over her chest as if she could suppress the beating of her heart by putting pressure on it, the way you press down on a wound. Saliva filled her throat and each time she swallowed, it came back faster.

"That was someone. That was someone."

"Stop. Please stop. Please."

"Will you hurry."

"Don't make me."

"Hurry. Please hurry."

The wood of the floor groaned with the weight of them shifting and Sophia felt suddenly that she needed to flex against the confines of her space, and pressed her knees up into the rough underside of the bench above her and pushed her spine down into the wooden floor that was still bending with the stop start motion of the shop girl and the boy who looked like her but wasn't.

And then there was a sound, a definite sound like a door slamming, and there were voices—new voices—coming from far back, from behind the stage.

"Casey!" the shop girl whispered.

"Go," he said. "Go, go."

While the voices behind the stage grew clearer, the couple's footsteps ran up the aisle, toward Sophia. She made her body rigid and straight and shifted herself so that she was completely below the bench. She closed her eyes tight as their footsteps came closer, as if her blindness might keep them from seeing her. The footsteps came closer and then they moved past. Once they had, Sophia noticed that her feet were flexed and her toes were pointed down.

My toes, she thought. *My shoes.*

"Casey," said the shop girl. The voices behind the stage were becoming louder, but the shop girl had stopped. "Casey, these shoes weren't here when we came in."

"Leave them," he said. "They were there. I remember. Right there."

"Casey—"

There were footsteps from the stage and the voices became less muffled, as if they'd come out from behind a curtain.

"Leave them. Let's go."

Sophia did not hear the door open, but she heard it shut. She laid there still, staring up at the underside of the bench while two men spoke on stage. They spoke loudly, and suddenly the place did not seem sacred anymore, as it had only moments before. It was as if some god had descended on the place and then flown off, like a passing oracular vision, and been replaced with a lesson on maintenance. The men on stage discussed the lighting and the switches, they spoke about the organ and cleaning the brass pipes. Sophia heard the buzz of electricity fill the hall like locusts when one of them demonstrated the switch, but there was no difference in the light she saw, and the hum went away as quickly as it had come. Sophia thought that it must have been lights of the painted flag, or of the words that flanked it on either side. HOLINESS TO THE LORD. SO BE YE HOLY.

The organ sounded as one of the men pressed several keys. At first, the sheer volume of it made Sophia jump, but beyond the first notes, the sound was a comfort—it was something like a shroud of darkness, and she felt that she could move freely and undetected once again. Sophia slithered back the way she had come—underneath the benches—and thought that her body must have shrunk because now her spine cleared the space beneath the benches without any trouble. On the floor just under the final bench she crawled beneath, there was a quarter that she had not seen before. She picked it up and moved it through her fingers; for her, there was the illicit thrill of handling currency on the Sabbath. She blew the dust from the surface and then held the coin between her lips while she crawled beneath the final bench and lifted herself up off her belly and onto her knees. She removed the quarter and tucked it into the waistband of her skirt.

Sophia peered over the back of the last bench and watched the two men on stage. One, indeed, looked like a janitor, in a white shirt and jean overalls, while the other wore a mustard-yellow shirt, the same color as the outside walls, tucked into khaki pants. Their backs were turned to her, as the one in the yellow shirt tapped out a simple tune using only one of the many keyboards, and the one who Sophia figured for the janitor looked up at the brass organ pipes in exaggerated awe. Sophia did not wait to see their faces, but picked up her shoes from where she had left them and ran quietly out the side door.

Once outside, Sophia ran quickly to the rows of tents, hid behind the first one she came to, and watched the Auditorium's side door to see if either of the men had followed her out. Satisfied that they had not, she turned around and found herself face to face with the boy who had given her an apple. All of the other apples were still stacked in their same pyramids on the table; Sophia was certain that none of the configurations had changed, and she wondered how long she had been inside the church.

"You're dirty," he said. "Are you really poor, then?"

She looked down at her blouse and her skirt; both were orange with dust. She brushed them off and then knelt down so that her eyes were level with the boy's.

"No," she said, playing with the waistline of her skirt until her fingers found the quarter. "In fact, I only came back to pay you for my apple."

Still looking at the boy, Sophia laid the quarter down on the laminated sign before him. Only when he had taken the quarter and turned to unzip his coin purse did she look down at the sign: Lodi Apples: $2.00/lb. Home Grown and Hand-Picked By REAL FARMERS in Acacia Grove, PA.

"Is that where you're from?" she said. "Acacia Grove?"

"Ah-*cay*-sha," the boy said. There was a gap in his smile where a front tooth was missing. Sophia smiled back at him and, feeling that she needed to touch something, reached over the table and ruffled his hair.

CHAPTER 10

. . . And My Sandals to Julia Swift

Madame K watched the white boy come in. She thought of him now as being white, which was funny to her. Mostly when she saw other white people she did not think of their whiteness; considerations of color were reserved strictly for others. When she saw a Black person, the first thing she noted was that they were, in fact, Black. Or brown or yellow. Everything else came after. If the "everything else" was something that she expected of their color, it deepened the shade; something unexpected and it whitened it. But the shade itself could never be escaped. She thought of Gabrielle as hardly Black at all—after all, the girl was very well-spoken and intelligent and had those sharp blue eyes like a glacier. But of course she was still Black, and in her Blackness she radiated a sort of color-cognizance around her that spread to anyone she interacted with before her old employer. And so when she was visited by a boy who was not Black the boy stopped being just a normal boy and became white. And here he was now, for the second day in a row.

It was a brutally hot day—too hot for many people to be out on the boardwalk. Each time a customer opened the door, Julie Kowolski counted the seconds and thought about the expensive, cold air that was escaping her shop. She sat on a high white stool behind the register, just below the AC unit, fanning herself with a stack of bills that felt almost damp with humidity. Trails of sweat worked down her back, and she shifted her shoulders to create a space between her shirt and her spine that cold air might find its way into. She felt personally affronted by the temperature, as if all the air had warmed only to draw out her sweat. A customer came in, and Julie's eyes thinned as the door opened and then slowly settled back into its frame.

If it had been any less hot, she would have closed in on the customer, or at least ordered Gabrielle to do it, but Madame K could not even think of being on her feet, let alone stepping out from beneath the wall unit and its stream of cold air. And besides, she was not much interested in the customer.

Julie watched Gabrielle and the white boy and decided that there was something strange in the way they interacted. It was as if they were children in love, who wanted desperately to touch one another but could not find a suitable pretense upon which to do so. The boy picked things up and then handed them to Gabrielle, and each time he did their fingers touched beneath the fabric. Madame K was sure of it, and she was sure that that was why he continued to pick things up in the first place. What she could not understand was why Gabrielle was tolerating it; it was by no means unusual for a male customer to come in and feign interest in order to flirt with the girls, but Gabrielle had a nose for them. She could smell them out and did not tolerate them. She never even allowed that boyfriend of hers to come inside the store. And she hated the extra work of refolding clothes.

The woman customer walked out without Gabrielle having noticed her. The door closed slowly, and Madame K felt the beads of sweat roll down her back.

"Excuse me," Madame K called as the door shut. "Excuse me. It's only women's clothing in here."

The boy turned away from Gabrielle. His shoulders were relaxed and there was nothing nervous in him. Julie Kowolski liked to inspire a certain respect, and she felt that it had not been inspired in this visitor. He walked up to the register slowly, smiling.

"I'm buying a gift," he said.

"Who for? What's their size?"

Beside one of the display tables, Gabrielle smiled as she refolded one of the pieces that her visitor had picked up. Madame K felt that she was being laughed at in her own shop.

"Alright," said the boy. "I'm not buying a gift."

"I knew it. I always know it and I knew it. If you aren't buying a gift then you've got no business in here. It's only women's clothing."

The boy nodded but did not leave immediately. He looked around, inspecting the shop. At least, thought Julie, he understands that this is a good store with nice things. I can see that in his face. It's an attractive face and he's got an attractive body. I wonder how he would match up to that boy who comes to see Gabrielle. They are about the same size but the Blacks always have an advantage in physical fights. Still, there is something dangerous in his eyes and really I would like to see them fight. He's got an attractive face that does not look as if it could be touched by another fist. Physically, yes. But something about the face would remain even if the skin went to pieces or the cheeks swelled up and exploded.

The face was close to her now. It was clear to Madame K that the boy was showing off for Gabrielle, and she wanted to break him or at least to see if he was afraid of being broken.

"Gabrielle," she said, looking at the boy all the while. "There's nobody coming in today. Why don't you take off early. I've seen that flirt of yours lurking around, and I'm sure he'd be glad for some company. Hot summer days were made for young love, after all. For the rest of us, all that matters is to find some shade. Isn't that right?"

The boy came closer, still looking around at the decor.

"What about those?" he asked, pointing behind Julie.

"What about what?"

"Those. You said that there was only women's clothing here, but look at those sandals. I'll take them. How much?"

Julie did not have to turn around, and she did not want to. She knew which sandals the boy spoke of. They had been hanging beside her register for a very long time. Her face went cold.

"They aren't your size," she said quietly.

"Well, let's try them on and see," he said. Gabrielle was smiling and folding shirts. "I think I could—"

"They aren't for sale. Now get out!"

Madame K was on her feet. She felt a hot flush rise through her body, but was uncertain of whether it came from her blood or from the effort of standing up. She looked down at her feet, as if unsure of how she'd come to possess them. She was wearing sandals, and the weight of her body pushed her skin out toward the edges of them. She breathed out and sank back onto the stool. It was a high stool and her torso did not move so much vertically to sit back down, but all of her body now seemed to sag. Gravity pulled on every inch of her, and she suddenly felt as if she were taking up too much space. She began playing with the antique register, and her painted fingernails shook as they moved between the vintage metal keys.

The boy understood that the game was over, and went to the door. He did not look again at the sandals on the wall.

"I think I will take off early," said Gabrielle, leaving the last shirt deliberately unfolded. She followed her visitor out from the store.

Madame K did not care. Her mind was elsewhere. She closed her eyes and leaned against the register. The doorbell jingled as a customer came in.

"We're closed," said Julie, without looking up.

"You should put up a sign." The customer stood in the open door while she waited for a response, and the hot air came rushing into the shop.

"I forgot," said Julie. She did not have the energy to fight. "Please, we're closed."

The door slowly shut. Julie Kowolski stood up and came out from behind the register to bolt the door. She flipped the sign to "closed" and pulled down the white venetian blinds, flipping them so that no sunlight could come through the windows. It came in anyway, but dim and cool, so that the room was colored blue and gray like early dawn. There was the hum of the wall unit and the fickle circulation of air that it inspired in the room, but otherwise all was still. And quiet.

Julie walked through the store on the balls of her feet so that she would not feel so heavy. She did not allow her hips to kick out but kept her motion in a straight, tight line, the way a ballerina moves across a stage. Her hands spread wide and pet the fabric of hanging shirts or dresses or pants, and Julie trusted all of her senses to her fingers; she would not look at her hands because she did not want to be reminded of what it was they looked like. Or maybe it was not so much what they looked like as what they did not look like, for she did not have bad wrinkles or liver spots, but her skin had nothing of the youthful glow it once did, and it was easier for her to pretend if unconfronted by a vision of reality. And so she watched the walls, the ceiling, the room that spun around her.

Eventually, she came to stand beside the register. There was the cold wind falling from the wall unit and there were the sandals pinned against the wall before her. She had not looked at them in a very long time. They were brown, simple sandals with worn leather straps that would cross over the top of a foot. And whose foot? The cork soles were only vaguely indented now, and there was only the slightest trace of an indentation left by the shape of the wearer's sole, of the wearer's weight. And whose sole? Whose weight?

She had not touched the sandals in a long time but now she ran her fingers over their edges, along the straps, up to the buckles. No portion of the sandals held any temperature; they had hung there so long that they were more like a cancer of the sheetrock than they were like separate things.

Whose weight?

His name had been Gal Marhabba. His family was one of the first Syrian Jewish families to come to New Jersey, and Gal had grown up spending his summers in Deal, much like Madame K's runner did now. Gal's mother had been proud in the way that only beautiful, first generation Americans can be. The grandmother, Julie remembered, had once come to the church to confront a speaker who was preaching about the need of Israel to open its doors to Palestine, to quell the Intifada. The grandmother had said, with such lovely, wrinkled dignity and an accent that sounded almost French, "My friend, I was a girl in Syria. I watched them pull my father from his shop by his beard and drag him through the streets until there was not a hair left on his chin. Let them in? You do not know of what you speak." The old woman had carried herself like royalty—such proud blood! And that same proud blood had been passed down to her daughter, Gal's mother, who had come knocking once on Julie's door . . .

Of course, she had been Julia, then—Julia Swift. She could not remember when the last syllable had floated off, or why, only that it had gone. But what she could remember was the night that Gal's mother had come knocking. She was called Adinah—what names these people had!—and Adinah had come knocking on little Julia Swift's door, because she understood that the pretty young girl held a certain power over her darling Gal. Gal wanted to go to the army—the American army—and Adinah wanted Julia to stop him.

Power, thought Julie, that had been power.

But it had not been power, for she had not been able to convince him to stay. At the end, he was doing it more for himself than for her, although she was certainly in his thoughts. And perhaps, she thought, if she had turned to him on that last night and tried, really tried, she could have pulled him close against her chest and kept him there. But when he came to call on her, to say goodbye, she had not even been able to look at him. It was nighttime and he was to go in the morning. She sat before her vanity, brushing her long, golden hair, and she could not even look away from her own reflection to face him. He had stood there for some time, neither of them speaking, and then he said:

"Well, goodbye then."

"Goodbye," she thought, but could not remember if she had said it. She did not turn to face him. He began to leave and then turned back to her.

"You're well on your way to becoming a flower," he told her.

"Thank you," she said. And then once he had left she said once more, to the mirror: "Thank you."

She never saw him again after that, although he wrote to her often in the months before he died. He was not supposed to die; the Gulf War was not a war that people died in. Julia's father had had friends who died in Vietnam, in Korea. Her grandfather had had friends who had died in the Second World War. But Iraq? It was not the kind of war that people died in. And yet Gal had died in it anyway.

He had eaten nothing on the morning that he died because he had heard that a bullet in the gut was worse if it shared the space with anything else, anything that bacteria might swarm to. Gal Marhabba had been terribly afraid of a bullet in the gut. At the end, whether he had eaten or not would have made no difference, because where they shot him was through the cheek, with a long, high caliber bullet that had come in so hard and so fast that there was a sharp dent in the back of his helmet that had been pushed outward by the force.

A black government car had come to deliver the news, along with the helmet and a flag to Adinah's home in Flatbush. Also, there was a letter. It was a rare thing to have a letter from a soldier that had not died in hospice, but Gal Marhabba had been such a morbid, frightened boy that he had written a letter in case of the worst and kept it on his person always. There was a will involved, too, and it was the last line of the will that made Adinah get in her car and drive down from Flatbush to Julia Swift's house on Deal Lake, only Julia Swift no longer lived with her parents, and she was not Julia Swift anymore.

". . . and my sandals to Julia Swift," Adinah read aloud. Before her she held a photocopy of Gal's will, with everything blacked out except the final line, not willing to allow Julia to read a single word that did not directly concern her, "and my sandals to Julia Swift."

"And you are not even Julia Swift anymore," said Adinah. Her dark, gleaming eyes shone with all the grayness of the sky.

"No," said Julie. "It's Kowolski now."

"Kowolski," said Adinah. They stood on the front lawn and Adinah looked behind Julia and dragged her eyes over the house and the shutters and the blinds and the red door and the porch. "Kowolski. Polish?"

Julia nodded.

"Why did he leave you these sandals?" said Adinah. Her voice was trembling and she took one cautious step forward toward Julie. A breeze came through the cool autumn air and one of the shutters rattled against the house. Julie turned her head slightly back toward the noise as if to listen, as if she thought that the house might offer some encouragement.

"I don't know," she said, still turned halfway back toward the house.

"Why did he leave you these sandals? Why did he go?"

"I don't know!" screamed Julie.

Adinah slapped her hard across the cheek. It was a small, sharp sound, as small and sharp as the din of wooden shutters against the house. Adinah's hand covered her mouth, and she looked surprised to have hit the girl before her. Julie's hand went to her reddening cheek, and she seemed to draw strength from the violence.

"I don't know," she said again. "I don't know, and I don't want to know. But if you don't get off my lawn, I'll call the police! That's what I'll do. This is a nice town in the fall. It's fall now. It isn't yours now, it isn't yours."

Julie swayed as if the wind had moved her. "It isn't yours," she said again, but all the meaning had gone out of her voice. She was only speaking to make sound, and she did not understand what she was saying. Adinah took a step toward her, no longer angry but afraid for the girl, and Julie stepped back, frightened.

"Alright," said Adinah. "I'll go. I would like to leave the sandals, even though they are not truly addressed to you anymore. I would like to leave them and one day if they remind you or suggest to you why my son went willingly to die, it would take a great question from my shoulders. Questions are the things with weight. Answers can be sharp but only questions have the real weight. I'm going to leave them here," she said, and laid the sandals on the grass in the small space between herself and Julie, bending at the waist and keeping her eyes on Julie the whole time, cautious as an animal feeder at the zoo. The grass was dry and hard and the sandals were not heavy enough to flatten it. "If you don't want them, say so. Otherwise I will leave them here and go."

No response came, and so Adinah left them there and went. The black car sped off and Julie watched it trace the perimeter of Deal Lake and then disappear into Allenhurst. Long after it was gone, Julie stood there, looking down at the shoes as if they were weeds that had impossibly grown back after careful removal. Eventually she picked them up and went back toward the house. Once she had climbed the three stairs up to the porch, she approached the red door and rang the doorbell. She rang it again. She seemed to have forgotten that it was her own house, that her husband was at work, that there was nobody else inside. She lifted the brass knocker and knocked three times, and then turned away from the door and sank into her rocking chair and looked out over the water. On days like this it was very still and flat and just before the far bank the surface held a near perfect reflection of the trees that rose around the houses on the far side of the lake. It was autumn and their leaves were red and yellow and the color kept in the dark water but mostly the leaves were gone and the branches were barren. She liked the trees best this way, when she could tell the real shape of them. A wind came across the water and she lost the reflection in the ripples. The birds flew very low above the water and cast dark and flitting shadows.

Strange, she thought, that it is not the news itself but the hearing of the news that makes you feel a certain way. Probably I would never have seen Gal again, and that was alright. The heartbreak of that was over. And it was not his dying but the news of his dying. Why had Adinah brought the news? She had come down in her shiny black car and shiny black eyes and given black news of Gal's death. Why had she done it? What did she care if Julia Swift knew? No, she thought, not Julia Swift.

Julie Kowolski remembered something that her own mother had done. Her son—Julie's younger brother—had gone everywhere by bicycle. He'd gotten a seven-speed for Christmas one year and rode it as if trying to wear out the tread marks on its tires. But he never wore a helmet, and Julie's mother was always on him about the helmet and threatened to take away the bike if he wouldn't wear one, but he wouldn't wear one and still she did not take the bike away.

The boy was crushed by an eighteen-wheeler—or, more accurately, he was touched barely by an eighteen-wheeler and thrown into the air and then crushed by the ground. Anyone reasonable could see that it would not have mattered if he had been wearing a helmet or not, but it was all that Julia's mother wanted to know. "Was he wearing a helmet? I am owed that knowledge. I am owed it." Of course he wasn't, Julia had wanted to yell at her mother, he never owned one to begin with. It would have been a remarkable coincidence if on the day he'd purchased one, a truck had flattened him. "Was he wearing one? I want to know—I *want* to know!"

Julie stared at the water and heard her mother's voice. It was as if the ghost of her mother had possessed the reflections of autumn on the lake.

What right did she have to come here? Julie thought. She tried to pick out the spot in the grass where Adinah had left the sandals but could not, and then turned finally to the sandals themselves. They were dark, and the shape of his foot was fresh in the cork, like a handprint left in asphalt.

Asphalt had been just as much a culprit in Gal's fall as the sandals. It was as if the two of them had worked together, whispered to one another across the baking summer air. Gal was proud of his Israeli sandals, and he wore them everywhere. Aside from the sandals, he wore only a bathing suit that hardly covered his thighs. He wore the same one each day, so that the tan lines on his waist and thighs where the skin turned from brown to white were sudden, almost violent. He was not very big, but he worked on his build and he was proud of it. He was proud in general. Together they would walk the beach and he would take his proud sandals in his proud, brown fingers and puff out his proud brown chest as they walked past the Syrian boys playing volleyball. Of course, he never showed Julia to his parents, or any adults in the community, but he liked to show her off to his friends, and he often walked her home, from Deal Beach south to Allenhurst, so that he might walk past them without walking past their parents or his own. Every day, he walked Julia to her door.

On the day that it happened, they had left the sand and were walking along the road. The blacktop was torn up by years of neglect, and it was baking in the late afternoon sun. They had barely stepped onto the pavement when they were suddenly surrounded by three boys on bicycles. The boys had been friends of Julia's brother when he was alive, and they swarmed now around Julia and Gal like wolves. They were younger than the couple by a few years; her brother would have been fifteen and they were roughly the same age.

"I don't think Evan would have liked his sister going around with some Jew," said one of them. "Everybody knows a Jew doesn't know how to take care of his girl."

Gal stepped in front of Julia, to protect her as best he could, but they were all around him and there was no way to adequately protect her; and anyway, it was not Julia that needed protecting.

"Well, what do you have to say. Running around with a kike."

But Julia did not have anything to say. And when they dropped their bikes she did not have anything to say. And when they feigned at him from different angles to watch how he reacted she did not have anything to say. And when the one at his back moved in toward her and struck out with his fist against the back of Gal's head, she screamed and ran out of the circle and watched from the grass, but still she did not have anything to say.

All she could do was watch, and she did watch, and she felt herself brave for watching. It had not been an easy thing to watch. On the sand, or on grass, Gal could have easily taken any one of them, possibly all three. They were so little, like children, and their fists did not amount to much. But Gal could hardly move. His feet slipped in the cork soles of his sandals, and soon they had fallen off. The asphalt was broken up and hot as a cast iron pan, and would have been nearly impossible to walk on in bare feet without wincing. The boys were all in sneakers. They spun around him and took turns punching the back of his head. After the fourth punch, he took one knee, and he winced as his leg lay flat against the hot and broken pavement, but as another boy rushed him, Gal grabbed the boy and got him into a headlock and lay down with his bare back against the pavement and the choking boy on top of him like a shield.

"I'll kill him if you don't go," Gal screamed. His voice was heavy with pain from the scorching tar against his back. "I swear to god I'll kill him."

It seemed for a minute that the other boys might really leave. Gal took the opportunity to relieve his burning back and he rolled over so that the boy he had in a headlock was flat against the pavement, his whole young cheek pressed down into the burning black asphalt, and the boy began to scream.

"It's burning, it's burning," in such wailing, violent cries that his friends forgot that they themselves had been the aggressors and now took on a mindset of vengeance. One ran and kicked Gal just below the ribs. Gal gasped but maintained his hold on the boy, still screaming, and so the other came and kicked him in the head. Gal rolled off and lay once more with his back to the asphalt and his face looking up at blue afternoon sky with not a cloud to block the sun, and the boys took turns kicking him. The one whose face Gal had held against the pavement screamed—"You don't get to burn me, you fucking kike. It's you kikes who are good at burning. Burn, you fucking kike!"

And Gal laid there while their small feet kicked him, and he laid there long after they had left. When finally he stood up, Julia was only half-looking at him. There were tears on her face that shone brilliantly with sunlight. She looked at him as if he were not a man, but a wounded dog.

"I'm not hurt badly," he told her. He walked toward her and she took a step back, and he could not tell whether it was because there was blood on his face or because she was disgusted. "You could have said something. It might have helped."

"They were boys," she said. "What did you want me to do? Hurt them? They were children."

"They didn't sound like children. They didn't act like children."

"You're nineteen! They're fifteen, if that! I thought you'd be able to defend yourself!"

"They were all in tennis shoes! How could I move in these," he said. He bent down and picked up the sandals. He had always been such a calm boy but now his hands shook with rage or something else. He had never spoken angrily to her but now he could not help it. "How could I move in these—how? And you—you scared bitch! You just sat there! Did you enjoy the show? Would your ancestors have been proud? Would your dead brother have been proud that you watched a Jew get beaten?"

Gal threw the sandals down at her feet, and one grazed her calf. They were light things, only leather and rubber and cork, and he did not throw it with so much force, but Julia began to wail. She bent down and held her shin as if it were in great pain.

"Maybe they were right!" she said. She picked up the sandals and threw them back at Gal. One missed and landed behind him, and the other he caught. "Maybe you Jews don't know how to take care of your girls!"

"You're not my girl," Gal screamed. "You're just a scared blond shiksa cunt!"

The air was very still between them and the heat rose off the pavement and boiled their blood. Gal turned away from Julia with his sandals in his hand and walked back to the beach on the path of sand that went between the dunes.

Julia had watched him until he disappeared. She had watched Adinah's car until it disappeared. Each morning she watched her runner as he came and went and came and went and disappeared. She was always watching things until they disappeared, she thought. It was simply her nature.

Madame K ran her fingers along the soft edges of the sandals. All that was left of a once-love was a depression left by his weight. On the wall above the sandals, the Mitsubishi unit hummed. Cool air fell down each time the pulsing cycle of its vents came to an end, and Julie felt that she was conversing with a ghost.

CHAPTER 11

Greetings from Asbury Park

It was late afternoon, almost evening, but in the dark room of the Saint bar on Main Street, the daylight outside made no difference. Gabrielle sat down at a little round table. She and the band had finished going through their set while the manager of the Saint had worked on the stage lights, but the show he'd been working on seemed to have nothing to do with the music and it had kept them at an arm's length from their own performance, had kept the rehearsal from being really satisfying. There was a feeling in the space now of something half-boiled; Liam put away his cymbals, the pianist sat at his bench, his fingers going through motions as if practicing on a phantom instrument but failing to come down on the keys. His eyes watched as the manager went around turning on lights, and then both he and Liam watched as the manager came and tried to speak with Gabrielle. He was always trying to speak with Gabrielle and always while he spoke with her they watched him.

"I always say that this place is like the opposite of Vegas," he said, nodding toward the wall of glass cubes that did deceivingly little to let in the daylight. He was holding a coil of extension cord wrapped around his forearm and with his other hand pulled out the seat opposite of Gabrielle. He did not sit down but she looked up at him. "In Vegas they've got ceilings that look like sky, so you never know that it isn't daytime. There they keep out the night. Here it's just like the opposite of that."

Gabrielle looked at the glass bricks but did not look up at the manager and still he did not sit down.

"Did I ever tell you that I was in Vegas? I worked on a show there. Everybody came there. I saw Keith Richards one time, up close. I saw Celine Dion, too."

Gabrielle finally looked up at him, but only with her eyes— nothing else of her moved.

"But I always say that this place is like the opposite of Vegas," he said again. He lifted his hand from the back of the chair.

"You mean that it's dark," said Liam, coming over with his cymbals in his hand. "You mean that it's a dark room. That's profound."

Liam sat in the chair that the manager had pulled out. There was bad tension in the room and it wasn't really the fault of the clumsy lights or of the manager who had produced them, but he was the easiest target now for their bitterness and he absorbed it all. He went out through the back and still the space remained constricted, wound tight like a steel string inside the chest of a piano.

As soon as the door closed, the pianist began to play. It was easier to play than to talk, and they all felt the necessity of keeping out the silence. Gabrielle watched what was visible of the pianist: his feet on the pedals beneath the piano and his shoulders and face above it. Gabrielle knew why he had waited for the manager to leave, he had vocalized the sentiment frequently enough.

His father had signed the list of twenty demands in 1970 and had later been arrested in the riots. That was when they had still been making arrests instead of simply abandoning the town as a lost cause, but that hadn't stopped them from keeping him in prison. And now he felt that every time he played in a white bar, where the owners and the managers were white, he was betraying a piece of his father's failed revolution. But all of the owners and the managers were white and so he played for them out of necessity, but only the jazz that they paid him to play; he was through now with jazz and onto something else, and above all he wouldn't play white music for a white manager; it felt to him in some way like pandering, like servitude, and he refused on principle to do it. But principle could not keep him from wanting to hear the sounds or wanting to play them, and as soon as they were alone in the room, his fingers came down heavy on the keys and the space—wound tight as coil, eternally dark—exploded and shook with the opening chords of Sonata no. 8, the *Pathétique*.

"Pathetic," said Liam. He liked this little joke, this little business of willful mistranslation, this resolve to interpret each word to its least generous form. He watched Gabrielle's face and she felt his eyes but kept her own pointed only at the piano— no longer at the pianist but at the instrument itself, this source of unseen radiation, a dark and different sort of sun. In the silent space between the first climb and the second explosion, Liam corrected himself: "really it doesn't mean pathetic," he said, rushing his words out so as not to interfere with the chords, "it means passionate."

"Really it means pitiable," she told him, but she had not waited for a silent stretch and her words were lost in space. She did not repeat them.

Pitiable, she thought. Look at the pitiable condition of this unrelenting anger, this slavery masquerading as defiance, this allowing of some other presence or absence to dictate what they will and will not play. Should I be honored that they'll play for me, and will they always? What is this "me" to them—is it white, is it Black? Is it rich, is it poor? Is it colleague, is it friend, is it hopeful future lover? Liam knows about Casey—in erasing the possibility of us, have I erased, in his mind, a part of me? What is left of me to give to him now, and what do I remain. Friend or failure? What is left of me now and what do I remain; oppressor with a downward weight that depresses him with its gravity, or part of the same depressed spring, united in our attempts to spread our coils? What is left: all, none, other? What a multitude of things you were forced to be in a little town! All these unlived memories that attached themselves to strange unintuitive things, like the color of your skin, or the last name of your father, or the sex between your legs. Could an excess of dark pigment recall the sharp end of a whip? Could a lack of it recall the guilty weight of having swung it? How many memories could squeeze themselves into a little cell! What a horrible inheritance that could make the world so small, that could pull the continents together so that here, in a little bar on Main Street on the shoreline of New Jersey, sat Ireland and Africa, impossibly at war!

Ella listened to the notes climb and then cascade, like rock slides down an octave. It seemed to her that she was stretched wide across some vast dark space and contracting all the time, just the opposite of the way that earth had pulled apart Pangea . . . The notes began to move fast and she thought of a rendering she had seen once of the supercontinent. She had only been a girl then, but had seen vividly in her mind the reversal of time and of space, so that the Atlantic, the Mediterranean were squeezed out into nothing and New Jersey approached and then kissed the northern coast of Africa. She had imagined then—as she imagined now—the two continents coming together like great ships colliding, the coast of either land lined with its people, all in their best formal clothes: dark suits and dresses in Asbury Park and then colorful robes and gold beads in Africa. And they stood apart like seabirds on their opposite shorelines with the oceans disappearing between them, sand coming onto sand, and the little figures shouted across the narrowing sea: "Greetings from Morocco!" and she in her funeral black returned "Greetings from Asbury Park!"

Liam's face in the darkness reflected the green lights on the stage and glowed like a sickly crescent moon. In his eyes there were tears. He gave himself over completely to sound and with the *Pathétique* now he was crying. Only the tears did not run down his cheeks but hung in the thick folds of his eyes like a reluctant, marsupial sadness. . . Or perhaps it wasn't sadness but the opposite of sadness but it looked enough like sadness in the dark. There was a rhythm to the climbing notes that infected Ella's thoughts and the moving stage lights—just a disco light now with the manager having gone—began to play with colors in the room . . .

Suddenly, Liam's face was no longer there against the shadow of the Saint, but instead in profile against the off-white sand of the beach in November. But aside from the background the face was the same—six years younger, but essentially the same—and with the same wetness in the eyes but now it fell down onto his cheeks and the green glow was replaced by a gray autumn light. It hung to his face and especially to the trail of tears, shining now like loose streaks of paint which fall from the ends of graffiti . . .

They were in their Sunday best, in their funeral black, only now there was no celebration, no banners, no slow-approaching Africa opposite them, but only the sea, gray-green in November with the clouds moving fast and hard above the choppy waves, left to right, from north to south, like a flock of migratory geese.

Liam's father had died and they stood there, a small group of them—no more than twenty—to scatter his ashes on the sea. "Actually," said Liam's mother as they had walked down from the boardwalk to the sand and to the salt and to the water, "actually he put a deposit down to have them scattered from an airplane." But it was not enough of a deposit and she could not afford the balance. "Actually," said Liam's mother, "it's really for the best because who in all hell would want to breathe in that poison? Who in all hell and in what hell would want that poison in their lungs. . ." She had thrown up these small barbed comments to defend against the reality of her husband's death, but as they approached the sea the stoniness in her face had cracked and then crumpled and—reflected above—the sky was moving fast and darker clouds were moving toward them on long fingers, or not exactly toward them but not away from them either. It was impossible to say whether the droplets on the air were the salt spray of the ocean or else rain. And as they moved toward the water and through a wide group of gulls that seemed to take up half the beach with their yellow eyes and orange feet, the gulls lifted up into the air and turned their bodies with the wind and the coming storm so that it took them no effort whatsoever to float quickly southward and then resettle on the sand, and Liam's mother had said "Why do they insist on coming down? It might be nice after all, over that big blue . . . it might be nice and they could simply float whenever their arms grow tired . . ." and Liam had corrected her and said: "Wings."

Liam's mother had then turned and held her son's face in her hands and then turned back to the sea and said: "He could have died in August," for the wind and the temperature of the water promised to make her task difficult. She took off her black leather slips and waded out into the wake, holding her dress up so that the hem would not be wet, shifting her weight from foot to foot to try to keep the blood flowing and so combat the cold. But she was so little and the ocean so vast that her warmth could do nothing, mean nothing to its infinite coldness and the preacher had tried to rush through his speech, but Liam's father had been very specific and there was much text to get through. In order to twist the cap from the little steel urn, Liam's mother had dropped her dress and the heavy cotton hem came down on the water where it quickly became soaked and then made a sound like a drum as it began to writhe and whip in the wind . . .

"Actually, who in all hell and in what hell would want that poison in their lungs," Liam's mother had asked, and now some conspiracy of ocean and storm gathered their answer around her feet going numb in the cold and threw the wind back into her face so that the ash flew up to meet her when she turned it out, and suddenly she was staggering back, stumbling out of the wake with her dress whipping and black as a storm cloud against the gray sea. She had dropped the little steel canister and it bobbed on the thin shining wake and began to move south, just like everything else and Liam began to run after it but then stopped and stood for a moment half-paralyzed, stuck between the living and the dead, between the ashes of his father and his mother, who was falling away from the ocean and had spun—as if by accident—to face the group. Her wet black cotton dress was stuck to her chest so that they could see her lungs heaving, breathing in and breathing in and then expelling the air by calling out "I can taste him, I can taste him," and she fell to her knees in the sand and took great fistfuls of it as maybe meaning to scrape the taste from her tongue and Liam had stood there frozen and then finally looked away from the canister and went to catch his mother and hold her wrists in his hands. The canister, unwatched now, picked up speed and moved south in the thin gray water just like the wind and the sand and the gulls and like everything else . . .

Everybody else had rushed then to Liam's mother, but Ella had stood very still, as if grief was a predator that detected only motion, as if by her stillness she could somehow avoid it. She looked up at the sky because she could not stand to look at Liam and his mother. Or rather, she could stand it but it made her feel embarrassed and unfit for the show she was seeing, like a blind man gone to an art gallery or a deaf man hammering clumsily on the keys of a piano. She had looked up at the sky and now the gray began to separate into white and black keys and she was back in the Saint and the *Pathétique* was still going and she had been watching Liam's face glowing green.

He felt her eyes on him and turned to her, and must have thought that she was watching his tears because his lip curled and he said:

"*Pathétique*," he said, as if it were necessary to excuse his tears, "passionate." He closed his eyes and their closing pushed the water to one side but still it did not fall onto his cheek.

Gabrielle understood that he was not speaking about the music. "Actually," she said, or perhaps she didn't say, "it means pitiable." She stood up and walked for the door. She heard him call her name but she did not turn back and she went through the door and out onto the street. Daylight was quickly failing in the sky and the door closed behind her, slamming into its frame like a cleaver coming down on a butcher block. "Gabby . . ." Liam had called, and it was as if she had severed the name from her person. It felt foolish, young, naive.

She had not gone to her own father's funeral. Why hadn't she gone? She tried to think now of her arguments but could not remember any of them. She could remember the stubbornness, but it seemed to her now like an act that she had put on out of necessity, like a sequined dress, or rouge. On the first night that her and Casey were together she had been wearing a sequined dress and rouge and he had slipped the straps off her shoulders and let it fall to the floor of the dark room where it somehow found light to catch and hold in its black-purple sequins and it shimmered like a pool upon the floor. He had not taken off her rouge—how could he have taken off her rouge?—but in the morning it was gone anyway when she looked in the mirror, and she had opened up the mirror in order to turn it, so as not to be watched by her own reflection, and in the medicine cabinet behind it had been her father's razor and his toothbrush, and some trick of the light made the bristles glitter as if he'd only just been there and she closed the mirror again and then rushed from the room and from the house.

She turned back to look at the Saint. How little it looked from the outside! How neat, how gross! How stucco and stale, how beige! Worst of all, how quiet . . .

She had gone to Liam's father's funeral but she had not gone to her own. Why hadn't she gone? The notion of death swirled around in her head where it mixed with the notion of love. For what was death without love? What did it matter when strangers, when seabirds, when dogs in the street, when coastal Moroccans with their Greetings banners died? And if that was so, and without love death was a thing without sharpness, then by refusing to love could one remove the fangs from death?

She had not gone to her own father's funeral. Why hadn't she gone?

She had crossed to the east side of Main Street as she walked south so that the cars came at her endlessly, their headlights glowing against the pink-purple evening sky, so that she could see them coming from far off and then glowing and growing in a steady crescendo until they reached her and then: nothing. No lessening, no gradual dimming, but only an eruption as they passed by her field of vision and then were gone, replaced for a moment by a red flash of brake lights, perhaps confused with evening sky . . .

Her eyes had been on the sidewalk before her, rolled out like a pale-gray tongue pointing south, but now she looked up at the evening, and it seemed that the lane of sky above her was a sort of median between west and east, day and night. She turned east, and from over the Atlantic came little streaks of darkness, evening creeping in on long fingers, rivulets of dark. They crossed the lane, the median above her—they crossed the afterimage of the pale gray sidewalk like a tongue that had stayed in her vision . . .

Ella remembered walking with Joseph as a girl. It was before she knew that his kindness was like an act (like sequins, like rouge), and one day they had been walking hand in hand down the sidewalk, when suddenly there was a screech before them and then a scream; three driveways ahead, a reversing car had hit a small white dog, so small that it had not even been hit with the bumper but crushed beneath the tire. She had looked for the body but couldn't find it. All there had been was a dark stained mop in a scarlet puddle, leaking down the pale pavement in long streams which sometimes joined, making oblong ovals of bloodless space between. All the streams stopped where the sidewalk met the street and began to ooze down toward the gutter, no rush at all . . .

They had stepped into the street to avoid the blood, but otherwise they said nothing as they passed it; Joseph, too, had been embarrassed by death. Only many steps later did he say: "a dog doesn't even know that it's alive. Which means it doesn't know it's got to die. Which means it doesn't matter when it does." She had accepted it then, had always as a young girl accepted Joseph's hyperlogic, his cynic's view of the world in which the only god was competition, the only heaven evolutionary success. But now she wondered: it felt pain, didn't it? What was pain but a promise that more pain might lead to death?

There was the screaming of a train and Ella turned left, turned east, turned away from the sound and toward the gathering evening. The sky was pink above her still, but then red and then purple and then black far out over the Atlantic.

There was nothing worse in her mind than thinking of a winning point only when an argument was over, and she was too late to this argument—far too late—but she wanted to throw back in

Joseph's face: What was pain but a promise that more pain might lead to death? Doesn't that fit with evolution, isn't that what it's really all about? Without pain, why do anything at all, why not simply move as little as possible and wait for the end, the way that water finds its way down a mountain . . . Only then there was still the problem of children; an avoidance of pain did not give oneself over to having children. Unless there was a piece of the brain that whispered in your ear to go out and seek novelty, and its only function was to tell you to go out and work your way down a list of new things and if it convinced you to accomplish enough on the list, then somewhere down it was the idea of having children and that piece would be passed down . . .

Liam knew about Casey and he had pretended that it had more to do with Casey than with him. He had pretended that it mattered to him about the children, about the kids. "The kids will be fucked up," he'd said. And she'd told him that they would never have any, and he'd said: "But they'd be fucked up if you did. Doesn't it matter to you that they'd be fucked up if you did. Doesn't that make you want to get away from him? Doesn't that kill any passion?"

The *pathétique*, the passionate, the pitiable . . . What was pain but a promise that more pain might lead to death? And then the children . . . What was love but a promise that failing to love will lead, if not to death, then to a severance of one's line and of one's blood . . .

The streetlights on Cookman Avenue were decorative; they split in two at the top and each branch curved so that the light could be thrown on both the sidewalk and the street, and the arms themselves curved and curled like raised hands, like shrugging shoulders:

Why hadn't she gone to the funeral? Why had she let her sequins slip off and fall upon her father's floor?

She went over one street so that she walked down Lake Avenue instead, to the side of Wesley Lake, outside the purview of the tourists and the shrugging lights. The lights here were unpainted steel and sensible, plain, and one-directional, pointed up but also to the side . . .

Her mother had said: "God doesn't care if it's only a dog . . ." and she pointed up and to the side, so that god was not directly above them—never directly above them—but instead somewhere to the east above the Atlantic, like storm clouds, like ospreys, like evening, like Greetings from Morocco. And Gabrielle had looked at her father and said to her mother: "But we don't believe in god," and it was the only time that her mother ever hit her, slapped her straight across the face and said: "how are you going to be good if you don't believe in god? You'll go straight down to hell if you don't believe in god. You want to go straight down to hell?"

But wasn't that just more avoidance of pain? What was so good about not wanting to be in hell. Her father had thought it too, perhaps, but he didn't say it: perhaps he didn't want to get slapped.

Across the gray-green water of Wesley Lake, there was the facade of Ocean Grove houses like a single wall of eyes, flickering on in yellow squares of window light. The water was so matte that you couldn't see the houses on its surface, but you could always see the yellow lights like eyes. On her left was the beer garden, the indoor sounds spilling out with each opening of the door, the rooftop pulsing with bass and with voices, with the clinks of glasses, laughter, time . . .

She crossed the street, which made the reflection of window lights shy back across the lake. In the green water there were geese or swans gliding along like ferrymen toward Ocean Grove. Following their retreat, her eyes lifted for a moment and then saw it, the roof of the church, of the Great Auditorium: yawning, huge, yellow beneath the roof like a window light always left on. A horrible color, she thought. And then: *So be ye holy.*

Why had she let her sequins slip off and fall upon her father's floor, so that they shimmered in a puddle in the darkness; and with what light did they shimmer, for in the room it had been dark . . . hadn't it been dark in the room?

She passed by a sign for paddle boat rentals, and the paddle boats were all the shapes of swans; they were huddled there, chained up on this side of the lake, protected by a little iron gate. The gate was more symbolic than protective, for it was small and could not wrap around beyond the beginning of the lake, but it was evidently of some use, for a group of teens was leaning against it, smoking, and she thought: they're the type to get into strange boats that don't belong to them and paddle off in green-gray water, among the birds, across the dark strips of shadows that stretch below the footbridge, away from the wall of brightly colored houses, ornate eaves, yellow squares of light . . . the little gate cannot keep them out, but they let it keep them out anyway. Perhaps it is more comfortable to simply lean against the iron. Perhaps they know that peddling the swan-shaped boats is work. Perhaps they know that it's a man-made lake and there isn't anywhere to go . . .

Past the iron gate was a walking bridge and on the far side of the bridge was Ocean Grove. Elevated above the town, as if held up by other roofs, stood the sliver of yellow wall, and above it was the roof, red-brown in the sun but now made darker by the evening. Its twin belfries jutted up like sentinels, one impaled with a cross too dark and too narrow now to see, like an eyelash lengthened by mascara, so thin as to be almost invisible . . .

In her father's mirror in the morning her rouge was gone, though Casey had never taken that off. Why had she let her sequins slip off and fall upon her father's floor, so that they shimmered in a puddle in the darkness; and with what light did they shimmer, for hadn't it been dark in the room?

Her mother had believed in god and tried to avoid hell and her father had tried only to avoid pain, and yet somehow her dark had reflected his light and she shimmered. Or his dark had reflected her light . . . But hadn't it been dark in the room?

Through two stone pillars sat the bridge to Ocean Grove, and upon one of them was written "Greetings from—" but where the greetings were originally from had been spray painted over, first with black as a background and then with "fuck your mother." *Greetings from fuck your mother.* And from the "r" hung a trail where the pale graffiti had run down and she walked through it and onto the bridge and kept her eyes down on the pale-gray concrete surface . . .

Gray November sky reflected in the wetness of Liam's cheek and Liam's mother asked about the seagulls "why do they insist on coming down? It might be nice after all over that big blue—it might be nice and they could simply float whenever their arms grow tired," and Liam had corrected her and said "wings" . . .

But what was really nice about the seagulls, Ella thought, was that they could make things small by floating up and floating up, whereas as soon as I can make out a face the thing is almost upon me and so everything takes me by surprise and without the defense of distance you learn to throw up other defenses. And I have good eyes now and imagine growing old so that as soon as you make out a face suddenly the thing is life-sized, face-sized, you-sized, so that it's like looking at yourself inside a mirror.

And behind the mirror were her father's razor and his toothbrush, as if the only things in life were plaque and shadow, and the toothbrush glistened as if it had just been used and her mouth felt dirty, hot and she closed the mirror again and there she was, without rouge, though he had never taken off the rouge, but he had taken off her sequins and they shimmered in a puddle on the floor even though—hadn't it been dark in the room?—and she turned and ran from the house but not before Casey, still naked in the gray bed with the gray morning ocean framed behind him, had stirred and sat up, but as soon as his eyes focused on her he made her small or threw up his other defenses and she counted the breaking waves behind him like chimes of a clock, one . . . two . . . and she could see in his face that she was small.

Casey with the gray morning ocean framed behind him.
So be ye holy.

Casey. He makes everything small with such impersonal negation, like multiplication by zero, so that he does not even afford you the custom harm of saying "One? Negative one. Two? Negative two," but only calls out "Zero, zero, zero." He throws up a wall not of stone but of glass, so that it's only your reflection there and suddenly it's huge to you, the size of your face in the mirror and he isn't anywhere around, and you look behind the pane for Casey but there is only a razor and a toothbrush still glistening, like a puddle of sequins on the ground. And if I only see myself when I look at him, then what does he see? And are our reasons necessarily the same? He goes at love like a sort of exorcism, as if by proving that we aren't really bound up together then maybe he isn't related to our father. Our father . . .

It was almost dark now as she stepped off the footbridge and into Ocean Grove and between the colorful houses and their yellow squares of light. You could not see the Auditorium from here, and she felt that the shadows mixed with light from the windows were a different sort of shelter, an in-between of dark and light without the full purity of either. Wasn't she something like this half darkness, like the lane between day and night? She looked up between the shadows of the roofs . . . the lane had gone, shifted west, and above her it was dusk now, nearly dark.

She'd had a room, and a house of her own, and a mother. What had Casey had? What memories could be squeezed inside a cell? What horrible inheritance . . . The same, the same, but not really the same. Why hadn't she gone to the funeral? A house of her own, and a mother.

Greetings from fuck your mother.

But now, on the far side of the bridge, there wasn't graffiti anymore. There was never graffiti in Ocean Grove, she thought. It was funny how a little man-made lake, a little iron gate, the necessity of crossing a little open footbridge could keep out graffiti or keep a group of teenagers from stealing some boats. It wasn't really barriers but the idea of barriers which kept in or kept out, which reflected Ocean Grove across Wesley Lake or Loch Arbour across Deal Lake and there was never graffiti in either border town but then always:

Greetings from Asbury Park. Greetings from fuck your mother.

Suddenly the houses parted and there it was, the vast yellow wall of the Great Auditorium, huge as soon as she could see it, life-sized, face-sized but there wasn't any mirror to turn away from. There were no lights in the windows but the whole wall was the color of light.

She felt naked before it and reached down to touch her dress, to make sure that it was there. Her sequins had slid down and hung in a puddle on the floor with what light and her rouge in the mirror was gone and behind the mirror there was only a razor and a toothbrush, shadow and plaque, bristles glittering with what water, with what light.

But hadn't it been dark in the room? And Casey with the ocean gray behind him. One . . . *So be ye holy.* Two . . .

The sea was almost too far to hear but she heard it anyway, counted seconds on the waves. Turning her back to the yellow wall she ducked back in among the houses, negating the thing if unable to make it small, heading back across the footbridge almost at a run, over the swans or swan-shaped boats, hidden by a little iron gate that could keep out nothing that wanted to get in, but perhaps nothing wanted to get in. Perhaps it was more comfortable to lean against the gate. She saw them from the bridge, still leaning against the gate, the red tips of their cigarettes pulsing and winking red-orange-white-orange-red as they breathed in and then blew out gray smoke into the darkness that caught the light of the beer hall behind it and seemed to catch the sound of it, too.

One . . . two . . .

In Ocean Grove behind her now the stone was clean, protected by the idea of a moat and a footbridge and an open iron gate. But now she slowed to a walk and touched the pillar. Her fingers could not feel the difference between clean stone and paint, but she saw the spray paint there: Greetings from . . .

A warm wind came rushing from the sea, around the shell of the Casino and the abandoned carousel, up over the gray-green water so that the swan-shaped boats tugged at their ropes, up so that the cigarette smoke scattered west over the continent, up so that it fluttered her dress, and she reached down to touch the dress and then shivered. And on the wind was the sound of the waves.

CHAPTER 12

Casey

"Was he looking any better today?" asked Meredith. I sat on her bed while she folded clothes.

"It's been a week," I told her. "He looks fine. It wasn't so bad to begin with."

"Wasn't so bad? He looked like he got the shit beat out of him and then slept in the gutter."

"Who do you know that can beat the shit out of Davey," I asked. "I'm telling you, he had one drink too many with his old college buddy and he's paying the price. He's had worse. He's a long way off from sleeping in the gutter."

"So where'd he sleep then?"

"It's Davey we're talking about. If I had to guess, he went home with some girl. Girls like to take care of him. Everybody likes to take care of him. Anyway, his face is almost healed. It's nothing to worry about."

"Well," said Meredith. "If you think he's really alright."

"I think he's really alright," I said. "He's drinking a lot but alright."

"You know that it isn't just drinking," said Meredith.

"Are we going to have this conversation again?"

"Are you going to keep doing nothing? There are ziplocks filled with painkillers around the house. Don't you think you should try to keep him away from all that?"

"You try keeping Davey away from something."

"You know what happens, don't you? They get started on the pills and then when they run out of money they move on to heroin. It's cheap. Ten dollars a bag. That's what kills them."

"Well," I said, standing up. "That's something we don't have to worry about. Davey isn't running out of money."

"I'm sorry," said Meredith. "Please sit down. It's just . . . Isn't that why you took the time off of work? To take care of him? Maybe he needs a little tough love."

I sat down again on the bed and Meredith went back to folding clothes. "What he needs is to learn how to take care of himself. He needs something to do but he doesn't see the sense in his taking a job that pays fifteen an hour when he's worth what he's worth."

"I guess he isn't wrong," she said.

"No, but there's more to it than being wrong," I said. "He shouldn't only think of it financially."

"And how are you doing?" she asked. I looked up at her. She was folding a shirt against her chest. "Financially, I mean. You're a bit of a bum, you know."

"Well, my month off is coming to an end," I said. "In some ways it'll be alright to go back to work. I won't feel so bad every time I spend money."

"It's been nice having you around."

Meredith smiled up at me and nodded her head.

"And how's Gabrielle?" she asked. She looked down at her fingers and tried to make her voice sound nonchalant.

"Why are you asking me about Gabrielle?"

"Oh, I don't know. I asked about the other two Larkin children and I figured I'd ask about the third."

"She isn't a Larkin."

"That's right. Well now that we're talking about her anyway, how is she?"

"She's alright. Goes off to school in a week."

"So you're going back to work just as she goes off to school."

"What do you mean by that?"

"Nothing," she said.

I could not tell what Meredith knew. Ella and I had been careful, but sometimes there were looks or phrases that people spoke that suggested something. She did not know how she was meant to act with a brother and I did not know how to act with a sister, and so neither of us understood how to pretend accordingly. I had picked her up from work on her last day and she had kissed me on the cheek. Madame K had looked at us strangely, and when Ella had gone to collect her things from behind the counter, Madame K had asked me, "Isn't she your sister?" and Ella, of course, had heard, and when she came back she kissed Madame K on the cheek as well to make it seem more a function of time and space than a product of affection. Because such a large piece of me was hidden, I constantly had the impression that anything occurring to me in the world outside Ella was only happening to a small piece of me, and so kept it from being real. It was as if the past month had been an act played out on a slow, expansive stage.

"Well," I said to Meredith. "If you want to know the truth, I'm not sure what to make of her. Sometimes she's like family and then sometimes she's as cold as her father was."

"*Her* father?"

"Yes," I said. "He was her father."

"He was your father too."

"Only in the biological sense."

"What other sense is there?" asked Meredith. She had been folding clothes but now threw the shirt in her hands to the floor. She seemed suddenly angry, but was determined not to let it show. She picked up the shirt as if it had slipped out of her hands. "Let's not talk about your father. You were telling me about her."

"There isn't anything to tell," I said. "I've promised her that I'll get tuition for her school from Davey. Joseph promised to pay for it, but he didn't actually leave them anything. I can't understand it. The mother, at least, seemed to really love him. She thinks that he probably just had not made changes to the will in a long time. God knows he never thought of himself as being on the verge of death."

"And what do you think about it?"

"It doesn't matter what I think," I said. "Anyway, I told her the tuition was a done deal, but I haven't managed to speak to Davey about it yet. I'm not exactly sure how to."

"Why not, if Joseph promised?"

"Because Joseph is dead. The money is Davey's now."

"But he seems to like her."

"He does," I said. "He likes almost everybody."

"You say that like it's a bad thing."

"It's not. I know it's not. That isn't Davey's problem."

"So what is Davey's problem?"

I laid back in her bed and looked up at the ceiling. "His father used to say that the problem with most people was that they died too old. He said that it would be kinder to die a child, with greatness visible in your distant horizon, than it would be to sail on toward it indefinitely only to learn that you've got a hole in the hull, or that success was only a mirage and a cruel trick of youth's light. He used to say that all children are great but few men are, and so the easiest thing to ensure greatness forever would be to die young."

"What a lovely, lovely man," said Meredith. She liked when I spoke to her about private things and she believed that I considered memories of my father to be private. It soothed her to hear them. "I see where you get it from. So that's Davey's problem? That he's lived too long?"

"Not in the same way," I said. "It's only that he had a wonderful childhood and nothing that he ever does in adult life is going to match it. I think he's beginning to realize that. When you're a kid, it's enough to be capable of doing something. Now he's actually got to go and do it."

Meredith had finished folding her clothes and came and sat beside me on the bed. She looked down at my hands on my thighs and clasped both of her hands around my own and brought it to her lips in a quick, sympathetic way. When she dropped her hands back to her thigh, my hand was with hers, too, and she flattened my hand against her leg and brought her mouth forward and kissed me.

I pulled my hand away and looked at her. She was staring intently at me and her jaw was locked tight.

"Why not?" she said. Her voice was quiet and she would

not look at me, but you could tell that the question had been on the tip of her tongue and she had been waiting to ask it.

"You and me?" I said.

"Yes. You and me. Me and you. Or are we really only friends?"

"I don't know," I said. "I just hadn't thought about it really. Besides, your mother is home."

"I don't mean right now," she said. She turned away, toward the window.

"She's home all the time."

"She can't come up the stairs. And there are places where she's not."

"Well, I just hadn't thought about it."

"Most men in the world have to work hard not to think of it."

"Maybe I'm not most men."

"That's for sure," she said. It did not sound like a compliment. We were quiet for a while. "It isn't that you don't want it, though. That's what you're telling me. It's just that you hadn't thought of it."

"That's what I'm telling you."

"Alright," she said. She tilted her ear to one side. "Did you hear that? I've got to go down for a minute."

I had not heard anything but Meredith went out. I checked my phone. Gabrielle had asked me when I'd be over. We were having dinner with Tamera. By the time I told her that I'd be there within the hour, I could hear Meredith's feet on the stairs. I quickly put my phone away; it felt heavy in my hands, like something that ought to be hidden.

Meredith walked into the room and without even shutting

the door, she moved directly toward me and straddled me with a leg on either side and wrapped her arms around my body and brought her lips to mine. There was only time for instinct and my instinct was the wrong one; I moved back, away from her touch, and watched her. Her face did not change; she had been fishing for that reaction and had expected it and now she had gotten it. She stood up and I reached out for her but there was no reaching out anymore. Meredith pulled her hand away.

"It's her, isn't it?" she said. She asked it, but halfway through the question it had become a statement. By vocalizing it she had cemented in her mind that it was a fact. "Isn't it." She was nearly in hysterics but the inflection of a question was entirely gone now. "Answer me."

"Yes," I said. "It's her."

She struck me hard across the face and began to cry. She hit me again but this time it was with the side of her fist against my chest and it was more a gesture of defeat than anything aimed at inflicting pain. She drummed the sides of her arms against my chest and eventually she was pressing her body against mine and I was holding her. I do not know how it happened.

"You'd rather kiss your sister than kiss me?" she asked.

"I suppose," I said. It would be easier to let it all go now than to keep her tethered on by some sinew and revisit the wound for a more complete separation down the road. The sooner it became scar tissue the sooner the nerve endings would go dead and it would be better for her.

Meredith stopped hitting me and she stopped crying. She took a step back and looked me up and down as if trying to remember the features of a thing she would never see again, or maybe like an adult who had come back to her childhood play place and was allowing herself to admit that the parapets and barbicans had only ever been the branches of trees, that the mighty stair she'd had to climb to mount the walls of her play castle had only ever been a stepladder.

"Thank you for telling me the truth," she said. Her voice was cold and steady. "I had heard it, but I wouldn't have believed it if you hadn't told me."

I nodded and began moving for the door. There wasn't anything for me to say.

"Casey," she said. I looked at her. "If I heard, then it's only a matter of time before Davey hears. It'll be better if it comes from you."

I stood watching her for a long time, trying to decide if she had enjoyed telling me that. No, she did not enjoy it. I nodded and went out of the room.

"Goodbye, Casey," I heard her say. I did not stop walking. It was not really me she had been speaking to.

* * *

After we had finished dinner, Tamera Walker stood at the head of the table and raised her cup importantly. It was bad rum, but she drank it straight with only a cube of sugar, and when she swung it up to shoulder-height, she flung the smell across the table.

"We are so glad to have had you here with us this summer, Casey. I can't help but feel that I'm losing not one, but two children next week."

She looked between Ella and me. The table was small and vaguely rectangular, but really it was more like a square. It could fit six people if they squeezed. Tamera always sat at one head, and Ella and I sat on either of the long sides.

"When my girl goes off to college, I beg her to remember this. Be careful. Be smart. Your mother will miss you dearly. And to you, Mr. Casey. Take care of yourself. This home will always be yours."

She said it so comfortably because she knew that it was not true. The home would not always be mine. I had sold it to Tamera Walker for $150,000; she would not let me leave it any other way, and it turned out that she had been left with something after all. I had been told that anything less would raise a flag of suspicion at the IRS, and if I'd had to pay a broker and lawyers, the net effect would have been something similar.

After dinner, Ella and I walked toward town. We were going nowhere in particular.

"I can't stand it when she talks about god," she said. "And then she lets it get in the way of her being really Christian. The woman wouldn't let you give her the house without a sale. Where's the logic in that? If her own pride was going to leave just her out on the street it would be one thing. But it was going to leave her daughter homeless as well. Isn't that against all the ideas of religion?"

"Is she really religious?"

"I don't know. They blend it down there with voodoo and somehow believe the two together. It's like those people who had models of the solar system with Earth at the center, and they believed that the sun and other planets would sometimes go the other way, and it was ridiculous but they kept on believing the things together."

"And did you ever believe in god?" I asked.

Ella did not answer for a long time.

"No," she said. "I don't see how anyone can. But what's more important is that I can't see how anyone can believe in anything resembling free will without him."

"So you don't believe in that either?"

"No," she said. "After all, if there's any choice at all then it means that if I were in your body I could choose to do something different than you. But if all I could do in your body is what you do, then there isn't anything other than the body."

"Like a soul?" I said.

"Yes," she said. "Like a soul. So if there isn't any god and then there isn't any soul, then how could anyone say that in someone else's body they could have chosen something different? No . . ." she said. Her attention trailed off and then came back and she repeated: "No."

"Don't be an atheist for the wrong reasons," I told her.

She stopped walking and I went one step ahead of her before turning around so that we could be face to face.

"And what are the wrong reasons?" she said.

"To absolve yourself of any responsibility."

"What's there to absolve?"

"Nothing," I said. "Nothing at all."

I turned to continue walking, but Ella did not move. I felt her eyes on my back and after a few steps I turned around. I had the feeling that there was a scab that I could not help but tear open.

"Are you alright?" she asked me. "You're acting strange."

"I'm fine."

"Casey," she said. "School starts very soon. I need the money for tuition. I'm not taking it from my mother."

"I'll talk to Davey tonight," I said. "Otherwise I'll give it to you myself."

Ella came up very close to me so that we were face to face.

"You haven't spoken to him yet?"

"You try telling him to fork over a hundred grand for the daughter of his father's maid," I said.

She slapped me hard across the face.

"Well," I told her. "That isn't the first time I've been hit tonight."

Ella looked as if I had slapped her back.

"Who else slapped you?" she said.

"Nobody. Forget it."

"Casey, who else slapped you."

"Meredith," I said. I breathed out and felt my shoulders sink. "She knows."

"She can't know. She can think, but she can't know. Isn't that right?"

I looked down. "She knows," I said.

Ella raised her hand as if to slap me again, but it went straight to her mouth. She began pacing back and forth in the middle of the street. I tried to think of what we would look like from any one of the windows all around us.

"If Meredith knows then everyone will know," she said. "She hates me. There isn't anything she wouldn't do to hurt me."

"This is Meredith we're talking about," I said. "And she didn't pull it out of thin air."

"What does that mean?"

"It means that she thinks Davey will have heard it too. Or that he will eventually."

"Well as long as 'eventually' is after he gives me that tuition, I don't really give a shit."

"That's nice," I said. "Real nice. It's a good thing you don't believe in free will."

"Oh, go to hell."

"I thought you didn't believe in god," I said.

Gabrielle took one big step toward me with her hand raised and I jumped back, but she did not come any further. She began walking back toward her house and I ran after her. I thought she might hit me when I grabbed her hand but all she did was stop walking. All the muscles in her face had gone dead and she looked as if she'd aged about six years.

"I was too nice to Joseph for agreeing to pay my tuition for it not to be true," she said. "He got my niceness without paying for it. That doesn't sound fair to me. It's got to be true."

"It'll be true," I said.

I put my arms around Ella and slid my hand up her spine to hold the back of her neck between my fingers and tried to pull her head into my shoulder. But she pushed away—she was looking now at all the windows around us, as if afraid that we were being watched. She began to walk slowly back toward her house and her gait had that awkward, forced nonchalance that is common among inexperienced thieves while leaving the scene of their crime. I liked that she didn't cry. It was always easier to talk to someone who was not crying.

We walked about half the way back to her house in silence, and she stopped when we got to the edge of her lawn. The street was dirty and all the other lawns were overgrown. There was a sharp, clean line in the grass where Tamera's lawn ended and the neighbor's lawn began. Far away, we could hear the beginning sounds of the night coming over the few streets between where we stood and the downtown, and it made us feel far away from the center of it all.

"Will it have been worth it if nothing comes of it?" she said quietly. "I'm afraid that all we'll be doing if we keep it up is proving to ourselves that it isn't wrong."

"It isn't wrong."

"It doesn't matter whether or not it was wrong."

"You said 'was' just now," I said.

Ella turned and looked at her house. I could not tell if she was thinking that she wanted to be inside it or that she wanted to be somewhere else entirely. It was clear that she did not like standing on the border of its lawn.

"It doesn't matter whether or not it was wrong," she said again. And then she turned to me and looked at me very directly. Her eyes were the same as Joseph's but they were soft now around the edges in a way that his had never been. "Do you understand what I'm saying."

"Yes," I said. "You could find that it's morally agreeable to jam your finger in a mousetrap, but that doesn't mean you ought to do it. Is that it?"

She smiled and reached out to hold my arm. For a moment I believed that she really was my sister.

"Yes," she said. "Something like that."

"And is that what we've been doing?"

"In a way," she said. I looked down at our feet and when I looked up, the sky had gotten darker. You never notice anything changing until you look away. "In a way," she said again.

"I'll go talk to Davey now," I said. "If he says no, I'll give it to you myself."

"I wouldn't want to take your money," she said. She looked down at her fingers the way some girls look at their engagement rings, with the arm stretched long so that the hand is far away.

Then she looked up at me and in the darkening light her eyes seemed darker. "That wouldn't seem right. We're the same, you know. David's the one who should pay."

I nodded. We stood very close to one another and though I could feel her breath on my face, it felt that there was something gaining form between us, like a third figure that had wedged its way between our bodies. Ella reached across the space and grabbed my hand very briefly, and then turned and walked inside.

* * *

When I got back to Joseph's house, Davey was out on the water. He had got into the habit of paddling a surfboard out to beyond the place where waves were breaking. I never saw him attempt a wave, but often he would sit there staring sometimes out at the horizon, but more commonly back at the house.

The front door was unlocked and I walked through the kitchen and saw that there was a bag of pills on the table. It was nearly empty. I took a beer and went onto the patio and watched Davey sitting on his board. The August days were long but it was too late and too dark for him to be out on the water if he was not sober, and I did not think that he was. I went down to the water and waved at him and he began to paddle in. A small wave carried him in and he rode it the whole way on his belly. When he got out of the water, he unstrapped the leash around his ankle and reached behind him to unzip his wetsuit. He could not grab the zipper immediately, and he spun in a circle like a dog chasing its tail.

"Here," I said. "I'll get it."

Beneath the wetsuit, his skin was pink and there were raised goosebumps all along his arms. He was breathing hard from the paddle in, and you could see the veins jumping in his shoulder. There were the remnants of a yellow bruise around his eye but really his face looked alright.

"You know," he said between breaths. "Until last year, I think I was getting stronger every day of my life. I was getting stronger and fitter and smarter. And then it started to reverse. I knew it would eventually, but it started sooner than I'd counted on."

He dug his board into the sand and looked out over the ocean and all its smooth, unsurfable waves that rose and fell like slight ripples in a sheet. He looked as if he had not shaved for several days, and the sun cast thin shadows of the bristles onto his jaw and chin. He looked back toward the house on its slightly raised ground and then down at his own feet. It was not that he was proud of falling, but there was something to be said for his accepting sea level as a destination. He wasn't bitter at the descent, but you could tell he was bitter to have started at some elevation which had made it necessary for him to fear the distance that gravity could carry him. It had carried him far and probably the collision had been painful. He had been promised advancement and the ability to grow past whatever terrace his roots had been planted on, but somewhere along the way a cruel trick had been played and all the railroads had been built, the oil was burned, the silver was mined, and there was nothing left for him to do. There were no more houses to build and even the ones that were standing could not be afforded. There was a cruelty in his having been so well provided for at birth; he'd been robbed of misery, robbed of loss, robbed of orphanage. There isn't anything worse than to be born both rich and proud. There wasn't any good direction in which he could go. We walked back up along the sand to the house.

"You look anxious," Davey told me once we had come back in. He always came in from the water by way of the kitchen because it did not matter if the tile floor was left wet.

"I'm alright."

"Well, I'm going to have a shower," he said.

He stopped for a moment to take one of the last few pills from the bag and he put it in his mouth. When he saw that I was looking, he quickly swallowed it and then rubbed his shoulder.

"I'm sore from surfing," he said.

I think the pill had stuck in his throat. He went over to the refrigerator and opened a beer and closed his eyes while he drank. There was nothing except beer in the refrigerator. He took out another one and put it on the table with enough force that I thought it might have broken and slid it toward me along the smooth countertop. I caught it and Davey turned to go shower.

By the time he came out, I had drunk three more of them. I sat on the couch in the living room, the same couch I'd first heard the sound of Ella's music coming from on that night that seemed like it belonged to another life entirely. I tried many different combinations of words in my head but none of them seemed correct. I spoke quietly but aloud to myself and searched for a delicate way to do it but there is no delicate way to do such things. Before Davey came out, I determined that I would say it to him immediately. If I let him speak first, I did not think that I would be able to do it.

"I was with Gabrielle," I said. I said it as soon as I heard his footsteps on the cold stone floor and only stood up from the couch and turned to face him afterward. His skin glistened from the shower and his hair was wet and stuck to his forehead. A towel was wrapped loosely around his waist and he wore nothing else. Davey was always his most confident when naked and he had better posture without a shirt on.

"I know," he said. He continued walking to the kitchen and I followed him to the sound of his wet feet slapping against the stone floor. He left a trail of footprints behind him. "You just had dinner there, didn't you?"

Davey opened the refrigerator and the silver door was between the two of us so that I could only see the top of his head.

"That isn't what I mean," I said. "I mean that I was with her."

Davey stopped moving behind the refrigerator, and I heard the sound of a beer bottle opening. He kept the refrigerator door between us for a long time.

"Well," he said finally. "I guess there isn't anything so wrong with it. Dad always said that the problem with the world today is that everybody digs so deep to find something offensive that they all wind up with their heads buried in the sand."

Any time that Davey was upset he went looking for comfort in our father's old wisdoms.

"I don't know if that applies," I said. "I won't think your head is in the sand if you don't like it."

There was still the refrigerator door between us. It was brushed gray steel and my reflection in it was only a blurred and formless shadow against the light.

"Were you drunk?" he said.

"The first time, maybe."

"It was more than once," he said. He closed the refrigerator door and turned toward the kitchen island. He reached out and took one of the pills from the bag and put it on his tongue and swallowed it down with a sip of beer. All the while he was nodding his head up and down. "How many times?"

"I forgot to keep count," I said. I didn't like Davey's calmness. It somehow would have been alright if he'd punched me but to have him just standing there and drinking beer as if we were discussing a football game was too much. He would not even respond to my getting angry.

"But she's our sister," he said. He finally looked at me.

"Only half."

"We're only half."

"That's true," I said. I hadn't thought of it that way.

Davey looked as if he was not sure what he was supposed to say.

"And here I thought that you were choosing her for other reasons."

"What do you mean, *choosing* her?"

"Oh, please, Casey. You stick around this summer and you tell Meredith and me that we'll be seeing you a lot, but it's like we're little moons. There isn't any question as to where your orbit has been focused. That goes for both of you. I'm just as related to her as you are, and she'll barely step foot inside this house."

"Her mother cleaned these floors for twenty years," I said. "And Ella was never allowed inside! And, in case you forgot, we're all just as related to Joseph as you are, but the house and the bank accounts and everything but the scraps are only in your name."

"I'm not dad, Casey. I didn't ask him to marry one woman and not another. In case you forgot, things didn't exactly work out for my mother either."

"Oh, please," I said. "I'll get a violin."

Davey looked up at the ceiling and tapped his fingers on the granite countertop.

"Alright," he said. "So you and Gabrielle. Why are you telling me this?"

"Meredith knew," I said. I was breathing hard. "I thought you'd find out anyway."

"But you wouldn't have told me otherwise."

"No," I said. "Probably not."

Davey nodded sagely. He spread his arms wide on the countertop and tapped his fingers in quick succession.

"Is that all?" he said.

"No."

I went over to the counter and opened the refrigerator myself. He moved aside so that I could get to the refrigerator without our bodies making contact. I took a beer and opened it and went to sit at one of the high stools.

"She needs money for tuition," I said. A wide, caustic smile spread across Davey's face and he dropped his chin to his chest. "Joseph had promised it to her but didn't leave them anything. He probably meant to. She starts school in two weeks."

Davey's feet were back, as if he was stretching his calves, and from where I sat I could see down his spine when his head was down. Now he lifted his head and looked like an osprey with his arms spread wide and the muscles of his shoulders rounded as if for attack.

"Dad promised," he said. "That's what you mean."

"That's what I said."

"You said 'Joseph.'"

"That was his name, in case you forgot."

"Was he only ever money to you?"

"Mostly he wasn't even so much of that."

Davey breathed out a short burst of bitter laughter. He curled his tongue up so that it sat against his teeth and then closed his mouth and swallowed.

"Am *I* only money to you? Is that all I am?" he asked. "Money?"

I put the beer down on the counter.

"Yes, David. That's all you are to me. Just money."

"I'm being serious," he said. Finally there was a trace of anger in his voice and it had broken out of the melancholy calm.

"Don't ask stupid questions if you don't want stupid answers."

"Well, look at you. You stay here all summer but are always out of the house. You haven't spent a dime of your own cash. You haven't even been back to work since it happened."

"I stayed here for you."

"Oh, thank you so much, Casey." He stood up straight and put his hand over his chest in mock appreciation. "Thank you for coming home and for staying in my house without paying rent, and for drinking my beer and eating my food."

"Send me a bill."

"How could you pay a bill?" he said. Our voices were louder now and his was becoming a yell. "You haven't even been back to work since it happened. You haven't spent a night in your own apartment, on your own dime, and you haven't been back to work. And now you want me to pay this girl's tuition?"

"She's your sister," I said.

"Well then maybe I ought to fuck her too."

We were quiet for a while as the sound echoed through the hard surfaces of the empty house. I looked down at the ceiling lights reflected in the dark granite countertop and then pushed my beer into the center of the counter and slid off of the stool. I walked out of the kitchen and up the stairs. I had not brought so many things with me from the city, and I wondered at how I had lived here for a month. As I started packing all of my things into a bag, I heard Davey's footsteps on the stairs. I did not look up when I saw him in the doorway. There were no lights on in the hall and his shadow went only the other way.

"Where are you going," he said.

"Back to the city. Like you said, I haven't been to work in a month."

"Casey."

"We can't all get by on inheritance alone," I said. He was still standing in the doorway when I closed my bag and he stood aside to let me pass. I walked until I reached the station at Long Branch and boarded the first train for New York.

CHAPTER 13
All the Perfumes of Arabia

Sam Besalel sat on the porch of his cousin's oceanfront mansion in Deal, reading news on his phone. It was the second Friday in August and somewhere behind him, the sun had dipped beneath the line of stucco houses and planted trees. There had been rain in the afternoon, but the clouds had dispersed in great dark clusters, purple now at sunset, and the rest of the sky was clear. Out over the ocean, the jet streams of evening flights shone white and orange, like small scars burning against the pale blue face of the sky. A layer of dark, wet sand covered the beach, and as the children ran over it, the layer was broken and turned over to the dry white sand beneath. Watching them, it seemed to Sam that they were like a colony of birds, congregating at the same summer homes the way that breeding albatross will swarm their nesting islands.

"Phone away," said his wife. "Sun down, phone away. Shabbat shalom."

Alanna kissed him on the cheek and sat down on his lap, draping her long arms around his neck. Against the top of his spine, he could feel how soft and loose the skin and muscle of her arm had become. "My wife is old," he thought. He had been thinking it all summer but he thought it now especially.

She was not really so old, but the vigor with which she fought against her encroaching age made the opponent seem all the more imminent. Sam constantly allowed the books he loved to do his thinking for him, and looking now at his wife and her age, he thought: "From the vehemence with which you deny my existence, I am convinced that you believe in me!"

Before they had married, he had believed that she would be one of those women who accepted age gracefully. He had believed many things about her before they had married, and immediately many of them had been disproved.

As an Ashkenazi Jew, Alanna had not been embraced by the Syrian community. They took it as an affront to their blood that their own young women were not enough to satisfy. Part of what Sam loved in Alanna was how fiercely oppositional she could be. She'd been a law school student then who wore thick glasses, torn Levis and oversized sweaters.

Sitting on his lap now, she wore white pants and a dark and sleeveless silk top. She looked like all the other women. When her eyes moved, contact lenses followed to keep up with her irises. She had never truly practiced law. They had married just after her graduation, and she was pregnant before she had been at work a year. The degree to her was something like jewelry. And what a marriage they'd had! On the beach in the summer, a house just like the one they were at now, perhaps even the same one. They were all the same one. He had expected her to fight, had thought she would be one of those women to demand a hyphenation, and a part of him had been disappointed when she had not demanded it.

His family had put her through hell; they checked three generations of her ancestors' bar and bat mitzvahs and genealogy. They interviewed rabbis, called Hebrew day schools. There had been a near-hiccup when her father's birth certificate could not be verified; he had come over on a secret boat from Austria in 1938. At every turn, he had expected her to refuse the gross inquisition, and had half-hoped that he could ball up her refusal and throw it in their faces. It would have given him a way out, a moral claim to exodus.

But she had not. She had acquiesced, like a lamb. She had more or less renounced her own family for his. Instead of practicing law, she planned Sabbath meals, cooked with all the other Syrian women—cooked, for god's sake, cooked! This woman who did not believe in god but spent her life a slave to him. He had confused shackles for wings, and now he sat with the same people he always sat with, at the same place they always sat.

His children approached. He had tried to fill them all their lives with strange ideas, had tried to make strangers of them. Of his son, there was no chance of it; the boy was straight as an arrow. He ran the same path every day. By any reasonable measure, Sam ought to have been a proud father of the boy, and in many ways he was, but there was a lingering disappointment with Jacob's inability to deviate.

In his daughter, though, he sometimes glimpsed the rebellion he hoped for. He had watched her walk the beaches, far beyond where most of the Syrians would go. He had followed her and watched from afar while she walked the length of the boardwalk, and he kept to the shadows because he knew that when he himself was that age, the tacit agreement of his parents seemed to soften his resolve and curiosity, and he did not want to soften hers.

"Are you having a good time?" Alanna asked the children as they came near. "It's the last one of the summer. I always try to really soak it in."

"It was a nice party," said Jacob.

"You should never have a party after rain," said Sophia. "All anybody can talk about is how lucky we are that the weather cleared up. Nobody ever talks about anything that matters."

"And who would you like to talk with about things that matter?" said Sam.

"Oh, nobody. But you might as well be alone as be here."

"That's a nice thing to say at a big party," said Alanna. "I'm trying to soak it in and all you can do is complain."

"But I like large parties," said Sam, smiling at his daughter. "They're so intimate. At small parties there isn't any privacy. Who said that?"

"Gatsby," she said.

"That's just what she needs," said Alanna. "A book about drinking and smuggling. Well, Jacob. Anybody of interest? What about the Levine girl?"

Jacob reddened in the cheeks, but his face was stern, almost stoic, as if he would be doing the girl a great dishonor to consent to such discussion.

"No," he said. "She's still young."

Sam did not like the Levine girl for his son, but her parents had made it clear that they considered the two a match.

"She's older than your sister," he said.

"Sophia's young too," said Jacob. He said it forcefully, as if to remind his sister of the fact, but she was not paying attention. Her eyes were far off to the south, where the evening haze was orange-brown and the shadow of Convention Hall jutted out over the sand.

"Anyone of interest for *you*?" said Sam.

"Maybe," she said. She turned back to her father. "In fact, yes."

"And can a father ask who?"

"No," she said.

"Oh, guilty! Guilty! I can smell the guilt on you!" he said. With a wild, smiling look in his eyes, Sam took his daughter's one hand between his two and brought it to his face, sniffing at the air around it. "Here's the smell of blood still! All the perfumes of Arabia will not sweeten this little hand! Oh, oh, oh!"

Alanna slapped her husband's hands away from their daughter. "She'll never find a boy here if you treat her like a child," she said.

Sam ignored his wife. "And do you know who said that?" he asked.

"I think it was Isaiah," said Jacob.

"That's Shakespeare," said Sophia.

"What Shakespeare?"

"William," said Jacob, while Sophia said: "*Macbeth*."

She smiled at her father, and then turned her head again to look at the figure of Convention Hall. 'Is that where your Daisy Buchanan lives?' Sam wanted to say, but he did not want to take away the sanctity of whatever secret she was holding. Discussing it here, as if it were a normal, approved-of thing, would take away its gravity, and he wanted more than anything for it to pull her. He was suddenly jealous of his daughter and thought that the greatest treasure of youth was in keeping secrets.

"Well," said Alanna. "Let's go thank the Levines and get home."

Jacob followed his mother immediately, but Sophia lingered behind. She sat down beside her father so that they both watched the ocean together.

"You're quiet tonight," she said. She leaned her head against his shoulder.

"Quiet is good," he said. "Treasure quiet. It is rare in life to find people you are comfortable being quiet with."

"I guess I've ruined our quiet with my question."

"You never ruin anything."

Sam tried very hard to commit each sensation to memory: the weight of his daughter's head against his shoulder, the golden film of late sunlight on the surface of the water, the evening gulls like white shadows against the sky.

"Sam! Sophia!" shouted Alanna from behind them. "Come on you two!"

Sophia took her head from against her father's shoulder. "Well. *She* definitely ruined the quiet."

"No," said Sam with a smile. "That isn't any way to talk about your mother."

They walked home down Ocean Avenue, out of Deal, through Allenhurst and into Loch Arbour. The four of them walked shoulder to shoulder, and the whole time Alanna spoke to her son while her son politely answered. Sam and Sophia heard them like white noise on a radio. The walk took less than half an hour, and by the time they all got home the sky was dark.

It was forbidden on the Sabbath to turn on a light, but it

was not forbidden to have left one turned on; the problem was in the spark created when a switch was hit. And so the Besalels had left two lamps on in the living room, as they did every Friday night in the summer, and they huddled around them and read. They had never assigned seating, but somehow it had become tacitly assigned anyway. Always the same positions.

Sam sat, as he always sat, between his wife and his daughter. Jacob would not read on the Sabbath, even by the light of a lamp that had already been on. He carried with him the old slaveries. Three thousand years of bondage, and bondage to what? To remember that once upon a time we were slaves in Egypt. And then to remember that once upon a time we were exiled from Spain. And then to remember that once upon a time we were butchered in Poland. And now, to pay homage to the way our families were torn apart like cotton, we chain our children so tightly to our houses and our histories that it squeezes the life out of them. Was it noble to swear off a light switch on Friday because all along the line they had sworn it off? Was it noble to sink back three thousand years in time once a week, to abandon the present for the cave?

A car passed by outside. Sam heard it and felt that he was hearing through a fog. Jacob stood by the window, and the car's headlights briefly shone on one side of Jacob's face. He quickly drew the curtains; in his face, there was sternness, always sternness, and now was there anger there as well? Is that what a passing car on Friday could induce—anger? And for what reason?

God, he thought. For the reason of God. And what was God, now? It was all the parts of the God from *then* that could not yet be disproven. Did he create the world in six days? No, they said, he did not mean six. He created it, but days were different then, and so the calendar was wrong. But if the days were longer, then how did Abraham and Isaac achieve such extraordinary ages? They became shorter. Everything moves in cycles. Did he create the heavens and the earth, separate air from water from land? Yes, but only not so directly. He did it with the help of quantum mechanics and the rapid expansion of mass, and did it in so sly a way that he left a microwave radiation like a signature all throughout the fabric of space. Did he part the waters of the Dead Sea? Not part, not part, but they could have walked through on a stepping path of salt pillars that the Pharaoh's horses could not follow. And did he freeze his heart or not? And if so, why? And should we love him still? If we knew such answers, they said, then we'd have no need for God! No, none indeed. He was perversions of science and acrobatics of logic, his powers were all the things that could not yet be explained and his purpose was that which could not be asked of him.

And who was asking and who was answering, thought Sam. Hadn't he now put his children in the same Yeshiva that he'd been in, dragged them through the same summers and the same sand? Was he supposed to tell them flatly: no? Had his own father explicitly told him: make this of your life? Or had it just happened that way? Had his own father seen him the way he looked now at Jacob?

Beside him, Alanna read recent issues of fashion magazines. The turn of her glossed pages was loud and almost vulgar to Sam. On his other side, Sophia read *East of Eden*. She had worked through the dryness of her summer reading list from Yeshiva, and was now onto things she had picked up herself.

Good, thought Sam, that was good. For the second time in the evening, Sam felt jealous of his daughter—for all the things she had not yet done but would. Compared to his wife, she was delicate with the turnings of her pages, almost silent.

Almost silent. No, there was no "almost" about it. She was silent—truly silent. Sam watched her for a long time out of the corner of his eye. Sophia's book was opened, but her hand was laid carelessly across the page. Her eyes did not move over the words; they were glazed over and far away. Her mind was somewhere else. They sat for an hour before all going off to sleep, and she did not turn a single page.

* * *

Sam could not tell if it was sound or feeling that awoke him, but only that he was awake. He had been dreaming, but he could not remember of what. It was half past midnight. Besides from the faint red glow of the digital clock beside his bed, the room was completely dark.

He had awoken with his back turned to his wife, but now he turned to look at her. She slept like the dead, with the sheet tucked in above her chest but below her arms—a heavy strapless dress. Something in her look of deadness made the notion of sleep unappealing, and Sam slipped out of the covers and left the room.

At night, the house felt strange to him. His wife and children spent the whole summer here, but Sam spent his weeks in Brooklyn and came down on Thursday nights; he was never as used to the place as they were. Even after twenty years, it never felt like home. He crept through it now like a stranger, with his hands groping along the unfamiliar white walls, his feet sliding along the carpet so as not to miss a step. He was careful with his weight, afraid to make sound.

When the dull thud of a door opening or closing echoed through the walls, he thought at first that it was his own clumsiness that had caused it. He stood very still and listened to the sounds of his own breathing. The soft finishes and white carpeting swallowed all the other sound. But there it was again, the echo of a door being carelessly flung open.

He climbed the stairs, one foot at a time. His toes traced the lines of the treads and he walked with one hand on the banister and the other on the wall, his body at an angle to his motion. The hallway where both of his children's rooms were was long, but a large decorative window at the end of it sent streetlights and moonlight into the hall through its crystal prisms, so there was more light here than on the stair, but it was spread on the walls in strange patterns. Also, the hall was not still and was not so quiet as the rest of the house. A wind seemed to move through it, as if the house was drawing breath.

Sophia's door was flung open. Sam thought he could hear a whisper, but it was only the sound of air moving through the hall. It pushed the open door gently, until it touched the doorstop with a polite, nearly delicate force.

"Sophia?" whispered Sam.

There wasn't any answer. He moved forward quietly, his chest turned slightly toward the right wall where the moving door was hinged, as if by directing his body that way, he might detect his daughter's presence.

"Sophia," he said again, louder now.

He turned out of the hallway and into her room. White

curtain liners fluttered back from an open window, and the wind was like a cool breath upon him. Outside, the moon was bright, and it curled through the thin liner fabric and shone white against his face.

"Sophia," he said again, although he knew she was not there. Sam came fully into the room and closed the door behind him; the door to Jacob's room was across the hall and Sam did not want to wake him.

Sam's fingers found the wall as if of their own accord and slid up it until they came to rest on the light switch. The plastic was warm and his whole palm flattened against it while his ring finger curled beneath the switch. He closed his eyes as he pushed it up and the room exploded in a yellow, dirty light. Sam turned it off as soon as he had turned it on, and realized then that he had been holding his breath. It had been bright, far too bright. Sam went and sat beside the pillows on his daughter's bed and turned on her small reading light; he had sometimes seen the light on beneath her door on Friday nights, and had been secretly proud of it. Only now, the light shone dully in an empty room, and Sam felt nothing like pride.

He went to the window and thought of closing it but did not. Pushing the dancing curtains aside, he looked down at the slope of the roof outside the window, and could see clearly the path that someone would take from here to the ground. It was such an easy, obvious path that he wondered how he had not seen it before, how he had ever allowed himself to purchase a house with such an obvious path and how he had put his daughter in a room at its trailhead.

It made him feel old to feel angry, but he felt angry anyway. He sat down on the bed and to calm his nerves he picked up the book from her nightstand. He tried to read by the lamplight the words that Sophia had, only hours before, tried to read herself, but had been too distracted with the thoughts of her imminent escape to digest. Like his daughter, Sam watched the page for a long time without reading a single word, and eventually he watched the window, sick with worry.

* * *

"Hi, stranger," she said to him. She put her hand against his shoulder.

"Hi, yourself," said Davey, without recognizing the voice. He sat on the same bar stool, with his shoulders hunched over, looking down into his glass and he did not take his eyes from his drink.

Sophia flicked the fabric of her yellow dress into his field of vision, like a matador who teases the bull with a glimmer of red. Slowly, as if waking from a dream, Davey looked up at her and a broad smile broke across his face as recognition struck. She thought that his smile matched his body—wide and somewhat shiftless, but powerful. On seeing her, the convexity of his figure changed and, like a flower blooming, he pushed out from his hunch into a round, inflected searchlight that drank her in. He looked her up and down, from head to toe. She felt powerful to have inspired the metamorphosis.

"Hi, yourself," he said again, but now with all his despondent quiet shaken off, so that the phrase seemed drunk with confidence. "I was wondering when I'd see you."

"Well, now you see me."

Davey's arm slid up the side of Sophia's body and curled

around her back. He pulled her in close to himself, spreading his legs out on the stool so that she could fit between them.

"Order me a drink," she said. She turned her back to the bar and shook her hair out to cover her face and, if possible, the back of her dress. Davey did not seem to remember it, she thought, but the bartender might.

"What do you drink?" Davey asked her.

"It doesn't matter. Anything at all."

"Two whiskeys," he said to Tony.

"And how about something for the girl?" said Tony.

They both laughed. Seeing Davey laugh, Sophia laughed, too. He had seemed at first to consider Tony's question as a joke, but now he reconsidered.

"Bring her a vodka soda," said Davey. He looked to Sophia, and she nodded.

The vodka was cold and she drank it through a straw so that it nearly skipped her tongue and went straight back to her throat. She drank slowly at first, determined to make her face still so that no trace of her dislike for the taste would show on it, but she did not dislike the taste.

"What's your name?" she asked him.

"David. Everyone calls me Davey."

"I like David better."

"So call me David, then."

"I will."

"You can call me John if you like. It doesn't matter to me."

"I like David."

Sophia thought of herself now as acting. On the whole quiet walk from Allenhurst to Asbury Park, she had hid her face from each passing headlight, had burned with regret at the brightness of her dress, how conspicuous it was against the night. But once she had crossed the southern side of Deal Lake, a washing calm had fallen over and she was no longer afraid; instead, the spaced lanterns of the boardwalk and the disco lights of Convention Hall had taken on the sportive quality of stage lights. *Greetings from Asbury Park* read the sign above the Hall, and it might as well have been the dimming down of theater lights; passing underneath its light was slipping into other skin. She felt that everything that might occur was scripted; every sound she heard she was supposed to hear; every person she saw was moving with purpose as if they had entered from behind the curtains on one side and were waltzing off to exit on the other; each car moved like a stage prop on wheels. And in her head was her father's voice, asking after every line—"who said that one? who wrote this one?"—to which her answer every time was me, me, me. She heard his dramatic recitation, saying in accent: *I love large parties,* or *Here's the smell of blood still!* And Sophia began to think in accent too. At first, it affected only her inner dialogue, but soon it seeped into her speech, so that now when she spoke to David, she was aware of a theatrical, supercilious accent.

"I like this drink," she said to him.

"Where are you from?" he asked.

"Nowhere," she said, and although he had not asked her name: "I'm no one from nowhere."

"Well, I'm David from—"

"I don't care where you're from. I don't want to know."

"What *do* you want then?"

"Another drink," she said. She had finished the one in her hands.

"How old are you?" he asked her, looking at the empty glass

and then at her face. He had brought his second whiskey to his mouth, but paused with the rim of the glass on his bottom lip. It stung her eyes, and she reached up from underneath so that her fingers pressed against the underside of the glass, encouraging Davey to drink it.

"Old enough," she said.

Whatever small worry had arisen with the question of her age went readily out of Davey's face. He had been eager for it to go. Now he let her fingers push the whiskey into his mouth. Sophia sniffed at the air.

"I don't think I'd like that drink," she said.

"Try it first and then decide."

"Alright."

David motioned to the bartender for two more whiskeys and they were brought over right away. He handed one to her and took the other. Smiling, Sophia wrapped her thin brown forearm around his like a desert snake, so that their arms were intertwined but each would drink from their own glass.

"It's how they drink wine at the weddings where I'm from," she said.

"I thought you were from nowhere."

"That's right. This is how they drink wine at weddings in nowhere."

They drank. Sophia watched David pour the whiskey into his mouth as if it were water, and she did the same. The taste of it nearly choked her, and she felt her face whiten, eyes grow wide. Davey had swallowed his whiskey and was laughing. Sophia felt that her throat would not work, would not open. She raised the glass back to her lips to spit some out, but Davey laughed and shook his head. He put his fingers over her lips.

"No, no," he said. "You don't need to. Just throw it down. Like water."

Fighting the urge to spit or worse, she tilted her head back so that her eyes were on the ceiling, and she managed to finally swallow. Davey watched her throat the whole time, as if to verify, and when she opened her mouth to show him that she had done it, he took her jaw in his fingers as if he were a dentist and looked inside before roughly letting go. She coughed twice and then raised her own hand to her mouth. Davey laughed and his hot breath rushed her.

"Maybe they stick to vodka sodas in nowhere," he said.

She was suddenly ashamed of the joke; it made her feel like a child.

"Vodka soda," Davey called to the bartender. He tapped his empty glass on the bar. "And another whiskey."

Sophia drank fast to rinse the taste of whiskey from her mouth. The bitterness had held all of her attention, but as it washed away, she felt the beginnings of what she had expected to feel. Consciousness began to separate; now this was light and this was touch and this was sound. The intensity of each sensation seemed to move independently. Her head swam in the light and the touch and the sound. All through her body was a warm feeling.

"Yes," she said. Her shame had melted away as if the cold drink had dissolved it. "Maybe they stick to vodka sodas in nowhere."

She took a drink and swished the drink over her teeth like mouthwash. She leaned forward into David and pressed her lips against his. She did not open her mouth, but she did not close it either, and his warm wet tongue pushed through and pried open her teeth. She could taste the whiskey there again, as if his tongue was soaked like bread, but now the taste was not so bad. She pulled her head away and was aware that the hand of Davey's that was not on the bar had curled behind her thigh and was pulling her in, toward himself. The hand was one of incredible strength, and she could feel the force of it half-lift her from the ground.

"You taste like whiskey," she said. She watched his lips while she spoke. They glistened with saliva. "You smell like it too."

"You smell like," he said, and sniffed at the air. "Something else. Not just vodka. I don't know what."

"It's perfume," she said, giggling. "I stole it from my mother."

"Do nobodies have mothers too?"

"Everybody has mothers."

Davey threw back his next whiskey. He looked at the bar and then at Sophia.

"Let's get out of here," he said.

Sophia looked down at her glass. It was half empty and her lips fumbled for the straw and then drank.

"Alright," she said, the straw still in her mouth. "Where to?"

"Let's go back to my house."

Sophia bit down on the straw. "No," she said. "Let's stay out. Where else can we go?"

Davey's cheeks puffed as he exhaled. "Well, there's Beach Bar and the Anchor's Bend over at Convention Hall. They've always got music."

"Good," she said. "I like music."

She put her drink down on the edge of the bar, but most of its weight was hanging off, and as she let go of it, it fell to the ground and shattered. Sophia and the bartender looked at one another, and she quickly turned away.

"Let's go," she said to Davey. "Let's go now."

"Hey," he said. "You going to clean that up?"

Davey looked at her, and then at Tony. "If she cleaned it up, what the fuck would you have to do for work?"

He stood up, and his giant frame immediately filled the space between Sophia and the bar. With one hand on her lower back, he pushed her toward the door with a touch filled with raw force and yet gentle in how little of his strength it required.

Outside, the night was warm and still. There was music all around. They turned left onto the boardwalk and walked hand in hand toward Convention Hall.

"Did you know that it was designed by the architect that did Grand Central Station?" Sophia asked him, pointing up ahead.

"Are you from the city?" he asked her.

"No. I only read about it. Or my father did. I can't remember which."

"Your father," he echoed quietly. "How old are you, really?"

"Old enough," she said again.

There was a crowd gathered on the small lawn between the boardwalk and the Stone Pony's Summer Stage. David and Sophia stopped for a while to listen to the music. All around them, children sat on top of their parents' shoulders in order to see over the high fence that closed around the ticketed area.

"Do you know who's playing?" she asked.

"No. But I'll give you a peek," he said. Davey dropped down to his knees behind her and put his head between her legs, and with no special effort at all, stood up, carrying her now on his shoulders. Sophia screamed as she was lifted into the air, but really she was delighted. She was higher than any of the children, higher than anyone. She could see the stage perfectly. Above it, a row of lights shone down and lit up oval regions of heads in the crowd, purple and orange and green. Between her legs, she could feel the hair on Davey's head. There was no fabric between him and her. Her fingers moved in his hair and then slid down to lay flat against his cheek. She locked her fingers beneath his jaw and tried to hunch over to see his face, but in doing so, set him off balance. He swayed and she felt the spinning pull of vertigo as her arms shot out to balance. When they stabilized, Sophia was breathing hard, but she could feel Davey's laughter beneath her. It came up through his neck and into her legs.

"Put me down," she said.

"No. Never."

"Please."

"Alright."

Davey dropped down to his knees and Sophia slid from his neck down off his back and to the ground. She felt the way she had felt once dismounting a camel. They walked on toward Convention Hall.

"It must be nice to be so big," she said. "I bet you never have to get in fights."

"Oh, that's a bet you'd lose," he said.

"But is it you that starts them?"

"No," he said. "I never start anything."

"I can't see who would fight you."

"Don't look too hard."

"I won't."

Davey lead Sophia by the hand to the entrance of the Anchor's Bend. Such was the difference in their respective strengths that he did not feel her pulling back as they approached the doorman. Her resistance meant nothing to him.

"Hi Dave," said the doorman. "Been a while. Who's your friend?"

"Nobody," said David. He seemed to want to show her off, and Sophia liked being shown off. David pulled her close to him, and then began to move into the bar, but the doorman stuck out his arm.

"Well, does nobody have an ID?"

Davey looked back at Sophia, waiting. She looked between the two men before her.

"I—I must have left it at the other place we were just at," she said. "I'm always doing that."

Davey nodded at her. His eyes did not seem drunk anymore.

"We'll go get it and be right back," he said. He pulled her back the way they had come, but they moved faster now.

"Wait," said Sophia, but he did not wait. Still moving fast, she spoke loudly to reach him. "I didn't leave it there. I'm sorry. I really did want to hear the music, but I didn't leave it there."

"I know," he said. "Come on."

"Where are we going?"

He turned sharply off the boardwalk, down the steps onto the sand. They went back the way they had just come, but now underneath the boardwalk instead of above it, where there wasn't any doorman.

"Here," he said. "Come on. Take off your shoes."

"But where are we going?" asked Sophia. She stopped at the bottom of the stairs, and undid the straps on her heels before stepping down onto the sand.

"Listen," he said. "Look. Convention Hall juts out here over the sand. Twenty feet this way and you can stand fully beneath it. Forty feet and I could have you on my shoulders and you couldn't touch the floor. That's where the Anchor's Bend is. Listen. We'll be just beneath it."

They walked barefoot along the side of the Hall. From the earlier rain, there was a firm and brittle crust over the sand, and with each step, Sophia felt it break beneath her feet. Once there was enough space for them to stand beneath the Hall, they ducked under it. Here, all the sand was soft.

"Be careful," said Davey. "There's broken glass sometimes. Watch where you step."

Sophia did not mind so much the broken glass except that it meant that the place was not a secret. People had to know about a place to break glass there.

"Listen," she said. "I didn't like that you told the doorman that I was no one. I don't want you to tell anybody our jokes."

"Alright," he said. He was looking up at the underside of the Hall, trying to determine where they were. "I won't tell anybody who you are."

"That isn't what I meant—"

"Listen," he said. "Do you hear it?"

"Not particularly," said Sophia. She could hear her accent again—*Here's the smell of blood still! Oh, oh, this little hand!*—and closed her fingers into fists. They were clammy and wet and she closed her eyes and tried to listen hard. All she could hear was the sound of rolling waves. They were close to the eastern extremity of Convention Hall, which almost jutted out over the ocean. She put her fingers against Davey's arm as they moved in the dark quiet space between the pillars, trying to slow him down, but he was like a magnet for the sound above—he wanted desperately to find it.

"There was a ship once that almost crashed into this Hall," she said. She spoke loudly. "Did you know that? It came from Cuba and was trying to reach New York in record time. The captain died during a storm and then there was a fire. All the crew abandoned ship and the boat nearly crashed right into this building."

Davey had stopped so suddenly that she walked into him.

"Watch," he said. "There's glass here."

He put his arms around her waist and lifted her up. She wrapped her arms around his neck. He took one large step over the glass that she never saw, and did not put her down afterward.

"We're directly beneath the band now," he said. "Can you hear it?"

"Yes," she said, "But mostly just the waves."

"Just on the other side of those rocks is the ocean."

"I know," she said. "They put the rocks there to protect the building. There was once a ship that nearly crashed into it."

"Was there?" said Davey. He held Sophia tightly against him as she loosened her arms around his neck. He turned himself toward the ocean, which turned Sophia's back to it, and took another step, and then another. Sophia gasped as her back came against one of the giant concrete pillars that held up Convention Hall. Vibrations from the music above traveled down through the thick beams and trembled against the notches of her spine. The surface was rough and warm, and it dug into the skin of her back, but she felt it as though it were happening to other skin, another body. Davey's face was just before hers and she kissed it and held onto the back of his head. Her fingers worked in his hair and trembled along the round outline of his skull as his lips moved from her mouth to her neck to her shoulder, from kissing to breaking to biting. Her ankles met behind his back and hooked around one another so that she stayed there, pressed between his body and the trembling bones of the boardwalk above, which dug like small knives into her shoulders. Davey's hands slid up from her calves over her knees and up her thighs and pushed up the dress as they went, as eager and unrelenting as a tide, and when they slid up over her hips the dress was pulled back and she heard it tear as its fabric moved against the sharp splinters of the pillar behind her, moved in small sharp angles and thin circles, jumped like a needle reading heartbeats in green lines across a dark monitor, and she gasped as she was squeezed from either side by his body or the warm sharp dark pillar and her lungs were squeezed and folded upon themselves like the skin of an accordion and the sound escaped her lips in low, guttural resonations until finally she formed the words, "be kind," but there was no space for kindness between their shifting bodies and his arms wrapped around the pillar so that he could compress the space further and she looked up at the trembling underbelly of the Hall and thought for a moment that he might break the pillar and bring the whole thing down on top of them, like Samson at the Philistine temple. Her fingers moved up along his neck and worked in his hair.

Everything was still. A small, childish sound came from David's lips, and her skin was wet with his saliva where his mouth had been pressed against her collar bone. He had kept his head buried there the whole time, never fully looking at her. And then there was another sound, the sound of applause. Sophia's eyes moved down the underbelly of the Hall above them, but the applause was too loud—it did not come from above. Her eyes scanned the darkness. In the shadows beneath the Hall, there were two homeless men watching. They sat on a tarp with sleeping bags and pillows, passing a glass bottle between them.

"Hooray," they screamed and laughed their drunken laughs. "Well done, well done."

Their hands clapped together without any rhythm and sent sharp violent pulses of air out into the darkness.

"Don't stop," they called. "Don't stop. Hooray, hooray."

Davey lowered Sophia slowly to the ground and her back slid down against the rough surface of the pillar, still trembling with the sound of the music above. Nothing above had changed. Her feet touched the sand but it did not seem soft any more. There was the sound of their clapping and of Davey's zipper—a comical sound, like one to accompany a cartoon injury, where all the speech was in bubbles or clouds.

"Don't worry about them," said Davey, grinning. "They're lowlives." He turned briefly toward their clapping and mimicked a shallow bow.

Sophia nodded and turned north, toward home. She began to walk. The sand was soft and dry beneath the Hall.

"But—your shoes," said Davey. "They're the other way."

Sophia nodded as she walked, and kept nodding, kept walking.

"Don't you want your shoes?" he said. His voice was far away.

She knew she had come out from underneath the Hall, not because the moonlight but because the sand beneath her was now crusted again, the way it was after a rain. There had been a rain that afternoon, she thought. This was how the sand felt after the rain this afternoon and there hasn't been a rain since then. The same sand, dried with the same rain.

"Hey," said Davey. He ran after her and walked beside her. He took her hand in his. She did not pull it away but she did not hold it, either. It did not feel like her hand that he was holding, and she could not think how she might do anything with it.

"Can I at least walk you home," said Davey.

Sophia did not answer and she did not slow. They came to the first jetty, where one beach led onto the next over a short wall of rocks.

"Let me carry you across it," he said, and she did not answer, but only kept walking. His hand let hers go, and it dropped to her side and hung there like a dead animal. She clamored over the rocks and slipped against the smooth side of one of them so that her knees came into the sand.

"Hey—are you alright," said Davey.

But she had already gotten up and kept on walking. He did not follow. She walked on the edge of the sea, on the wet sand that glistened as the water slid up it and down it and shone like white glass under the moon. Each time her sole pressed into the wet sand, all the sand around it moved and darkened and the water squeezed from the sand crawled up and over her foot. "If I stop moving," she thought, "I'll die." She thought of the water crawling up her legs and knees and thighs and hips and covering her body like the strangling vines of a poison fig.

"If I stop moving, I'll die," she thought, and kept moving north along the water and then turned in and walked up the sand and off the beach when she saw the familiar silhouette of the house at the end of her street and she walked through strangers' lawns and then onto the road and did not feel the rough pavement beneath her bare feet. She walked onto the sharp grass of her own lawn, through the sprinklers, and her eyes fell on her window and the slanted roof going up to it and the windowsill below that she had used like a ladder and she could not see how the climb back up was possible but knowing that if she stopped moving, she would die, continued on and clamored up the roof and through the open window.

She did not notice that the lamp beside her bed was turned on, but went straight to the full length mirror and stood before it. She looked at herself like a ghost in the mirror, and slid the straps of the yellow dress down around her shoulders so that the thing fell down into a puddle at her feet. Below the knees, her legs glistened with seawater and they were covered in sand. There were light spots along her thighs where white sand had clung to the wetness of sea or of blood or of him that had stuck to her skin.

Her reflection was still, impossibly still, but something moved in the shadow behind it. Sophia turned around and looked at her bed, where her father sat up with his back against the pillows and her book laying flat and open across his chest. He looked as if he had only just woken up, and his eyes widened as they drank in her figure. He blinked several times, and slowly stood as he closed the book and put it back on the bedside table.

They watched each other without speaking, but between their bodies played a conversation.

"So this is it," hers seemed to say. Small, thin. Emaciated by choice, browned by the sun, trembling by the coolness of the night.

And his was heavy, old, unworkable. His eyes were soft but knowing. His fingers rested on her nightstand and fingered the corners of her book, and his eyes turned down, away from her. *What's done cannot be undone*, his body seemed to say in someone else's words. *To bed, to bed, to bed.*

"Go," she finally whispered. "Please go." And then: "Please don't tell mom."

And she turned back to the mirror and her father walked slowly from the room. Pausing for a moment as he passed near her, he reached out his lips toward the side of her head, but she shrank away from the vulgar comfort of them, and instead he kissed the air, and breathed in the smell of his daughter, which was the smell of his wife's perfume blended with the smell of the sea and of the night, of the dark space beneath the boardwalk.

Once he had gone from the room and closed the door, she collapsed before the mirror. And slept all night on the floor with the torn dress like a sheet or chain around her. And the thing was stained and torn along the back, and the sound of it tearing was like an echo in her memory that persisted all throughout her night of sleep, like a dream of noise and nothing else. And the other half that had been torn away hung like a flag against the post where it had happened. And it fluttered in the wind that came off the sea at dawn.

CHAPTER 14
The Runner, Again

Two silver bells jingled as the door to Madame K's shop swung open. She did not mind that the outside air was coming in. It was the first Sunday in September, the first truly cool day of the year. In the air there was the feeling that the summer was over. Besides, Madame K would not have minded the door's being open even if the air had been hot; her mind was reeling and ecstatic with the gossip she had heard.

Gossip, to Madame K, was something like an analgesic. She loved to hear of other people's dramas because they made her feel that she was lucky to have none. But this one, in particular, concerned a slight to her—a girl that had worked in her shop. All of a sudden, she had stopped coming to work, and Madame K had worried that the shop was becoming unfashionable. But no, she laughed to herself. No, no, no.

"Madame K?" said the man who came in.

"Yes, yes," said Madame K without looking up from her

phone. She was copying her news to anyone who would have it. "Welcome to my shop. If it's a present you're looking for, my girls will help you find a gift for any occasion."

Madame K waved her hand toward the empty store before remembering that she no longer had an assistant. She finally looked up, bitter to be distracted from what she saw now as her moral duties of dissemination and saw the man. He was dressed simply, in a white tee shirt and jeans, and she had a difficult time telling how expensive his clothing was.

"Or," she said, "if you have something in mind, I'll be happy to—"

"That's alright, Madame K," he said. "I already have what I came for. I only came to pay for it."

"Already have it?" asked Madame K. "But you've only just . . ."

Her voice trailed off. She noticed now that the man held a paper grocery bag in one hand, and as he approached her, he pulled from it a yellow dress and laid it across the counter. He spread the fabric out before her eyes. The back of the dress was badly torn and frayed, and the skirt of it was stained with something dark.

"Oh no," said Madame K. She smiled up at Sam Besalel. "You know how careless girls can be."

"My daughter isn't a careless girl," said Sam.

"Well," said Madame K. Her smile faltered. "Un—unfortunately, you see, we don't take returns . . ."

"I'm not making a return, Madame K. I've come to pay. Didn't you hear what I said?"

Sam looked straight ahead at her and she could not meet his eyes.

"Well I—I suppose we could make an exception, the dress is really badly torn. How did it happen?"

"You aren't listening to me," said Sam, looking down at the dress. His fingers moved along the counter as if to touch the fabric, but then they stopped and he put his hands in his pocket. "I don't mean to return it. I only mean to pay for it. As for how it happened, I can only guess."

He opened his wallet and took out two one-hundred-dollar bills.

"You—you can't pay for it," said Madame K. She seemed angry with him, and folded the skirt of the dress over so that the stain was covered. With his free hand, Sam unfolded the skirt and smoothed the yellow fabric against the counter.

"Was it more or less than two hundred?" said Sam. "If it was more, I'll leave more. If it was less, I'll leave less."

"It was less," said Madame K quietly. She sank down onto her stool and her whole figure seemed to shrink.

"Good. Was it much less?"

"No." Her voice was hardly more than a whisper. "Not much less."

Madame K looked down at the crisp, hundred dollar bills in Sam's hand.

"We—we don't have any change," she told him. Her voice was shaking. "We only take credit cards."

"I don't need any change," he said. "My wife wouldn't like to see a bill from Madame K's on our account."

Sam looked at her sternly but said nothing.

"I only thought," she said. "I only meant. She looked so pretty in it."

"Yes," he said. "She's a very pretty girl."

Madame K stared down at the ruined fabric and wished that she had turned the wall unit on today, or that something would occur to break up the awful silence. When she spoke, her voice was hardly more than a whisper, and Sam had to lean in to hear it.

"I wanted to do something nice for her," she said. "I live across the lake from you. I practically watched those children grow up. Your son runs in front of my house every morning, at just the time that I take coffee on the porch. I . . . I watched them grow up, in a way."

"Madame K," said Sam. He had not meant it cruelly—there was even a strain of sympathy in his voice now for the old woman crumbling before him. He had not meant it cruelly but it sounded cruel to her. The name suddenly embarrassed her, mocked her, laughed as quietly as the rustling of fabric. She nodded. "Stay away from my children."

He laid the money on top of the dress, careful not to cover up the spot where his daughter's blood had dried and stained the fabric. Sam walked from the store and out onto the boardwalk. Once the door had shut, Julie snatched the money from on top of the dress and, feeling suddenly outraged, she went forward, around the counter and out of the shop brandishing the two bills before her.

"Look here," she cried out. "Look here!"

But it was a bright Sunday in late summer and the boardwalk was filled with people. Sam Besalel was nowhere to be seen. Instead, people looked at the strange figure of a woman, running wildly about with cash clenched in her right fist, screaming. All along the outside of her shop, the moving crowd began to laugh. They did not stop to stare and laugh, but only laughed in passing as they kept moving all around her.

* * *

Five doors down the boardwalk from Madame K's shop, David Larkin sat where he always sat, with his elbows on the bar and his back to the door. It was evening now and the red neon lights inside Pop's Garage made all the surfaces glow with a soft pink haze. The music inside the bar was always loud because it had to compete with the waves.

With his middle finger and thumb, Davey spun his empty glass on the bar while Tony poured another customer a drink. The bar was crowded for a Sunday night, mostly with the young summer crowd whose summer was over, who were drinking to prepare for the return to school or work.

"Jesus, Tony," said Davey. "What's a guy got to do to get a drink in this shithole."

He spoke loudly and a few heads turned toward him, but mostly the crowd knew Davey and they did not pay him much attention. To Pop's Garage, David Larkin had become like a piece of curious decoration or a bar game that nobody plays. The only people who paid him serious attention were the girls who he bought drinks for and the bartender, Tony; he turned now away from his mixing glasses, where another customer's drink was half-made, to refill Davey's glass of whiskey.

"Another of the same?" he asked. He did not wait for a response to start pouring.

As soon as his glass was filled, Davey turned on his stool. He put one elbow on the bar and rested his head in his hand. A girl came up next to him to order a drink, and he looked at her for a long time while she waited for a drink.

"Don't I know you?" he yelled to her.

She looked taken aback at first, but then smiled. "Sure you do. You're Casey Larkin's older brother."

"Older half brother."

"I didn't know that," she said. Her voice brightened: "Well, we met . . . it's got to be two months ago now. You remember, we played pool? Me and my friend and you and your . . . well, your Casey. We all played pool and then got split up. My friend's name was Steph. You remember Steph, don't you? She said you had a nice time together."

Lena gave Davey a slight wink, but subtlety was beyond him, and he did not remember much about the night of his father's funeral.

"I remember playing pool," he said.

"You were good. Better than Casey, anyway. Is he around tonight?"

Davey looked at Lena without saying anything and then turned back to the bar and looked down into his drink.

"Well," said Lena. "It was nice running into you."

Lena walked to the far side bar and sat down at an empty stool.

"Nice try," said Tony when he went to take her order. "But it's wasted effort on that one."

He nodded his head back toward the far side of the bar where David sat alone. Even though Davey was much too far to hear, Tony kept his voice low, and Lena needed to lean over the bar to hear him.

"What do you mean?" she said.

"I mean," he said. "That if you're trying to meet someone, you're wasting your time on Davey Larkin. Rumor has it that he's switched teams."

Lena looked past Tony at David. "I'm not trying to meet anyone," she said.

"Well, if you are—"

"Thanks," she said. She said it harshly enough so that the ugly smile went out of Tony's face. Something in the smile had reminded Lena of her mother. "I'm not. Just a PBR."

"Suit yourself," he said. He put a can down in front of her and did not even bother to open it. "And what are you having?" he said to somebody who had taken the empty seat on Lena's left.

"Just water."

"Well," said Tony. "You want water, there's a whole fucking ocean out there. When you come into my bar, you drink."

From across the bar, Davey Larkin was calling for a drink.

"Better scoot," said Lena.

"I'll be back," said Tony, and he left them. Lena watched him rush to pour Davey Larkin another whiskey.

"You know him?" said the man who had sat down next to her. She did not turn to face him but looked down to check the time on her phone. It was getting late.

"Who," she said. "The bartender?"

"Not the bartender. Him—David Larkin."

"Is David Larkin all anybody wants to talk about tonight?" she began to say, but she did not make it past "anybody." In anger, she had turned to face her questioner, and now that she saw him, she felt the blood go out of her face.

Sitting beside her was the Runner. His face looked strange out of motion. When he ran, his eyes were numb and far away, on the places he was going to; now, they were sharp and focused across the bar on David Larkin.

"Yes," she said. "I know him."

It had been a long time since Lena had felt nervous speaking with a boy, but she felt nervous now. Time seemed to be going fast, emphasizing how long the gaps of silence were between their words. A breathless, anxious feeling filled her stomach and pushed words into her mouth.

"I know you too," she said. She looked down at her can of beer and quickly drank. She could feel the Runner's eyes on her. "Not your name. Or anything about you. Only that you run every morning in front of my house."

"Oh," he said. "You live on the Lake?"

Lena nodded and felt the silence forming between them again.

"What do you want with David Larkin?" she asked him.

"To kill him," said Jacob. He gripped the edge of the bar and said it again, as if to convince himself that he really meant it. "To kill him."

The Runner tried to make his voice sound serious and dangerous, and something about the effort put Lena at ease. When he ran by her house each morning, he looked like a machine and she had really considered him to be one. She had built up the idea of him as a machine and had wondered how a machine could be spoken to, or flirted with, or loved. But now she could see that he was anything but a machine; he was only a boy. She noticed how cleanly shaven his jaw was, and how nervously his fingers played with the corner of the bar.

"And why do you want to kill David Larkin?" she said. A lightness had come into her voice.

"What," he said, turning to her. "You don't believe me? You don't think I could do it?"

"I didn't say that," said Lena. They faced each other fully

now. "I only asked why you wanted to. Look at him. Look at how much he's had to drink. He's on the verge of killing himself. I just can't understand why you'd want to."

Jacob seemed to be noticing for the first time how close his face was to Lena's. As he opened his mouth to speak, Tony came back and leaned over the bar between them.

"I thought you weren't trying to meet anyone," he said to Lena with a wink. "Well, this is more like it. So what are you two drinking?"

"Two more beers," said Lena before Jacob could speak.

"Coming up," said Tony. "And our friend over there says they're on his tab."

Lena looked over toward Davey. "No," she said. "These ones are on me."

"I'll buy them," said Jacob. He began to fumble with his wallet, but Lena laid her hand against his arm.

"You'll get the next one," she said. "How's that?"

Jacob looked over toward Davey and then looked down at his own knuckles. He was badly afraid and wanted something for his nerves. "Alright."

They drank quietly. They did not look at Davey while Tony went to tell him that they had not wanted his drink. Lena turned to Jacob so that he would turn to her. She spoke to him like a snake charmer.

"Now," she said. "You were telling me why you wanted to go and do a thing like kill David Larkin."

Jacob took a sip of his beer, and Lena could tell by his face that he was not accustomed to drinking. He read the label on the can.

"It doesn't matter why," he said. "But I've got to."

Lena nodded and took a sip of her own beer. "Did he do something wrong to you?"

"Yes. Or no. Not to me."

"Who then?"

"It doesn't matter. I've got to."

"Alright. So you've got to kill him. And killing him is going to make it right for this other person?"

Across the bar, Davey watched them with eyes that seemed dull and out of focus. Tony had an ugly smile on his face. Jacob seemed almost embarrassed to be caught staring and looked down to read the label of his beer once more.

"I've got to," he said quietly. "It's what's right."

"Alright," said Lena. "And just say that you can't do it. Just say that he beats you instead. Will that make him right then?"

"No," said Jacob, but he did not seem so certain. "Nothing can make him right. What— you don't think I can do it?"

"No," said Lena. "I don't think you can do it."

Jacob looked down at his knuckles. "It's what's right."

"I believe that it's what's right. But that isn't going to help you in a fistfight, and being wrong isn't going to hurt him in a fistfight. So why do you think that a fistfight is the best way to settle it?"

Jacob opened his mouth and then closed it again without speaking. He took a drink instead.

"What other way is there?" he said.

Tony came back to their end of the bar. "Mr. Larkin wants to know why a 'pretty lady' like you won't let him buy you a drink. His words."

Lena was struck by how similar the two of them were— David Larkin and her Runner. One sat alone at an oceanfront bar with his back turned always to the ocean, and the other ran every day around an ugly, man-made lake while the boardwalk was right there, and somehow they had found each other here and were on the brink of violence. It was all a game, she thought—a childish, unintelligent game. "Alright," she thought. "I'll play."

She turned away from the bar and leaned in close to Jacob. She whispered to him, and then closed her lips around his earlobe before turning back to the bar.

"I'm buying her drinks," said Jacob. His voice shook. "You can tell David that I'm buying her drinks."

Tony raised his eyebrows and shrugged. "It's all the same to me," he said. He took away their empty cans and replaced them with two full ones.

They drank the beers that Jacob had bought for them while Davey watched them from across the bar. He watched them with the shameless stare of someone who is only partly conscious. When they had finished the second beer, Lena took Jacob's face in her hands and kissed him. He flushed and stuttered and looked over at Davey to make sure that he had seen.

Across the bar, David's head was heavy in his hand.

"Well," Tony said to him. "Looks like you lost that one. It's a shame too. I know how much you like a pretty girl."

The words were like an alarm bell in David's ear, and he raised his face and looked at Tony.

"What do you mean by that?" he said.

Tony had thought that he was teasing something that was half-dead, but now the drunkenness seemed to go out of Davey. He partially stood up in his seat and grabbed Tony by the collar. "What did you mean by that?"

"I didn't mean anything, Dave. Let me get your next round. On me, on the house."

Davey inspected the bartender's face for what seemed like a long time before releasing his grip on the collar.

"Alright," he said. "On you."

David leaned back away from the bar and back into his stool, but somewhere in the shifting of weight, he had miscalculated; the barstool tipped beneath him and Davey's whole great body came crashing to the ground. Tony jumped over the bar to see what had gone wrong, and by the time he had landed on the other side, Davey was already on his knees. He was wearing a short sleeved, button-down shirt with an open breast pocket and, when he fell, loose pills had fallen from his shirt pocket and scattered on the floor.

"You're bleeding, Dave," said Tony.

David did not answer. He was scrambling now to collect his pills, his thick fingers trembling over the dirty barroom floor like censors. Tony kneeled down beside him.

"Let me call you a cab," he said.

Davey did not try speaking. He stood and looked back to where Lena and Jacob had been sitting only moments before. They were gone now. Tony followed Davey's stare and then looked slowly back at Davey.

"Let me call you a cab," he said again, but Davey shook his head and walked out the door and onto the boardwalk. He walked straight to the railing that separated the boardwalk from the sand below and then looked back at the bar. Now it seemed to him like a small rectangle of red-yellow light against the evening, and Davey wanted to put as much distance between himself and the light as was possible. He climbed over the railing and jumped down into the sand. He staggered upon landing and sank down to his knees before getting up again. The sand was soft and his great weight shifted it from side to side and made his going slow as he walked toward the ocean. A strong wind pulled the white sand north along the beach, and it gave Davey the impression that the world was tilted and running off toward the left. There was the sound like rain against a roof as the grains of windswept sand struck against his jeans. When strong gusts came, the sand flew up above his waist and above his shoulders, and each grain was like a dart as it struck him in the arms and in the face. He turned north, so that he was moving with the wind and then the grains of sand would only hit against his back. He walked on for a long time, and only after he recognized the back entrance to his father's house did he realize that—by providence of chance and wind—he had been walking in the right direction.

* * *

It was nearly 9:00 a.m. now and Julie Kowolski was beginning to get nervous. Her coffee was cold and she had not had more than a sip. It sat on the table beside her and long ago it had stopped letting off steam. Sitting upright, she held a newspaper flat against her lap and did not even pretend to read it. Her eyes quickly scanned the lake and the road that ran around it. She watched the sky for signs of bad weather, but it was overcast and cool, with a light morning breeze coming off the sea. The gulls tilted their wings toward the ocean and hung frozen in the air, nearly blending into the sky, and on the lake the water had lost its glasslike stillness and the surface was broken and gray.

No, the weather was not the reason why her runner was not running.

Perhaps, she thought, their father packed them up after he came to the shop yesterday. The thought made her sick, and in her mind she thought of the Marhabba boy who had gone off to war, who had come to say goodbye and who she had been unable to turn away from the mirror to face. "You're well on your way to becoming a flower," he had told her. It played in her head like a skipping record. "You're well on your way to becoming a flower." The lake was too broken to reflect anything but the color of the sky.

Suddenly, there was a sound that came from around the house. It sounded like voices, but they were bent and dragged by the wind, so that all that reached Julie was a vague, droning hum. The sound made her sick. Everything made her sick. Julie lifted the mug to her lips and sipped the cold coffee and nearly spit it out. It was the temperature of air. And then there was the voice again. It sounded near, and almost familiar despite the wind's distortion.

Julie rested the coffee mug down again and stood up, the paper clenched tight in her hands. There was a nervous, trembling feeling, as if she was walking down unknown stairs into a dark basement. She went to the edge of her porch, from where she could see around the side of the house, and her fingers tightened into fists on the edges of her paper.

The voices were clearer now. They were coming from just before the garage that Lena lived above, and there were two of them. One of them was Lena's and the other she did not know. She walked further on the porch, toward the side of the house from where she would be able to see the garage and to properly hear the voices. The newspaper crumpled in Julie's fingers as her hands closed into a fist. At the end, the thin gray paper curled and flexed into a point and she held it up as if she were brandishing a knife.

Julie could see the garage now. Leaving it was Lena, dressed in only a bathrobe, and with her was her runner.

"Yes," she thought, "my runner. Mine."

Julie watched silently while her daughter held her runner by his face and kissed him on the mouth. Without seeing Julie, they walked together down the driveway, their fingers interlocked.

Julie took two steps sideways to follow them as they moved down the driveway. When she came to the place where the stairs led from the porch down to the lawn, she took the first stair down in two heavy steps, her left first and then her right onto the same tread; it was all her knees could handle. She could feel her stale weight shift against the fabric of her nightgown and her heavy breasts sway side to side.

"No," she called out to them as her bare feet came onto the lawn. She did not know exactly what it was she disagreed with, but was only certain that she disagreed. Neither daughter nor runner had noticed the old woman yet, but now they turned their heads and noticed. They looked at her not as one human looks at another, but as two humans look together upon a charging animal. In the moment before they recognized Julie Kowolski, they clutched to each other with all the instinct of doomed lovers, and their touch made Julie charge faster.

"No," she cried again.

At the second yell, the runner began to pull away and move independently down the driveway. Lena's arms remained stretched out toward him.

"Don't," she called out. "Please don't."

But the runner was already moving. He took awkward steps as he ran off the driveway, and his face contorted with the discomfort of running without his usual clothes or proper shoes. There was an unfamiliar pounding in his head and what felt like a weight in his gut, and he grunted each time his feet came down against the pavement, but each sound was softer than the one before, each contortion of his face less pronounced. By the time he had crossed the street to be on the lakeside of the road, his face had regained its mannequin calm, his breath was even and light and his tread had all the steady of a metronome. His thoughts had stopped completely, and everything that there was in the whole universe converged like light through a magnifying glass until there was only his feet and the road, and the next step, and the next.

Lena had not taken her eyes from him or dropped her hand, even as her mother had approached with the rolled newspaper brandished like a sword. They stood side by side, watching Jacob Besalel's figure shrinking as he ran on. Once he had become so distant that they could no longer hear his footsteps, Julie turned to her daughter and struck her across the face with the newspaper.

"You little slut," she cried.

The thing tickled more than it hurt, but Lena raised her hand to her cheek and looked down on her mother, not with anger but with pity. The old woman sat down on the driveway, which was dark and wet from the sprinklers having passed over it. The water soaked through her nightgown but she did not feel it. She sat there and looked at the surface of the lake, still white with the gray morning sky. Julie dropped the newspaper onto the pavement and watched it darken as the pulp drank in the wetness like a sponge. She did not feel anything until there was a hand on her shoulder.

"Mom," said Lena.

The old woman turned around swiftly toward her daughter and her face was hot and wet. She tried to pick up the newspaper again to lash out at the girl, but the thing was soaked through with water and the pulp came apart in her fingers.

"You slut," she said again, but softer now. Her voice was hoarse and there was a lump in her throat. "Don't you understand that it's all your fault? Don't you understand?"

Lena's hand came slowly away from her mother's shoulder and then the shoulder began to shake. Julie leaned all of her weight toward that shoulder as if the hand was still there and could support it—but it was not, and could not—and without it there, Julie lay down in the driveway with her shoulder against the pavement, soaking in the morning water as if she were a flower on the lawn.

Lena turned and walked back toward the garage—there was no instinct left in her to return to her childhood room in the house. The place seemed strange and foreign, and she did not stop moving until she stood at the window of the room above the garage. Looking out, she could see her mother rising in the driveway, as if emerging from a bad dream, and far, far beyond her, was the runner going home.

CHAPTER 15
St. Kolbe's

The Atlantic hurricane season runs from June through November. The early ones are not so strong once they cross the Carolinas, but in August the bad storms begin forming in the Gulf and when they claw their way north along the Eastern Seaboard they bring more than only rain.

It was early October and they had just had their first real one of the season. Nobody wanted to admit that it had been a real one because Sandy had devastated the coast only four years before and the quiet years in between had built up everybody's idea of what a real hurricane was supposed to look like. It had become a point of pride to be unimpressed by storms, and if you had moved to the coast after Sandy there was a condescending attitude that persisted all through hurricane season toward your lack of resilience to the weather. The houses, too, had adopted this sentiment; they were all on stilts and fortified such that the conditions would not affect them so seriously.

But whether anyone wanted to admit it or not, a hurricane had come through. Some power lines had been snapped by fallen trees and soil dried where it had run in thick, dark streams across the sidewalks and the streets. Large swaths of beach had been reclaimed by the ocean, and to hear people speak of it the waves had not really been so large, but what they had been was gluttonous and they had taken all the sand with them when they receded.

The communal effort toward restoration in the wake of a storm was always something of a spectacle to behold and it made you almost grateful to have had the hurricane in the first place. But now two weeks had passed and the sentiment was beginning to turn. If you had not made a serious attempt at restoring the way that your house or your lawn looked by now, you would get a sort of prodding from your neighbors that became less and less gentle as time went on.

It was Saturday, October 8, and I had taken the first Seastreak Ferry from Thirty-Fifth Street in New York. Meredith had called me early in the morning and asked me to come. We had not spoken since I had gone back to New York and she would not have asked if it wasn't important. I had no plans to see Davey, but the house was on the way from the ferry landing to Meredith and so I had stopped in. The shape it was in did not surprise me and I did not stop there for very long. It had taken a beating in the storm. The hedge between the street and the house had been nearly downed in its entirety, and the house looked accidentally exposed, like something shameful that had failed at being hidden. On the lawn leading up to the house, small trees were knocked down, and the whole thing was covered over by a blanket of leaves. It was a kindness to only see it now, because it probably had not been well-maintained before the storm either and at least now it had some excuse for its decrepitude.

"Is this where we're stopping?" the driver asked me.

"No," I said. "I only wanted to pull in and see it. We can go now. To Allenhurst."

The Hawthorne lawn looked as immaculate as it always did. Meredith was not home when I arrived at her house. It was Evelyn who answered. She looked older than I remembered, but it had been a very long time since I'd seen her.

"Casey, dear," she said. She had a thick Irish accent and it seemed sometimes that she was speaking a different language. Her arms had been one of the earliest things to go after her sickness and she could not do very much with them, but they reached up toward me and I bent forward to give her a hug. Despite everything, her eyes had not lost any happiness. She avoided looking beyond me toward the lawn. "Come in, come in. What a treat to see you, dear. Are you back for good? Meredith mentioned that you were in the big city now."

"That's right," I said. "Staying here too long doesn't agree with me."

"If you haven't changed much, Mister Larkin, I'm struck by the memory that not a whole lot seems to agree with you."

"I haven't changed much," I said.

"That's good. Nobody ever got anywhere by being agreeable."

"Nobody gets anywhere anyway."

"Ah," she said. "The youth is turning awfully morbid. Will you make an old lady a cup of tea?"

We sat and had tea. Evelyn asked me to only fill the cup halfway because her hands shook so violently.

"So tell me," she said. "What's become of you?"

"Oh, nothing so much. I came into a little bit of money and I'm slowly losing it all."

"Better slowly than quickly," she said. Words did not escape her lips that weren't accompanied by a smile. "But yes, I was sorry to hear about it."

"You sounded like Meredith when you said that. I can hear her saying the same exact thing."

"Well, it is the thing to say, isn't it? And besides, you know, I really was sorry to hear it. Your father wasn't the most popular man but he had a little place in my heart. Did you know he was the only one along Ocean Avenue who wouldn't hire me?"

"I thought you did his lawn."

"I did, eventually. But he wouldn't hire me. I detested his lawn—detested it, you know. So I decided to do it anyway. He threatened to call the police—he really did, too—for trespassing. I was taken off his lawn three consecutive days straight. He never pressed charges, mind you, and after three days he figured that he could not help it and he stopped calling the police on me. It was something of a victory for me, dear. You know, even enemies are remembered fondly when you beat them."

"I didn't know that."

"Yes. Well, I'm sure there are a lot of things you don't know."

"I'm beginning to find out."

"Mind you, about three weeks after I had finished your father's lawn, I received a check in the mail from him. It was more than I would've charged and so I mailed it back and told him the correct amount. And do you know what he did?"

"What'd he do?"

"He sent back a new one worth a cent more than his original. So I didn't deposit it, and then he sent another one a week later with another penny added. He sent five checks in total and finally the last one had a note on the memo. 'Beat me once. Don't push luck. JL.' Well, when you put it like that. As if it were a telegram."

Evelyn smiled and took a sip of her tea.

"A few weeks later I was down in his area and I was passing his post box and I left a nickel inside—to pay him back for the pennies added, you understand. The next morning the nickel was in my mailbox. He had colored half of it with a red marker."

"Why did he do that?"

"I don't know," she said. She shrugged her shoulders to the extent that it was possible for her to do so. "I never understood it. I wanted to ask but it never seemed like the sort of thing to bring up in public and I never saw him privately. Something like a secret between us. Something like a scandal, you understand."

"Yes," I said. "I understand scandals well enough."

"Oh, I bet you do, Mister Larkin. Well, I still have the nickel. Here, go and take it."

Evelyn smiled and moved her hand to vaguely point toward a drawer.

"That's alright," I told her. "I got all the inheritance I can manage out of him. You keep your nickel."

"You'll manage, dear. We all manage. Only try and not get used to living on inheritance. Nothing ages a man quite so fast as idleness."

"I've heard that before."

"Well now you've heard it again. Consider acting on it. Meredith is beginning to act on it. I'm very proud of that girl, Casey."

"There's a lot to be proud of," I said. I looked down at my hands. "Where is she?"

But even as I said it, I could hear Meredith's car pulling into the driveway.

"Well," said Evelyn. She rolled forward and handed me her teacup. "Do me a favor and go and rinse these out. I'll leave the two of you be."

"Alright," I said. I was nervous to be seeing Meredith and wanted something to do. "Tell Meredith I'm cleaning the cups and I'll be out in a minute."

"Like I told you," she said sternly, "just a quick rinse and leave them. If you rinse a thing quick there isn't so much cleaning to do later. It's only if you let it sit that you truly need to scrub. Leave the soap to Meredith, dear. Go on. She's good with soap."

"Alright," I said. There was the sound of Meredith's car door closing.

"Oh, and Casey?" said Evelyn. Her voice had lost its gaiety. "Whatever was the matter with him, I was sorry to hear about your father. It's a little late, I know."

"That's alright. Punctuality isn't important for that sort of thing."

"I suppose that's true. Well, when I pass on, do try and be a little more punctual about it for Meredith."

"Don't talk like that, Miss Hawthorne. You'll outlive us all."

"Dear god, I hope it isn't true," she said, laughing as she left the room.

When I came out of the kitchen, Meredith was standing in the front door. My eyes had adjusted to the darkness of the house and I could only make out a silhouette of her figure against the bright gray sky.

"Let's go," she said. "Get in the car."

* * *

St. Kolbe's Inpatient Center for Drug Addiction and Rehabilitation is located in the Township of Toms River. It was the sixth addiction center to open in Ocean County that year, and it was very nearly full. It was a private center that did not accept medical insurance and the brochure emphasized the tranquil views of the Atlantic in bold font and stock photographs that had not been taken on the site. Even from the best rooms, all you could see was the inlet before the structures of Ortley Beach, obscured all but a sliver of the distant views of ocean.

Davey had one of the best rooms. He was asleep when we entered and I looked between the brochure I had taken at the front desk and the windows, where the nurse was drawing the curtains.

"They must have taken the photos from this room," I told her.

"I didn't make the ads," she said. "I wouldn't know where they took the pictures from."

You got the sense that the nurses were accustomed to managing the discrepancies between visitors' expectations and reality. She was neither apologetic nor defensive and waited patiently to see if I would say anything else about it. I would not. She was middle-aged and very kind and exactly the type of person you would hope to be caring for your brother. If it had not been her, I might have insisted that he find another place. Perhaps that was only her job and she was not even a real nurse.

When she woke Davey up, he looked for a moment like a child. It was wonderful to see him wake up as if he were getting up for grade school, without fully remembering where he was. He quickly remembered and all that hopeful innocence dissolved and you wondered if it had ever been there in the first place. His eyes darted quickly between the three of us and then he turned his head toward the window where outside it was gray and overcast.

"Will you give us a minute?" I said. The nurse bowed her head and left the room and Meredith followed.

I pulled up a chair beside the bed and we sat for a while without saying anything. Eventually I put my hand on his shoulder. I knew there was nothing physical in his injury but I touched him as if he were made of porcelain. He half turned to me and smiled. There were dark rings beneath his eyes and his voice was tired when he spoke.

"Remember when you had that sledding accident on Cemetery Hill?" he asked. "When you went straight into a tree?"

"Sure."

"I remember coming to see you in the hospital after. The nurses let me give you your food. I thought hospitals were nice, then. I liked it better when you were in the bed and I was sitting there."

"I liked that better too," I said. "It seems like a lifetime ago, doesn't it?"

"Yes," said Davey. He looked at the ceiling above him. "Like a lifetime. Everything seems so obvious when you look back at it."

"That's why it's best to never look back at it."

"Easier said than done."

"That's true," I said.

We were quiet for a while. I tried to listen for the ocean, but either the glass was very thick or it was very far away.

"Listen," I said, "is it only the pills? They aren't sure. Apparently, the tests don't tell the difference so well."

"You mean am I shooting up?"

"That's what I mean."

"No," said Davey. He laughed.

"Don't laugh. I'd only laugh about something like that if I were lying. Are you lying?"

"No," he said. "It isn't that. I'm nervous about needles. Always have been."

"I've done a whole mess of things that make me nervous," I said. I looked at him to see if he was lying. "And I'd guess that you have too. Now is it only the pills?"

"Yes," he said. He was serious now. "Only the pills."

"They think it's a good idea if I take control of the finances."

"It probably is a good idea."

"It's just for a while, until we can be sure that you're out of it."

Davey nodded. I had expected a little fight out of him, and I had been prepared for it. What I had not prepared for was this overwhelming sense of defeat.

"What are you doing them for, Dave? You've got so much good going for you."

"Do I? Like what?"

"You don't have many problems, you can do anything you want to do. You've got about twenty million—"

"See," he interrupted. "That's what it comes down to, isn't it. That's what everyone has said. Why am I doing this? I have so much going for me, so much money. But whose money is it really? I didn't make it. I've never had to worry about it before. Actually, I worry about it more now. Maybe I want to have something besides a lot of money. Having a dead father does not seem like much of an accomplishment."

"You've got time, Dave. You're four years from thirty. Go travel, go learn something you've wanted to. You've got so much time and you're lucky enough that you can do anything you want to with it."

I wish that I had thought of something better to say, but I could not. He had a point. What he had was time and money. They are two good things to have but perhaps they are not enough.

"You're right," said Davey. He nodded but his voice was unconvinced. "Of course you're right. You always had that, being right."

"If you really think that, then maybe pills really are your best option."

Davey laughed and this time it was real.

"Listen," he said. "About you and Gabrielle. I've thought about it lots. Maybe I don't like it, and maybe nobody will like it, but people haven't liked things before that turned out to be alright. A hundred years ago they wouldn't let whites and Blacks get married. Now they're even allowing gays to do it. Maybe in fifty years it'll be alright to do what you're doing."

We were quiet for a while and I sat down on the side of the bed and patted him twice on the thigh.

"You'll be a better man than your father was," I said. "But don't think about this too hard. There isn't anything to think about. Even if it is alright in fifty years. Sometimes it's easier just to do things the way that everybody else is."

David looked down at his hands. "Don't you see her anymore?"

"No," I said. "She's been in college. We thought it would be better not to keep in touch."

"How did she pay?"

"I gave her the money."

"I should have paid," he said. "I'll pay you back."

"No," I said. "It's alright. I didn't want the money anyway."

A knock came from the door and the nurse poked her head inside.

"It's time for group meditation," she said. "You can skip it if you like."

"No, that's alright. I'll go," said Davey. He peeled the sheets off his bed and the nurse closed the door to wait outside. Davey grinned at me. "There's a twenty-two-year-old girl who's been committed by her family for a love affair with blow. If she manages to kick it, I think I'll try and be her sponsor."

"There's the Dave we know and love."

Davey moved toward his dresser and then stopped and turned to me. "Thanks for coming, Casey."

"You're my brother."

"All the same."

"I'll come again to get you out. And then hopefully we'll never be here again."

"No, hopefully not."

I left him to dress. Meredith was waiting outside and she did not say anything until we were out of the building.

"How is he?" she asked.

"I don't know. It's difficult to tell with him."

"Is he going to be alright?"

"He's alive, if that's what you mean."

"It's not," she said. "Is he going to be alright?"

"I don't know. How do you tell if someone's going to be alright?"

We walked back toward where the car was parked and did not speak again until we stood before it.

"Casey," she said. "Where have you been the past month?"

Meredith was looking at me very directly over the hood of the car.

"I had to work," I said. "And then I had to settle something."

Meredith looked to the door of the rehabilitation center and squinted her eyes.

"Well," she said finally. "Is it settled?"

"It's settled."

Meredith nodded and exhaled deeply and walked around the car and got in abruptly. I stood outside uncertain whether or not I was meant to join her. The car rumbled to life and very quickly the radio was turned up so loud that you could feel the bass's tremors in your ribcage even outside the car. And then another sound joined the stereo; Meredith screamed and it was something like an explosion of anger. I saw the roof of the car pulse up three times and figured that she must be hitting it with her fists. When the radio cut, there were several seconds of relative silence, interrupted only by the rumbling of the engine. The passenger side window slid open.

"Are you going to get in or am I leaving you?" said Meredith.

I got into the passenger seat and only chanced a furtive glance at Meredith as I fastened my seatbelt. Her makeup was running slightly around the eyes, but she did not really wear very much and it did not look so bad, even in the aftermath of tears. It was the only way to tell that she had been crying. She reached down and raised the volume on the radio slightly, so that it was barely audible. It was the same tune that had been blasting only moments before, but scaled down so significantly that it was barely recognizable. It sounded like elevator music or the music you hear at the beginning of a film while a large carnival is happening and suddenly you understand that something is going to explode because the music is too happy to inspire emotion beyond the feeling of loss when it is inevitably cut short by tragedy. It kept going. I could not help but laugh.

"Don't," said Meredith. "Don't laugh. There isn't anything to laugh about."

"No," I said. "There isn't anything to laugh about at all. It's good to finally agree on something. Will you agree to a cup of coffee?"

"Alright," said Meredith.

I watched Meredith's face while she drove. She became more attractive the longer you were with her, like a song that you did not care all that much for but now you'd heard it so many times and could not get it out of your head.

We followed Route 35 north along the coast. To our left were the inlets and bays where all but the largest boats had been removed for the winter season and to our right was the ocean. When we reached Point Pleasant, Meredith kept going straight onto Ocean Avenue instead of turning with the highway. There were faster ways to go but we were not so interested in speed. We got caught at the open bridge in Belmar and watched the fishing boats returning from their mornings on the deep sea back to the harbor.

"I always liked watching the bridge opening and closing," said Meredith. "When I was a little girl I used to think that when I finally got my license I'd drive through the gate and try to jump the span. It always seemed so plausible."

"Does it seem plausible now?"

"No," she said. "There's too much weight in the car. I'll get out and walk while you give it a go."

"That's alright," I said. "I wouldn't want to keep you waiting."

"Wouldn't you?"

After the bridge we cut up a few streets and drove along South Main until we reached Frank's Deli and Restaurant in Asbury Park. It was something of a local institution and they took tremendous pride in not having changed very much about their menu or decor. In summer there was always a wait to sit because people who had come down for the weekend wanted to try the local favorite, but in the off-season months the same regulars came and sat at the same spots at the same times every day. The restaurant achieved a universal appeal by not trying to cater to anyone at all. Even the waitresses did not seem particularly interested in you but there was something charming in their indifference that kept everybody coming back.

We sat at a small table in the back of the restaurant. Pork-roll is a type of processed ham indigenous to New Jersey and whenever I returned to the Shore after I'd first left it, I felt a certain obligation to order it for meals wherever it was available. Except that now I did not feel as if I was required to have it. There is something in visiting your brother at a local care center that makes you not feel like a tourist anymore. We ordered coffee and I had one of the preset breakfasts and Meredith ordered an omelet.

"I've never understood those girls who order bacon, egg and cheese to only pull apart the bread and pick at what's inside."

"No," I said. "You wouldn't."

"Do you?"

"I think so. Or at least I did, once upon a time."

"Me too. But I'm glad I wasn't ever one of them. I felt bad for them, really."

"Yes, you would."

"I don't mean it in a condescending way."

"I know that."

"Only you shouldn't feel ashamed to eat healthy. There isn't anything wrong with it."

"No, there isn't."

We were quiet for a moment while the food came. Meredith fingered the plastic corner of the menu and then stirred her spoon inside her coffee glass. She was drinking it black and there was nothing in it to stir. Suddenly she stopped and spoke.

"You never owed me anything, Casey," she said. She looked down into the coffee and then up at me. "But you were a shitty friend. I have no right to be angry at you for what happened, and I even understand it in a way. If you could reason that there was nothing to hold the two of you back, then maybe you could reason that he wasn't really your father. Well, he was, and I guess you've figured that out by now or you wouldn't be here. It doesn't make sense to me, but I understand it in a way. Everything up to the point where you left without a word. The quiet nearly killed me."

"I know it. It nearly killed me too."

"That isn't any excuse."

"That's true," I said. "I'm sorry. You're probably the only person who's ever cared about me without having to."

"Davey cares about you."

"Davey has to. And we aren't talking about Davey."

"No, we aren't."

"You deserved better from a friend and I wasn't better."

"Do you think you can be?"

I lingered on the silence for a moment before answering. I thought it might give the answer some gravity and make it seem as if when I answered it was not an impulse but something I had really thought about. It was something I had really thought about, but I had done all that thinking well before.

"Yes," I said. "I can be."

"Don't say it if you don't mean it," she said. "I'm not in the business of forgiving twice."

"I mean it."

"There isn't any shame in ordering healthy if that's the way you want to eat. Only don't order something you don't want and then pull apart the bread."

"No," I told her. "I'm not pulling apart any bread."

Meredith raised her cup of coffee and smiled at me over the brim before drinking. We ate our meal in relative silence and we both finished our portions fully. The food tasted the same as it had always tasted. The restaurant was not going to win any Michelin stars, but it was not going to go out of business either. It would be standing there for a long time and you got the sense that the old woman who collected cash at the counter would live forever.

CHAPTER 16
Marble

There were two deaths of consequence in the first three months of 2017; the first was the passing of Evelyn Hawthorne.

It was an unseasonably warm morning in late January and all around the earth was wet from a light snowfall that had melted. When I arrived at the Hawthorne house, Evelyn still lay in bed. I had never entered her bedroom before. It was the only piece of her gardening that she had been able to keep up herself. Plants were hung from the ceiling and surrounding the bed there were many flowers. On either side table was a different orchid, and both were enjoying multiple blooms. The windows' panes were old and warped and sunlight fell through in uneven waves that lent the whole room a sense of motion. Evelyn's nightgown was white with floral print and she seemed at once to be a part of the room, like some rare flower that was the centerpiece of this very peculiar greenhouse.

"It almost looks like she's smiling," said Meredith. I could see what she meant but I did not necessarily agree. You could not call her expression a smile. It seemed simply to be there as a feature of something incapable of emotion, like a strange pattern that might manifest in the bark of a tree. It was not a smile but it was an expression of contentedness, nonetheless. I was suddenly envious of her. She had maintained a garden and it was enough to bring her happiness and that was something to be envious of. She had planted the correct garden—a small garden, but the correct one. If you're going to spend all that time tilling the soil and watering earth, you ought to make sure you've planted the right seeds. You ought to make sure they are the seeds of fruits you enjoy tasting or flowers you enjoy watching or high stalks of grass you enjoy running your fingers through. Otherwise, questions of the soil's fertility, of the patterns of rain, of the habits of vermin, of everything and anything are entirely irrelevant. Everything is irrelevant if you are tending the wrong garden.

"Yes," I said. "Almost."

Over the past several months I had come back often on weekends to check on Davey, and I saw Meredith each time I did. It was as if we had skipped over the initial stages of a relationship and gone directly to the part where we relied heavily on one another for many things, but physical gratification was not one of them. We did not touch each other. It was almost too serious for that. And yet nobody could say that we were only friends. Meredith spent most of her time either commuting to or working in New York and she would have stayed at my apartment, but she was never able to leave her mother alone. She had been accepted to a teaching degree program that would begin in the fall and she was trying to save up as much as she could before commencement. She would be helped by her inheritance, which was everything her mother had left behind. This included the house, her bank accounts, and her defunct gardening business. Neither the business nor the bank accounts were worth much but the house would be enough to get Meredith through school without debt if she were willing to sell it. She did not seem to have so much a problem with selling the house, but using the money so quickly and so explicitly gave her pause.

The funeral would set her back some, but she was helped by knowing that Evelyn Hawthorne would not have wanted anything lavish and she respected those wishes. We held a small gathering at the house after the service, but many more people arrived than we had anticipated. It seemed that everyone had maintained a secret correspondence with Evelyn Hawthorne, even long after she had receded into the isolation of her home. This one had brought her scones every Thursday evening and this one had continued to solicit Evelyn for gardening advice. Mourners wore these fabricated relationships on their sleeves and when they saw that everyone else had worn them as well, they ripped them off and waved them like flags. It was disgraceful to watch but Meredith would not let me say anything.

"Let them have it," she said. "Soon enough they'll believe it and in a year it will be as if it really happened."

"If you say so," I said.

"I say so."

The food and drink ran out quickly and after that the people ran out too. Eventually it was only Davey and Meredith and me. Davey's left forearm was in a cast and he'd been forced to cut into the sleeve of his dark suit in order to make it fit. Six weeks earlier, he had broken his wrist in an accident at the boxing gym. He claimed that it happened while hitting a bag without gloves, but the X-rays seemed to indicate that the bone had been crushed by weights. In any case, they would not allow him anything for the pain beyond high doses of acetaminophen.

Still, he looked better than he had, although not necessarily happier. Perhaps happiness would come later. He had gained back much of the weight he had lost and was keeping himself busy despite his resistance to employment. He was not allowed to drink for a period of six months that would be ending in April, and sobriety had been good for him. He had taken up reading and politics and he liked to paddle surf in the mornings. Oftentimes when I arrived on a Saturday morning, he would be paddling in. The weather did not bother him; he had a thick winter wetsuit and he enjoyed the feeling of having people see him and suppose that he must be crazy for venturing into the water given the season. He gathered a strange manner of pride from their speculation.

"It's getting late," he said. "I should get going."

Meredith nodded. "Thanks for helping with everything. I'm just going to clean up and get to bed."

She rubbed her eyes and gave Davey a kiss on the cheek and went into the kitchen. I spoke quietly to Davey once we were alone.

"If you give me a minute, I'll drive you back."

"Stay here, Case," he said. "She wants you to. You shouldn't let her be alone."

"You can drive?"

"Being able to drive is the one advantage of sobriety."

"It isn't the only one," I said.

"I didn't realize you were such an expert on the subject."

"There was whiskey that had to be drunk," I said. "I only had one."

"You had three."

"See, being able to count is another advantage."

"I guess it is. Anyway, I'll be alright. Stay here."

"You're sure?"

"I'm sure. Goodnight."

Davey went out and left Meredith and I alone in the house. She came out once he exited, as if she had expected him to go. She probably had. I was glad to be alone with her and she came up to me and leaned her head into my chest and I wrapped my arms around her.

"Will Davey be alright alone?"

"Sure," I said. "Let's not talk about Davey."

"But will he be alright? I mean you don't need to have an eye on him now?"

"I don't give him enough money to buy any pills. Let's not talk about Davey."

"All right," she said. "Let's not talk about him."

"How are you?"

"I don't want to talk about me, either."

"Alright. What should we talk about then?"

"Let's talk about nothing," she said. We were swaying side to side, almost like a slow dance. "Today was not supposed to be very sad, but I didn't like that everybody took for granted that it was only a celebration of life and that there was nothing sad in her dying."

"They didn't know her very well."

"Once upon a time they did. Everybody knew her once upon a time."

"That's true," I said, "but what effect does once upon a time ever have on today?"

"It ought to."

"Maybe," I said. "That never seems to help anything much."

"I suppose not. I thought we weren't going to talk about anything."

We continued to sway side to side and I began to hum. I do not know what it is that I was humming. Meredith pulled away gently and brought her lips to mine and then she turned away and moved toward the stairs. Along the stairs there was an electric rail that moved a chair up and down between floors. Evelyn used it once, when the disease was only just beginning, but it had not been used in the long time since she had moved her bedroom downstairs. Meredith paused at the base of the stair and ran her fingers along the seat and then moved up the stairs. She stopped on the landing and turned back to me.

"I feel like I need a shower before going to sleep," she said.

"It helps sometimes."

"Do you want to come join me?" she asked.

Meredith did not wait for a response and I did not move up the stairs until I heard the water. It seemed important that I should not seem to be following her too directly. I do not know what the logic was. The thought crossed my mind to undress before entering the bathroom, as sometimes the ungainliness of undressing can disrupt the solemnity of the reason for it, but when I stood outside the door it did not seem any longer to matter.

The water had turned hot and it was beginning to let off steam. Meredith stood with her naked back to me, and watched me enter through my reflection in the mirror. She tilted her head slightly side to side while she removed each earring and placed them together beside the basin of the sink. They were pearl earrings and the only ones I had ever seen her wear and between the white stone of the sink and the steam rolling off the shower they became invisible as soon as she put them down. Meredith turned to me and then stepped into the shower and was obscured by the steam on the glass wall. There was a wide glass door without any footing on the floor because it was designed so that a wheelchair could pass into the shower. There was no difference between the stone of the floor inside or out. It was roughly textured and even when it was wet you felt that you had a grip.

Meredith stood in the center of the space, directly beneath the showerhead. It was wide and mounted directly to the ceiling and dropped water in a perfect vertical as if to give the impression of rain on a day without wind. I joined Meredith in the water. Her hair fell over her breasts and I pushed it back behind her ear and behind her shoulder. Beneath her right breast was a small tattoo of dark figures in flight. I had never noticed it but I had never had much opportunity. Perhaps I had noticed but had never paid them much attention. They were either crows or the shadows of happier birds. Thick streams of water raced over the ink and it was impossible to tell. We pushed back out of the stream of water and all the breath escaped her lungs as they were pressed between my body and the smooth warm tile. All the breath echoed and seemed to be a thing no longer of our choosing but a natural order of events bent on equilibrium, like steam falling from hot water.

Meredith's hand found the valve and turned it toward the right.

"I don't want so much steam," she whispered. "Do you mind?"

"No," I said, unable to think. "I don't mind anything."

The water lost its heat and then it felt like ice. The rough stone of the floor moved from our feet to our knees and our elbows and our backs but it seemed the whole time that we remained upright and the room around us spun, or as if maybe there was not any room at all and gravity had lost its constitution. The cold did not numb our bodies but only demanded that every cell of skin stretch out toward the other to combine their urgent and radiant heat, and afterward there was no more steam.

We sat with our backs against the wall and our knees tucked into our chest. Our feet extended toward the center of the space, where the cold water landed, and eventually Meredith reached up and turned the water off completely. Without the water the room seemed very quiet. When she spoke, her voice was quiet but not a whisper. There was no reason to whisper anymore.

"Do you want to hear about the worst thing I ever did?" she asked.

"No," I said. "Never."

"When I found my mother, when I realized that she was gone, the first thing I felt was relief. I can't tell if I smiled or not, but I think I may have. I certainly didn't cry." She looked at me. "Do you think it's inhuman not to cry at such things?"

I looked at our faded reflection in the glass wall. The water had been cold for long enough that there was no longer any fog on the glass.

"No," I said. "Nothing a human ever does is inhuman. We are human, aren't we?"

"Yes," said Meredith. "I suppose so. Sometimes you want to be something better than that, though. Human doesn't seem to be a very high benchmark."

"It isn't," I said. "And thank god for that."

"Do you thank god often?"

"Never."

"Good," said Meredith. "I don't trust anybody who thanks god."

* * *

There were two deaths of consequence in the first three months of 2017; the second was that of David James Larkin.

I found him with a needle in his arm and a belt tied just above his elbow. His head was turned out the back door toward the ocean and I checked his pulse twice to be sure that he was really dead. I sat with the phone in my hand but I did not call the police for a long time. Or maybe it was not so long. I could not forfeit the notion that each time I looked away from him directly, his chest seemed to rise and fall. Eventually I dialed for the police but got Meredith instead and when she answered I hung up. This happened two more times and two more times I hung up and I only told her when she called back, as if it were a thing of her prompting: Davey is dead. I could hear myself say it and could hear the sound roll off my tongue, nothing more than fact; Davey is dead, as if I were mentioning the weather. It was the first warm day of the year and the seagulls lined the dunes and took to the sky above the sea but did not yet dive. The water was still too cold for that. It was the fourth such death in Monmouth County that year and it was not yet April.

The strand of heroin was called China White and he had gotten it from a boy he'd met at St. Kolbe's. It was a good deal less expensive than the prescription pills he had fallen into and he'd been able to pay for it with valuables from the house. They found the boy two days later, hiding beneath the elevated porch of a house three doors down from Davey. He had been attacked by a raccoon that lived beneath the porch and ran out screaming until he tripped on the sidewalk and spilled into the street. By the time the police came, his palms had stopped bleeding and he sat on the curb, clutching his knees to his chest and rocking back and forth. They said the smell of urine was so strong that the police drew sticks for who would return him to the precinct.

Aside from Meredith, I only called Davey's mother. She was an abhorrent woman who was probably made worse by her marriage to my father. She lived in Palm Beach with a new husband fourteen years her senior and had not seen her son for many years. When she heard that it was me on the other end of the line she knew at once. She was silent for a moment.

"Oh," she said quietly. "When?"

"Yesterday morning."

"I meant—"

"I know what you meant. Sunday, at ten."

"Where?"

"The same place they did Joseph's."

She was silent on the other end of the line.

"Meyer's Funeral Home, Neptune."

"Are there hotels nearby?"

"Many," I said. I hung up.

If you want to know who loved the dead, save the funeral for a weekend. If you have it on the weekday everybody only comes to get out of work. We buried Davey on the last Sunday in March and not so many people came. You could not have asked for better weather for a funeral. It was cold enough that there were no insects but warm enough to wear a suit and nothing else.

"Casey," said Meredith. She looked over toward the cemetery gates. There was Gabrielle walking toward us, and with her were Liam and Tamera.

"I didn't even call her," I said.

"I know," said Meredith. "I did. David was her brother, too."

As Gabrielle approached, Meredith nodded to her but did not say anything. Tamera hugged me and then went over to stand with the few others who were there. Meredith went with her. Liam took my hand very firmly and nodded and then went to join them. Suddenly I was alone with Gabrielle.

It was unclear to me what Liam knew, but I could see now that it would not have mattered. As Gabrielle approached, I could not feel any quickened beating of my heart or any tension. It felt as though I were seeing an old friend that I had been to war with. There was the mutual shame of having witnessed a certain kind of violence in one another's presence, but it did not seem now as if either one of us had been the perpetrator of it or in any way involved except as unwilling spectators. We looked at each other for a long time without speaking, but it was not so much an awkward silence as a pleasant assessment and there was nothing left of the spark between us. We had each had our fill of that.

The service would not begin for a few minutes and we walked together away from the small gathering.

"You look good," I told her.

"I look good?" She smiled and her eyes widened toward the edges.

"Yes," I said. "Me, on the other hand—"

"You look awful."

"That's true," I said.

"You and Meredith?"

"Yes," I said. I looked back at the small group in dark suits and picked out Meredith immediately. She was speaking with Tamera. "It's a long story. It goes way back."

"Well," she said. "Keep it to yourself then. I've had all the long stories a girl could ask for."

"And Liam?" I asked.

"Yes," she said. She smiled at his name and leaned her weight slightly against mine. "Yes."

"That's good," I said. "I thought so from the beginning."

"Did you?"

"In a way. He'll be good. He'll give you anything you want." We walked for a while without saying anything and I felt that all the lightness had left the conversation, the way that alcohol will evaporate even at room temperature. "You should have anything you want."

"You seem practical, like when I met you for the first time. I'm glad you're being practical again."

We walked for a while without saying anything.

"How's Tamera been with you away at school?" I asked.

"She's alright. She has her hobbies and her rum and house." Gabrielle stopped walking and turned to me. "You've been very good to me, Casey. To my mother too. I know we never talk, but you've been very good to me. I won't forget it."

"You ought to," I said. I looked back at the gathering. "I'll certainly try."

"It's funny," she said. "Now I feel like we're really his children. Joseph's."

"Something about David's being alive made that impossible," I said. "It was like we were second-class citizens and now without any first-class ones left we've been promoted."

Gabrielle looked around. "He didn't have such a rosy time of it either."

"No," I said. "I don't think he did. Probably he wanted to be us in some ways."

"Well, he isn't jealous anymore," she said.

"That's true," I said. "He isn't a lot of things."

"In my mother's country, they have a song. I don't know all of it but it ends: and the grass is always greener on the grave."

I looked around to see if it was true. Mostly there wasn't any difference between the grass before headstones and the grass that was everywhere else, but some of the paths were worn with foot traffic and you could see how somebody thought it might be true from far away. Over by David's grave, the service was about to begin.

I looked back to where everyone had gathered around the grave and I felt suddenly that I could not breathe. Gabrielle was looking at me. My hand slid out of hers and wrapped around her body and her hand on the back of my head pushed my face down into her shoulder. I was shaking all over and I could feel the cotton of her shirt sticking to my eyes. I had not cried since I had found Davey, or for a long, long time before that. Gabrielle brought her lips to my forehead and held them there for a long time. When we broke away it was clear that we would not touch again. I nodded but did not try to speak as we walked back to start the service. There wasn't any use in speaking.

Davey's mother came. She tried to stay toward the back but there were not really enough people present to constitute rows and eventually she wound up, as if by mistake, to be standing next to me.

"Strange that they should be so resistant here to mausoleums," she whispered. Her second husband was British and his accent had affected her speech. Everything she said sounded scripted and fake. "The weather so terrible. You forget how terrible the weather can be."

"It isn't so bad," I said.

She was quiet for some time. I liked her better when she was quiet.

"No, it isn't so bad. Are they granite, do you think?" She was looking at the tombstones. "The make, I mean."

"What else is there to mean?"

"I asked if it was granite," she said. She had been quicker to anger than I'd expected and I looked sideways at her. There were tears on her cheek and they ran black with her mascara. She dabbed at them with her sleeve. It was all very delicate.

"Marble," I said, as if the opulence of it could be in some way a consolation. "Maybe marble."

"I hope not. It's far too porous. Stains with oil. We have it on the countertops at home. The surface looks like the skin of an African cat."

"Nobody carries oil in the places it will be."

"Only one place," she said. Her voice was like a wisp of smoke and it sounded as if she was reciting poetry.

"Yes," I said. I wanted her to stop speaking. "And nobody carries oil there is my point."

"There are many kinds of oil, though. Burning, cooking, dipping. The kind for bodies and the kind for bread." She was quiet for some time. "Let's not speak of bodies."

"No," I agreed.

And that was all, we did not speak after that, of bodies or of anything else. When the funeral was over, she left. There was no reception or lunch or even an open tab at the bar. There is a certain age at which such things become acceptable and Davey had not yet reached it. Many people had not come. The ones who did were old friends of Davey's from his football days in high school. I recognized some of them but did not recognize more. Very few recognized me, and I think that they probably would not have recognized Davey either.

* * *

Everything Davey owned had come to me and I split it down the middle with Gabrielle. There was enough to go around. There had never been a will and, by technicality, we were both his next of kin.

By the end of April I had sold the house. I fantasized and even entertained the prospect of bulldozing it and building something unrecognizable on the empty lot but that was not the way to go about forgetting things. You bulldoze the houses you want to remember; the ones you want to forget you sell below their market value and let another family come and possess their halls and their kitchens and their bedrooms. In doing that, you've also sold the house's memories. Meredith had decided to sell her house, too, but first she uprooted the garden; you bulldoze the things you want to remember and keep them for yourself.

We stood on the balcony of her house and now without the rhododendrons it felt naked and exposed. It was early in the morning but there was no dew on the grass and the empty flower beds looked dry and gray, almost crumbling. It was nothing like the place where Meredith had grown up, and there was the feeling that she'd torn up one house with shears and a shovel and had now found another to sell. Meredith was breathing hard from having spent the hour since sunup raking over the vacant soil, and there was dirt on the knees of her jeans.

"Well," she said. "That about does it. And I've got movers next Wednesday to take everything to storage. Have you wrapped up yet with yours?"

"I have until the end of the month to get out," I said. "But I'll be back next week to finish cleaning out the place."

"You'd better get going if you want to catch the nine o'clock."

"Why don't you go get dressed and catch it with me."

"Some of us still have to work," she said. "I've got bills to pay."

"I'll pay your bills. I've got too much money and nothing to do with it."

"I don't want a loan from you, Casey."

"So don't pay it back. Then it isn't a loan."

"I don't want a loan from you," she said again. I understood that she was not speaking about money. I stared at her for a long time and put one hand on either hip. Her jaw was tight.

"So marry me," I said.

Meredith looked at me to see if I was being serious. I had never been so serious about anything in my entire life.

"Marry me," I said again. I felt the way I had when I had told her that Davey was dead. There was nothing of desire or resistance behind the words. They were not a reflection of how you wanted things to be or how you wanted them not to be;

they were simply the way things were. But suddenly there wasn't anything in her eyes; they were stripped of all their depth, as if she'd taken the shears to them after tearing up the flower beds.

"A girl expects a boy to take a knee when he proposes," she said, and it was like she was trying to erect a wall between us.

"Would you like me to take one?" I asked her.

"No," said Meredith. She did not come any closer and her jaw was still tight. "A girl expects a ring when she's proposed to."

"You'll have a ring," I said. "Any ring you want."

Still her eyes were flat. You could tell that behind them there was something working hard but it didn't reach the surface. It was rare for Meredith to allow quiet.

"I never liked the idea of a ring," she said finally. "And I never liked the idea that only one person bought into it. Especially you. If I were ever to take a ring from you, I'd make you split it down the middle. You wouldn't care half so much about protecting your investment as protecting mine."

"That's a hell of a thing to say to a man you've agreed to marry."

"I haven't agreed."

"But you will. And anyway, you don't have any money."

"Then I guess it wouldn't be a very big ring."

We had moved closer together and Meredith locked her arm around mine and took my fingers in hers and held my knuckles to her lips. Then she took them away and put her hand to my face.

"I suppose you're somewhat saved by the size of your hands," I said. "A large ring would overwhelm them."

"They're big enough to leave a mark across the whole of your cheek, Casey Larkin."

"I haven't forgotten it."

"No," she said. "Don't."

"Well," I told her. "I'd better go if I'm going to make that train."

Meredith had been looking at her hands but now she stuck them in the pockets of her jeans and looked at me and squinted her eyes.

"You know," she said. "Every time you go away, I wonder if you'll ever come back."

"Well you're going to have to stop wondering, considering that you've agreed—"

"I haven't agreed," she said quickly.

I reached out to take her hand but it was still inside her pocket and so I held her wrist.

"I'm coming back Saturday," I said. "I'll be here."

"I know," she said. "And you know I'll be here, don't you?"

"Yes," I said. I did know it too. All throughout the week I knew it and when I drove down the following Saturday I knew it and I didn't stop knowing it until I parked outside the strange flowerless house with the empty flower beds like moats around it and walked up onto the porch and tried to open up her door. It was locked. It had never been locked before but now it was locked. I rang the bell twice and could hear its muted chime come through the walls or door or windows. I put my ear to the door and rang the bell again, but as soon as the chime died out the house inside was empty, and it was like putting your ear to the chest of a cadaver. I thought of Davey lying on the floor with his dead eyes looking out at the sky above the ocean, my fingers pushing down on the soft skin beneath his jaw, searching for a pulse that wasn't there.

I took a step back and crossed my arms, looking at the door as if its inertia were a thing that could be stared down. It couldn't. I stepped down off the porch and spent some time looking between all the windows, but I gave it up quick. There wasn't anybody there and you could sort of feel the vacancy. So I drove back to Joseph's house. To David's house, to mine. The front door wasn't locked and when I opened it I saw that there was a pile of mail that had been pushed in through the brass slot, and on top of the pile was an envelope without any address that said Casey across the front in small blue letters. Casey. The handwriting was Meredith's and it said Casey across the front, but as I read my own name I heard again the last thing she'd said to me: "And you know I'll be here, don't you?" and then: "I haven't agreed."

I took the letter and left the rest of the mail on the floor. In the kitchen I opened it up, and because my head was in a fog, I put the letter in the garbage and held onto the envelope and read my name again in the neat blue ink. There was no liner in the trash can and I had to reach far down to get the letter and then flattened it against the table and began to read.

She had left it on my door instead of hers because she didn't know which house I'd go to first. If I went to hers first then I'd still have to come back to mine, and so she'd left it on my door to save me the trip. Nobody was ever going to take being considerate away from Meredith.

When I finished reading the letter I stood for a while in the kitchen, listening to the quiet of the house. It was still very early and the water would be calm and so there weren't any waves to listen to and time felt unraveled like yarn loosed from a spool, with its ends buried somewhere in its folds. It seemed that everything that had ever happened here was happening again and all at once. There was Joseph's bloody face and Davey on the floor and Ella swaying like a reed upstairs with the black vinyl spinning and Meredith's note lying flat against the marble.

I was desperate to find something to count time with, some pulse or progression, and I found it in a blinking red light. It came from the corner of the room, steady as a drum or a siren, and only after I'd been staring for a while did I realize that it was the answering machine. I went and pressed the button without out really knowing what I was doing and the automated voice blended in with the messages and at first I couldn't understand what it was saying because the only voice I could hear was Meredith's and it was reading the note in my hand.

Casey . . .

And on the machine all the messages were the same and they were all saying:

"I'm calling for David Larkin. Call me back. It's very urgent."

There were seven of those messages and they were more or less identical. I had the phone in one hand and Meredith's letter in the other and I crumpled up the paper and almost threw it in the garbage but then I smoothed it out again against the marble countertop. With the answering machine empty now, the red light had quit its blinking and time was in a tangle once again. I wanted to speak to Meredith but she wasn't there and so I called back the number that had left the voicemails. It rang twice and then somebody picked up.

"I didn't think you'd call," they said quietly. "Hold on."

There was some static on the other end and you could tell the phone was moving, rustling in a pocket, and there were footsteps going fast and hard, and then a door closing and foot-steps again and then it was quiet and there was only breathing.

"It's Saturday," the voice said finally. It was hardly more than a whisper. "We don't answer the phones on Saturday."

"Well," I said. "You answered."

"I answered."

I've spent my whole adult life taking care of one person and I'm going to be a little selfish before signing up to take care of an-other. You'll say now that you don't want or need to be taken care of, but you do, really you do.

"It's against our religion to carry burdens on Shabbat and so I'll speak to you now and let one go. If I met you in person a month ago, I might have killed you. You don't know me, Mr. Larkin, but I know all about you. I know where you live and where you go drinking. I know your mother's maiden name . . ."

His voice was so quiet that it took on a nebulous quality and it was like speaking with a cloud.

I've given you about a hundred chances and if you're serious you'll give me two.

". . . she's seventeen. Did you know that? I bet you didn't know that. To tell you the truth, it doesn't matter if you knew that. Because very few people try to be bad; they're only careless and don't try so hard to be good. Well, the two are the same, exactly the same . . ."

I don't know when I'll ask for my other chance but when I do . . .

". . . but you're lucky. If my daughter wasn't alright you wouldn't be so lucky, but she's alright. A little smarter but al-right. It's a thing you learn about having children is that you want them to stay as far from smart for as long as possible.

When they get too smart it's like they've lost something. So my daughter has lost something but she'll be alright . . ."

I wanted to say it to your face but I couldn't. It's bad of me and I'm a coward but there you have it, at least I know what I am . . .

". . . but some people aren't careless. I'm not careless, and I'm not going to drag my daughter's name through the mud just to get revenge on you, no matter how bad I might want to. And I'm not going to keep us from coming back to our summer home because of you, or let you matter in any way to our lives . . ."

I'm not going to be one of those girls that says I want you to be happy without me. The truth is that I want you to be miserable without me and come crawling to find me, only don't do it so fast. It'll be good for you to need something and to want something and not to get it right away . . .

". . . I'd tell you to stay away from her, but I don't need to. She'll stay away from you on her own."

So goodbye, for now. Don't call, don't write. M

The man's voice kept going. I had the sense that there was water pouring into the house through the speaker, on the vehicle of his whisper. It was like the kitchen was being filled up with an invisible something. And then suddenly it ended and still there wasn't the sound of waves or the red blinking light and again it was like time had stopped, that I was sitting in a great pool of it among bodies, words and voices.

"Hello?" the man said finally. "Are you there? David, are you there?"

"This is Casey," I said. But my voice sounded strange and I hardly believed that it was really mine. "Casey Larkin. Not David."

"Casey Larkin," said the voice. It echoed the name without

really digesting it. In his mind he was still speaking with David. "You're his . . ."

"His brother."

"Well," he said after some time. "Is your brother there?"

"No," I told him. "He's dead."

"Oh," he said. He went very quiet on the other end of the line and all that I could hear was his breathing. It was more or less the same volume as his voice had been, but the difference was that now it didn't feel like anything was pouring in. He was silent for so long that I began to reread Meredith's letter, and by the time he spoke again it was as if I was half-speaking to her.

"Well," he said finally. "I'm sorry."

"No," I thought of saying, "I don't think you're really sorry," but then I looked again at Meredith's letter in my hand and I thought of Meredith's face. Maybe he was really sorry and it was possible to believe that somebody had wronged you but still not really wish them to be dead. Maybe there were sort of gradations to revenge that should exist and some things you shouldn't do. In my mind Meredith's face changed to Ella's and I was staring at the place on the floor where Davey's heart had stopped.

"Me too," I finally told him.

"Alright," he said.

"Alright."

He hung up the phone and I kept it pressed lightly to my cheek until it started to make its disconnected tone, pulsing very fast like time rushing to catch up. I held it there a little longer and then finally put it down and went out the sliding back door and onto the sand. It was gray out over the ocean and the water was still and flat like glass and shining. A wind came across the water and you could hear it, almost like a whisper, and the ripples that it caused were not like waves but more like the way that skin shakes when the muscle spasms from having worked too hard beneath it.

A fishing boat went by a little way from the shore. It was at a good distance but the sound carried on the water and you could hear the engine pulsing. The slow slap of the hull against the surface of the water was a heavy sort of rhythm and it pushed out little waves which moved and then broke on the sand and very quickly the idea of motion seemed to spread across the whole gray surface like a pebble splintering the glass of a windshield.

I took off my shoes and the sand was beginning to warm in the sun and now there were little waves. The ocean was as cold as it would be all year and it would not be at warmest until autumn. Already the gulls had come back and sat high on the dunes. They scanned the horizon with their eyes and pulled their heads in close to their bodies to stay warm. Along the shore-line, whole colonies of storm petrels ran up the beach when the white wake chased them away from the ocean. When the water reached its apex they stopped and turned back to face it, and when it receded back toward the ocean they chased it downhill. It was like watching a metronome whose motor was fear and whose cadence kept time for no purpose; but purpose or not, the waves kept coming, higher and higher in their climb up on the sand, and the small yellow feet kept on running.

Acknowledgments

I'd like to begin by thanking my agent, Michelle Tessler, who never stopped believing in this book. Similar gratitude is due to Haila Williams, the acquiring editor, as well as the entire team at Blackstone, including Megan Wahrenbrock, Ember Hood, Alex Cruz, Josie Woodbridge, and Samantha Benson, without whom this book would not have been possible. Special thanks also to this book's editor, Michael Signorelli, for sharing a vision for this book and helping to make it a reality.

Endless gratitude is owed to the Faulkner Society, and especially Rosemary James and her late husband, Joseph J. DeSalvo Jr., for their early encouragement and support.

Thank you to my many, many writing mentors along the way, including Julia Glass, Austin Rattner, Michael Malone, as well as my peers and professors at Duke University and The New School. And I would probably not have been writing at all if not for the early mentorship of the late Oscar Hijuelos.

Finally, thank you to my parents and brothers, whose support has meant everything to me and who were most decidedly not the inspiration for any of the characters in this novel.